DEADMAN OF THE BOARD

Giving my arm a squeeze, Sol bent down to pluck a reed from the very Jersey jungle of baby sumac trees and ragweed clumped around a fragment of knee-high stone wall at the base of the incline. When I followed him, I could see that some graffiti artist had emblazoned the wall's pitted surface with the names of rappers Ice-T and Snoop Doggy Dogg in silver script. Sol stood up and presented the blade of greenery to me with a flourish.

But this courtly gesture was marred by the scowl that darkened his features and the anger when he said, "Jeez, the trash here pisses me off. Some people just won't rest until they've turned the whole world into a garbage heap. Would you look at this? Somebody's shoe!" Sol spoke now with that special disgust he reserved for those who littered, and he aimed a sharp kick at the offending object protruding from behind the makeshift mural.

The shoe barely moved. "Uh-oh." Sol walked around the bit of wall, bent down again, and parted the weeds. I leaned over for a closer look at the obdurate oxford.

We exhaled in unison, grabbing for each other's hands. It was Frank Si̲̲̲̲̲̲̲d as a doornail a̲̲̲̲̲̲̲̲y-five.

ATTENTION: ORGANIZATIONS AND CORPORATIONS
Most Avon Books paperbacks are available at special quantity
discounts for bulk purchases for sales promotions, premiums, or
fund-raising. For information, please call or write:

Special Markets Department, HarperCollins Publishers, Inc.,
10 East 53rd Street, New York, N.Y. 10022–5299.
Telephone: (212) 207–7528. Fax: (212) 207-7222.

MOOD SWINGS TO MURDER

A Bel Barrett Mystery

JANE ISENBERG

Jane Isenberg

AVON BOOKS
An Imprint of HarperCollinsPublishers

This is a work of fiction. Names, characters, places, and incidents are products of the author's imagination or are used fictitiously and are not to be construed as real. Any resemblance to actual events, locales, organizations, or persons, living or dead, is entirely coincidental.

AVON BOOKS
An Imprint of HarperCollins*Publishers*
10 East 53rd Street
New York, New York 10022-5299

Copyright © 2000 by Jane Isenberg
ISBN: 0-380-80282-1
www.avonbooks.com

First Avon Books paperback printing: December 2000

Avon Trademark Reg. U.S. Pat. Off. and in Other Countries, Marca Registrada, Hecho en U.S.A.
HarperCollins® is a trademark of HarperCollins Publishers Inc.

Printed in the U.S.A.

10 9 8 7 6 5 4 3 2 1

*To my former students
in appreciation for all you taught me*

Acknowledgments

This book, written as I prepared to retire from teaching and move away from Hoboken, is, in a very real sense, a love letter to my students, colleagues, and neighbors. That said, I wish to thank some of the many people who helped me to write it: the reference staff at the Hoboken Public Library; the guides of the Hoboken Historical Society's Sinatra tour; Jimmy Shamburg, Deputy Police Director, Jersey City, for providing information I sought; Mildred Aluotto, Elaine Foster, Johanna Hagelthorn, Lourdes Hallock, Liliane MacPherson, Stephen Nuding, Joan Rafter, Denise Swanson Stybr, and Ruth Tait—dear friends, for answering questions on demand; Laura Blake Peterson, my agent, for mentoring me in the writing business and Jennifer Sawyer Fisher, my editor, for mentoring me in the business of writing; Susan Babinski, Pat Juell, and Rebecca Mlynarczyk—members of my writing group, for giving me nine years of inspiration, affection, and honest re-sponses; Rachel and Brian Stoner, my daughter and son-in-law, for being on-call in Seattle with feedback and support; Daniel Isenberg, my son, and Shilyh Warren, our friend, for consulting on the manuscript in Hoboken and whisking me to book signings; and Phil Tompkins, my husband, for creating and maintaining my website, *www.Jane*Isenberg.com and also for helping me at every phase of the writing process with unfailing intelligence, patience, and wit.

Chapter 1

To: Bbarrett@circle.com
From: Rbarrett@UWash.edu
Re: Awesome news!
Date: Sun, 28 Jun 1998 09:35:42

Dear Mom,

Keith and I figured we'd better e-mail our big news so you'd have a chance to digest it before we talk, but he's still at work and I can't wait another second to tell you. Keith asked me to marry him! It happened yesterday right after he finished the Seattle-Portland bike race! I saw him ride through the tape at the finish line, so I elbowed my way through the crowd to hug his sweaty body. Just as I got to him, the announcer yelled, "Keith Roche, twenty-eight and a first-timer from Seattle finishing in one day! Keith has a very important question to ask Rebecca Barrett." I thought I was hearing things. Keith got down on one knee and said, "Rebecca, will you marry me!" right there in front of everybody! He didn't even take off his helmet. It was totally awesome. All the guys he trains with were there with their girlfriends or wives. They were taking pictures. They all knew he was going to propose. Can you believe Louise and I drove to Portland together and she never said a word? Anyway, we're getting married out here in January, during my mid-term break. It's so happening.

But that's not all! Are you sitting down? We're having a baby. Mark says you'll be psyched. But if I know you, you'll be worried about how we're going to make it. Don't get your undies in a wad, Mom. Everything's cool. Anyway, gotta study. Summer school is really condensed. We'll call Monday around seven our time 'cause I have to work tonight. That way you'll just be getting home from your evening class.

Love,
Rebecca

For the first time in fifteen years, I wanted a cigarette. This was a moment beyond chocolate. When Sol walked into the room ten minutes later, I was still sitting at the computer, staring at the monitor, tears streaming down my face. "Jesus, Bel, what's wrong?" In a few strides, Sol was by my side, reading over my shoulder as I leaned my head against him. "Okay. I get it. She really caught you off-guard, didn't she?" I nodded, allowing him to pull me to my feet. "Come on. Sinatra Drive's closed to traffic on summer Sundays. Let's go for a walk. You just need a few minutes to get used to Rebecca's news. Come on."

Sol believed a walk along what was left of Hoboken's waterfront was the cure for everything from IRS audits to prostate trouble, hot flashes, and mood swings. And usually I too found even a glimpse of the Manhattan skyline therapeutic. But this time even those spires glittering like marcasite in the June sunshine failed to raise my spirits. As I trudged silently beside him, Sol gently pressed me, "So what's bothering you? Rebecca and Keith have been living together for a few years now, right? They're clearly nuts about each other. And you told me last time you were out there that you thought they were in it for the long haul. And I know you like Keith. So are these tears of happiness, or what?"

"She didn't even tell me. I thought we were so close." I let go of Sol's hand to swab my face with a soggy Kleenex. "Even Mark knew about the baby. And they've decided everything already." I snorted miserably into the wadded Kleenex and jammed it into the pocket of my khaki shorts, a pair Rebecca had picked out for me the last time we'd gone shopping together. I could feel my throat tighten and new tears forming.

"Oh, now I see where you're coming from. Jesus, Bel, get over it. This is not about you. It's got nothing to do with you. It's not even about you and Rebecca. It's about Rebecca and Keith and their baby." Sol's words were harsh, but he grabbed my hand again. He was used to my bratty bouts of narcissism. "Besides, she's probably not more than a few months pregnant. What did you want her to do, e-mail you at the moment of conception?" We had paused at Frank Sinatra Park, Hoboken's new athletic field, a square patch of green partly edged by a brick walkway overlooking the Hudson and the world's most famous skyline. Leaning on the fence and shading his eyes from the glare of the sun on the water, Sol asked, "Want an iced tea or something?" He jerked his head in the direction of the snack bar that was crowded with young people in running clothes. A leggy blond with a long ponytail carrying a cup of coffee and a Sunday *Times* was striding over to a table. For a second she looked exactly like Rebecca. But no, my daughter was three thousand miles away. *Damn.*

"No thanks. Listen Sol, I don't want to beat this to death, but what am I anyway? The proverbial chopped liver?" Sol put his arm around my shoulder and pulled me to him. "They probably named the baby already too." I was still pouting in that la-la land somewhere between anguish and acceptance where mothers of adult kids spend a lot of time. "Besides, you know as well as I do that this is ludicrous. Rebecca has another whole year to go in physical therapy school and Keith . . ." I sputtered, picturing my future son-in-law, whose idea of career planning was getting work that didn't interfere with his training. He lived and breathed to qualify for the Ironman Triathlon in Hawaii. At the moment he worked in a bicycle shop and spent most of his spare time running, biking, and swimming. Rebecca attended classes by day and waited tables weekends and some evenings. "Listen, Sol, I know what I'm talking about here. I see how some of my students struggle. They can't afford good child care. They have to work to pay the bills. They have no time to study."

"Bel, let's look at the bright side. You're always going on about how motivated and determined your community college students are and how so many of them make it in spite of all these obstacles. Well, Rebecca and Keith are smart, resourceful kids. They'll cope. They'll have to. After all, we know there's nothing like a hungry, wet, cranky baby to shortstop a prolonged adolescence." We had resumed our stroll and were headed uptown. Sol was completely into his glass-half-full scenario now, so he said, "And Bel, you're getting what you've wanted so much for so long. You're finally going to be a grandmother!" Having made this dramatic pronouncement, Sol took my hand again and squeezed it as if he could squeeze me into seeing Rebecca's double-barreled fusillade as a good thing.

"Not only that, Bel . . ." The man was relentless. He was going to turn this sow's ear into a silk purse for me if it killed him. "You've finally got a wedding to plan. You've been mentally marrying off that daughter of yours for years, so this is your chance to do it for real." Sol was right. Rebecca's nuptials had occupied a disproportionate amount of space in my otherwise feminist fantasy life for over a decade. I had pictured her waltzing in a cloud of white chiffon through countless wedding scenarios. However, none of them had taken place in Seattle in January. In none of them had she been pregnant.

"Sol, give up on the Pollyanna crap for a minute and just explain to me how somebody with access to foolproof methods of birth control and who has been drilled on how to use them at home and in school can have an unplanned pregnancy. Rebecca's been putting condoms on cucumbers in practically every class she's had since the sixth grade. I just don't get it. This is 1998, not 1958. What's wrong with this picture?" My voice was getting shriller as I vented, and another Sunday stroller turned to stare. I didn't care. I was angry. How good it felt to sound off to Sol about my pain and disappointment. Even then I knew that I would never share these feelings with Rebecca. Somehow by evening I would summon the restraint to be tactful and supportive. And venting to Sol now would make that easier. I felt myself developing new empathy with King Lear.

"Bel, why do you assume they didn't plan this pregnancy? Maybe they did. After all, Keith and Rebecca have a very nineties relationship, not a fifties one, remember? And they have a lot of nineties choices too. As a card-carrying, pro-choice feminist, surely you know that. And they have chosen to have this baby."

Thank God, I thought before I even realized what I was grateful to the deity for. I hated when Sol, or anyone for that matter, implied that I didn't practice what I preached. But was he right?

Before I had a chance to respond, he went on, his deep voice tinged with irony, "Hello Bel. Because it's 1998, what you so charmingly label an 'unplanned pregnancy' no longer has to be cataclysmic the way it would have

been when we were young. Think about Alexis and Xie."
Sol was reminding me that his daughter had delivered
her baby without benefit of marriage on the very night of
her doctoral defense and two weeks before her longtime
boyfriend Xie left to do research on ecosystems of the
Yangtze in China. At the time, Sol had been wild with
concern for the little family's physical and fiscal well-
being. I had talked him through it, smugly confident all
the while that neither of *my* kids would ever put *me*
through that particular wringer. And now I was going to
be a mother-in-law and a grandmother and Sol was feeding my own riff back to me. I knew my own party line
when I heard it. Sighing, I reached into my bag for a
Post-it. I wanted to be sure to ask Rebecca about her
OBGYN when we talked later. And I'd better save my
personal days, my frequent flier miles, and my spare
change. We had a wedding to plan and a layette to buy.

"What's this? A trace of a smile? Perfect timing.
We're right under Sybil's Cave." Sol had stopped walking and was pointing across the road to an opening
barely visible behind a tangle of weeds and wildflowers
halfway up the palisade. In an earlier century when
Hoboken was a summer playground for Manhattanites,
Sybil's Cave had been the site of a spring whose waters
were reputed to have healing power. Sol loved that
snippet of local lore, at least partly because my full
name is Sybil, and because, in tender moments, he
claims I healed his hurting heart. "Maybe some healing
karma from a long-ago wise woman will drive off that
drama queen who takes over your body every now and
then. What do you think?" Giving my arm a squeeze, he
crossed the road and bent down to pluck a reed from the
very Jersey jungle of baby sumac trees and ragweed
clumped around a fragment of a knee-high stone wall at
the base of the incline. When I followed him, I could
see that some graffiti artist had emblazoned the wall's

pitted surface with the names of rappers Ice-T and Snoop Doggy Dogg in silver script. Sol stood up and presented the blade of greenery to me with a flourish.

But this courtly gesture was marred by the scowl that darkened his features and the anger in his voice when he said, "Jesus. The trash here pisses me off. Some people just won't rest until they've turned the whole world into a garbage heap. Would you look at this? Somebody's shoe." Sol spoke now with that special disgust he reserved for those who littered, and he aimed a sharp kick at the offending object protruding from behind the makeshift mural.

The shoe barely moved. "Uh-oh." Sol walked around the bit of wall, bent down again, and parted the weeds. I leaned over for a closer look at the obdurate oxford. "Jesus Christ," we exhaled in unison, grabbing for each other's hands. It was Frank Sinatra, dead as a doornail and not looking a day over twenty-five.

Chapter 2

To: Rbarrett@UWash.edu
From: Bbarrett@circle.com
Re: Double mazel tov
Date: Sun, 28 Jun 1998 13:05:12

Mazel tov to you and Keith! Sol sends love and congrats too! When do you think we should begin shopping for a wedding dress? I'll start looking for a cheap fare, or do you want to come here and shop? We can probably do better in New York. There's such variety, even out of season. But if I fly to Seattle, we can look for a place for the wedding, maybe on the water. That's probably more important, don't you think?

Right after I got your e-mail Sol and I took a walk on Sinatra Drive and then celebrated with brunch at Tania's. We would have brought Uncle-to-be Mark along, but he wasn't up yet. He had a late night jamming in the East Village again. I didn't tell Grandma Sadie, so you can call her yourself. She'll be really impossible when she's a great-grandma. Have you told your dad?

Got to go now. Have to take care of something that came up

unexpectedly. This day has been full of surprises! Can't wait to
talk with you tomorrow evening.

Love,
Granny or Nanny or Nana or Grandma Bel
(Which one do you like?)

Finding the corpse of a dead ringer for Old Blue
Eyes as a young man certainly had qualified as a surprise to both Sol and me. "Bel, if I hadn't seen his obit-
uary in every paper I picked up last May, I'd swear this
was some kind of back-to-the-future version of Frank.
What are you doing?"

While Sol stared fixedly at the ashen face and blank
blue eyes of the body at our feet, I had retrieved the cell
phone from my purse and was dialing 911. "Reporting
the body. You know, Sol, calling the cops. What the hell
do you think I'm doing?" Honestly, for a brilliant man,
Sol could be extremely obtuse sometimes. "Yuck.
Watch out." I shifted my foot quickly to avoid stepping
in a patch of rust-colored ooze that outlined the upper
torso of the corpse. The seepage was hard to see in the
weeds, but I was willing to bet that the back of the
white shirt the dead man wore was now blood red.
Without thinking, I began to cast my eyes around the
area.

As if reading my mind, Sol said, "Yeah. There could
be a gun or a knife somewhere around. This poor bastard must be one of those impersonators. Like the guy
at the dedication, remember? What was his name?"

"Sol." The way I dragged out that syllable reminded
my beloved that I did not appreciate being asked a
question which he should have known I would not be
able to answer. Not anymore. Life had become one long
senior moment. As a result, names that my brain used to

file away until I signaled for them to be zoomed to the
tip of my tongue were no longer on call. But I certainly
did remember the party Hoboken threw to dedicate
Frank Sinatra Park. And hearing the young man dressed
in the manner of the Chairman belt out "New York,
New York" on a starlit spring night with the skyline sil-
houetted in the background had been the highlight of an
evening of highs. A master showman, he'd first written
and then performed for us an extended monologue
called "The Little Town Blues Years," about, of course,
the years Frank had spent growing up in Hoboken.

My reverie was interrupted by Sol announcing,
"Here they come" and pointing at a police car weaving
between the joggers and strollers. The driver pulled to a
stop at the sight of Sol waving him over.

"Shit, man," exclaimed the shorter of the two officers
as soon as he parted the weeds and glimpsed the corpse.
"That's Louie Palumbo."

Hoboken's always been a family town in spite of its
colonization in the eighties by condo owners who now
overflow the suddenly trendy eateries and bars. It's literally a "mile square city" and the B&Rs, those born
and raised here, know one another. As soon as the officer spoke, I recognized the name I had been struggling
to recall. As the officers cordoned off the area and a
photographer arrived and began taking pictures, I heard
Sol explaining how we had stumbled upon the body.

Hearing the officer name the corpse had also brought
home the fact that the dead man at our feet had a family,
a mom and dad, a sibling. In fact, we had met the Palumbos at the dedication. They had turned out in force to see
their Louie pay homage to Frank, the original native son.
I felt my eyes fill up for the second time that day as I pictured the senior Palumbos, proud and humble at the same
time, a stance characteristic of immigrant parents whose
offspring have made their American dream come true,

and so validated the older generation's struggle. Wearing a green linen dress, Mrs. Palumbo smiled modestly and repeated, "From when he was little, Louie always loved Frank." Apparently the Palumbos had another son who had made good, because she beamed at the bearded, ponytailed man standing next to her and said, "This here's Louie's twin brother, Danny. My Danny, he's a teacher." Mrs. Palumbo uttered the word *teacher* with the same solemnity and reverence she would have used had her offspring grown up to become the Pope. The young man at her side rolled his eyes, clearly a time-honored response to his mother's unabashed pride. I remember noting how his low-key response contrasted with that of the youngest Palumbo, a knobby-kneed little girl of about four. Clutching a Beanie Baby leopard and yanking on Mr. Palumbo Sr.'s hand, the child whined over and over, "Nono, dance with me. Come on, Nono, puhlease," while her grinning grandpa gave left-handed handshakes and one-armed hugs to a circle of his son's admirers. The Palumbos' universe was about to be shattered forever.

I blotted my tears with Kleenex, relieved that Sol was talking to the cops. Even after another police car arrived, tears continued to wash down my cheeks. I had been like this for a few years. Unlike people of the Renaissance who believed that during pregnancy, menstrual blood was transformed into breast milk, I was convinced that mine had all been distilled into tears because my postmenopausal body secreted tears at the slightest provocation. But, I reminded myself, a dead young man was not "slight" provocation. Not to the Palumbos anyway. A final glance at Louie Palumbo's corpse, seemingly afloat in blood and beginning to interest early summer flies, was all the attitude adjustment this mother needed. Rebecca and Mark were alive and healthy. What else mattered?

Chapter 3

To: Bbarrett@circle.com
From: ToniD@venus.net
Re: Conference
Date: Sun, 28 Jun 1998 13:44:07

Dear Professor Barrett,

I'm sorry but I won't be able to make the conference we are supposed to have tomorrow. I'll let you know when I can reschedule. I'm really sorry for the inconvenience.

Toni Demaio

After promising the police we'd stop at headquarters later to go over their report and sign it, Sol and I walked home, shaken and a bit dazed. "Christ, Bel. We haven't even had breakfast yet and we've already weathered a parental crisis and found a corpse," he said quietly, taking my hand. "Let's get something to eat at least."

Actually I really wished we could go back home and leap into bed and make passionate life-affirming love to refute the grim reaper who had dared to surprise us on our stroll. Death may be an aphrodisiac as they say, but if you have adult kids living at home, sex has to be scheduled. A spontaneous Sunday afternoon session in the sack was bound to inspire embarrassing scrutiny. Besides, Sol looked pale. We'd better get something to eat. Anyway, eating was right up there with sex as a life affirmer. We could both use a little comfort food. "Good idea. Let's have brunch at Tania's."

Tania's is an Eastern European restaurant in run-down downtown Jersey City that has recently opened its courtyard to diners. There beneath shade trees you can sit sequestered from the grit and noise of the neighborhood. And you can eat a real breakfast, not what Sol disparagingly labels "yuppie food." We made a pit stop at home and I e-mailed Rebecca. That's when I saw Toni's message. A blip sounded in my brain. Something about Toni Demaio. And that's when Sol suggested, "Hey, let's ask Sadie and Sofia if they want to join us. I told them I'd take them grocery shopping later today anyway. Your mother loves Tania's." I sighed. After my dad's death, Sol and my mother had made peace and were now best buddies. Most of the time this was a blessing I was smart enough to appreciate, but that day I really didn't feel like sharing Sol with anybody, even Ma and her housemate Sofia.

But Sol was right. The Sunday schlep to the super-market had become a ritual, replacing leisurely brunches in the Village and gallery browsing. If we didn't do it sooner, one of us would have to go later. The price of wresting their car keys from these two octogenarians who turned into demon drivers for Satan behind the wheel was a willingness to chauffeur. At least today we'd have something to talk about with them besides how they had or had not beaten the one-armed bandits in Atlantic City this week or how Sofia's granddaughter's latest effort at breast pumping was going. It was going to be hard not to spill the beans about Rebecca's revelations, but I figured I could do it if I kept my mouth full of breakfast. Sadie could wait a few hours to learn that in a few months she too could chat casually about her own granddaughter's lactation.

When I called Ma, she said, "We ate breakfast already, but we could do with a little lunch before we go shopping. Are you sure we won't be a bother? Is Mark coming?" Even though her words were equivocal, the lift in her voice let me know how pleased she was to get the invitation, and I instantly regretted my reluctance to extend it. I left Mark a note, and then Sol and I picked up the Odd Couple. That's what he had taken to calling Ma and Sofia. Sofia had initiated their friendship by passing Ma a roll of toilet paper under the partition in the ladies' room of the Grand Street Senior Citizens' Center two years ago. In less time than it takes to feed a coin to a one-armed bandit, the two inveterate gamblers had bonded, and Sofia invited Ma to share her apartment in the row house where she had raised her family. Each brought to their friendship the same ritualized bickering she had enjoyed in her marriage. Sofia Dellafemina and Sadie Bickoff squabbled constantly. In that sense, they were probably no odder than most other couples.

They sure didn't look odd. They looked great. Every silvery strand of Ma's close-cropped hair was in place and her denim wrap skirt and floral print blouse were as crisp and bright as they had been in 1978 when she bought them. She carried a straw bag that matched her vintage straw wedges. There was little trace of the deranged widow crippled by arthritis and grief who had moved in with us just a couple of years ago. Modern medicine, companionship, and time had conspired with Ma's gutsy grit to heal her body and mind. Sofia was equally splendid, her blond curls gleaming, her deep pink linen sheath hugging her tiny waist, and her white high-heeled pumps showing off her still shapely legs. In spite of the fact that Sofia looked spiffy enough for lunch at the White House, I knew that in her white clutch bag there would be a detailed grocery list and a cache of coupons. And so we drove to Tania's, where I hoped to recover from the morning's events over fresh OJ and challah French toast with a slab of ham and eggs over easy on the side.

". . . so there he was, the poor bastard. He must have been stabbed. And then, whoever did it pushed him over the rail up at Stevens. That's what happened, don't you think?" Sol inquired between slugs of juice and forkfuls of French toast slathered with syrup. He had just finished recounting the tale of our discovery, correctly assuming that the gory story would fully engage his audience. Breakfast had been a good idea. Much of the color had returned to his face, but Sofia's cheeks had paled and she had stopped eating, resting her fork delicately beside the plate of cheese blintzes she and Ma were sharing.

"Louie Palumbo. That's one of Tess and Joe's twins. He grew up by me." She crossed herself quickly. Of course. I should have realized that. Sofia was B&R. After living over twenty years in Hoboken, Sol and I were still considered as transient as tourists by those born and raised here. The story of Louie Palumbo was more than just gossip to Sofia. It was a neighborhood tragedy. I knew that in a matter of hours she would be home, an apron over her dress, padding about the kitchen in her slippers, making sauce and stuffing shells to take to Tess and Joe. I saw Sadie reach over and pat her friend's arm even as she snapped, "The trouble with you is, you know everybody." As I savored the fresh orange juice, another image suddenly displaced the one of poor Louie Palumbo's bloody body that had relodged in my brain. It was the face of Toni Demaio.

"You know, one of my students—" I began by way of an admittedly oblique response to Sofia's distress. I was working on my eggs first so I could sop up the yolk with the toast.

"Jesus, Bel. Give it a break. Let's leave your damn students out of this for a change. This poor guy wasn't ever your student, was he?" I had to smile. Sol looked so pained at the possibility that the deceased just might have been one of the legions of my former students who popped up almost everywhere we went and whom I talked about the rest of the time. Like many people married to teachers, he got a little tired of hearing about students.

"No. I never taught him. But listen. I think one of my students was involved with him. Seriously involved." I pictured the angelic Toni Demaio. With black wire-rimmed glasses, shining brown hair, and glowing complexion, she looked like an intellectual Madonna. When Sol didn't cut me off, I continued. "She's actually doing an independent study with me in summer school. Remember I told you I was working with a student who needs to take Intro to Women's Studies in order to graduate but that it isn't offered during the summer?" Sol nodded and sipped his coffee, a resigned expression vying with one of total satiety on his face. He leaned back, waiting for the inevitable saga. "Well, she's very bright, very creative. And she's doing a really original project. I'm excited about it. She has most of her research done, so I'm just helping her put the paper together. Actually, I think she met Louis Palumbo while she was doing her research." I paused, watching the sunlight turn the mug of tea I was holding into liquid amber. Tea in glass mugs was another Tania's touch I especially appreciated.

"What's she researching? The Three Hundred Wives of Frank Sinatra?" I was grateful for Sol's interest, so I forgave him his snide tone. I even forgave Ma for honoring his remark with a smile. At the time I didn't notice the withering look Sofia shot him. He didn't either.

"You're not far off the mark. She's doing a paper on the most important woman in Frank's life. She's writing about Dolly Sinatra as a prefeminist icon," I replied, again picturing Toni earnestly explaining her project to me at our first conference.

"Who the hell is Dolly Sinatra?" I reminded myself that Sol's favorite musician was another Italian named Domenico Scarlatti, and I didn't know beans about *his* mother.

"Frank's mother." When Sol looked as if he were about to laugh, I held up my hand. "Before you crack up, let me explain." Sol had yet to come to terms with the fact that in the wake of the ideological hurricane otherwise known as the sixties that swept through academia, no subject was too domestic or too quotidian for scholarly study and analysis, including Frank Sinatra's mother. Looking up, Sol signaled our waiter for beverage refills, settled back in his chair, and almost succeeded in repressing a smile.

"Just what is so special about Frank Sinatra's mother?" Sol sputtered, his mouth straight, but his eyes teasing.

"I'm telling you. Just listen." Fortified by another swig of English Breakfast tea, I began. "You see . . ."

"No, you listen. I'll tell you what was so special about Dolly." It was Sofia, her pale cheeks suddenly flushed, her words crisp, her voice sharp. "You newcomers think you're so smart. Think all us old-timers are just a bunch of geezers and babushkas, don't you? What do you think? All us Italian mamas spend all day by the stove stirring gravy and got our kids tied to us with umbilical cords of linguini?" I blushed since a few minutes ago I had, in fact, been picturing Sofia stirring sauce. And, in fact, her kids and grandkids always leave her house staggering beneath the weight of huge trays of ravioli and manicotti and other goodies. As Sol and I sat there, two trays of Sofia's incomparable eggplant parmagiana graced our freezer.

"I actually thought it was just you who did all that cooking," said Ma facetiously.

Oblivious to my guilt and ignoring Ma's tweak, Sofia went on, "Dolly Sinatra was different. I remember Dolly." Sofia paused, pushed away her half-eaten blintz, and sipped her coffee. Satisfied that she had our attention, she put the mug down and continued. "Dolly was before her time. My mother said even as a kid, Dolly used to dress up as a boy so she could get in to watch her brothers box. And she was from a really comfortable Genovese family. That's in the north of Italy," Sofia added for the benefit of an audience she clearly considered ignorant. "But she eloped with Frank's father who was from a working-class Sicilian family. She married him in a civil ceremony without her parents' knowledge or consent. That was pretty daring for a nice Catholic girl in those days." She cast a glance at Sol, checking to see if he was taking her seriously.

And he was. Sol was always intrigued by people who flouted convention. Ma was hooked also, always intrigued by tales of family tension. Braced by another infusion of caffeine, Sofia spoke quickly. "And after she was married, Dolly didn't sit home and stir the gravy either. She went overseas and worked as a nurse during World War One. It wasn't till after she came back that she had Frank." Sofia pronounced the star's given name as if it were a magical incantation. Then she leaned back in her chair and smiled, savoring the moment of pride and pleasure that articulating that syllable evoked in almost all Hoboken natives. For once unconcerned that her bright pink lipstick had disappeared, Sofia took up her narrative again. "But Dolly still worked outside the home. She was a chocolate dipper in a factory on weekends. The best dipper in the plant from what I heard. But even that wasn't enough for her. She also became a midwife." Here Sofia looked down for a second and then, squaring her shoulders, continued. "She performed abortions when poor women who couldn't afford one more mouth to feed came to her. Believe me, this was hard on the family. A lot of people disapproved. Not that it was any of their business. But she did what she thought was right."

"Seems to me I did see something about that in the paper around when Frank died," Sol added, sipping his coffee. "I didn't think much about it."

"So get to the point already. Honest to God, you tell a story like we're going to live forever," Ma fumed. But she was as intrigued as the rest of us by Dolly's adventures.

Shrugging her shoulders at Sol's obvious lack of insight and Ma's impatience alike, Sofia said, "There's more to Dolly though. She knew all the different dialects spoken by Italians living in Hoboken." Sofia tapped on the table with the bright pink nail of her index finger, emphasizing Dolly's linguistic prowess. ". . . and she got herself a political career from that. She could bring in votes for whichever Irish pol was running city hall. In return, she got jobs for her husband, other relatives, friends, neighbors, whoever." Sofia stopped for breath.

"Sounds like an early version of the superwoman, right?" interjected Ma, clearly impressed by Dolly's many talents.

"Yeah. She must have been a real ball boosteh," Sol exclaimed, using the Yiddish term reserved to describe strong and accomplished women. " 'Cause back in the thirties and forties, Hoboken was an Irish town. Italians in Hoboken couldn't risk being seen east of Willow Street for fear of being picked up by the Irish cops and maybe even deported."

"That's right." Sofia was obviously pleased by Sol's and Ma's reaction to her story because she kept right on going. "But Dolly didn't look Italian. With those blue eyes and that light hair, she could pass." Sofia paused only a second before continuing. "On top of all that, Dolly ran a saloon too. It was in her husband's name, but that was just because back then women weren't allowed to own bars. Believe me, Dolly ran it. She was a little bit of a thing, but she tossed out anyone who was too drunk to behave." Finally Sofia stopped talking and sat back, a satisfied smile hinting that perhaps her own self-worth had expanded as she recounted Dolly's accomplishments.

I took out a Post-it and scribbled a note reminding myself to suggest to Toni that she interview Sofia, clearly an untapped mine of information on Dolly Sinatra. "Poor Toni," I said, again envisioning the bloody body we'd left by the side of the road. "She seemed pretty serious about this guy. Toni lives in North Bergen, but she grew up in Hoboken. Her last name is Demaio," I added primarily for Sofia's benefit. I was rewarded by a nod. "Actually, her family originally comes from Genoa too," I elaborated, remembering Toni laying out her project, her face full of excitement, her words bumping into one another.

"So why isn't she doing her paper on salami?" Sol's crude dig didn't stop me but it did earn him another dirty look from Sofia and a groan from Ma. I tossed my crumpled-up napkin at his chest. Catching it adroitly before it hit the ground, he said, "So go on."

"Well, Frank's mother's family and the Demaios lived in the same neighborhood."

"Right around the corner on Adams," Sofia inter-jected. "The Demaio family has a butcher shop. It's still there." The waiter began clearing away our dishes.

"I've never understood how there can be so many neighborhoods in a town that measures only one square mile," Sol remarked as the waiter left carrying our scraped and swabbed plates.

Ignoring Sol's aside, I continued, "Anyway, Toni grew up listening to stories about Frank her whole life. And when she got older, the stories she heard about Dolly made her curious. So she decided to do her women's studies project on Dolly, and that's how she met Louie Palumbo. They met in the Hoboken Public Library while she was doing research in the Sinatra archives there." Sol winced at the notion of Sinatra archives anywhere. "Because Louie Palumbo's an imper-sonator, he's become a Sinatra expert. He helped Toni find information and got people to talk to her. He defi-nitely is the local Sinatra guru."

"*Was*, you mean," added Sol, walking behind us as we made our way to the front door of the restaurant and into the street. "Poor guy."

Sol and I arrived home from the shopping expedition and the police station much later that afternoon. Mark was lying on the couch in the living room in his boxers feeding himself Froot Loops straight from the box with one hand and flicking the remote with the other as he channel surfed on a portable TV. Because Sol and I don't own a TV, Mark had persuaded his grandmother to buy him this one for his birthday years ago. "Easy, Bel," muttered Sol, giving me a squeeze on the shoulder and disappearing upstairs. There was no way he was going to get caught in the crossfire that often passed for conversation between my son and me since Mark had moved back home.

Sol knew only too well how walking in on this domestic diorama featuring Mark in his natural habitat affected me lately. The kid was pushing at least three of my buttons. Television was the invention of the devil. Every nanosecond a person spent in front of the tube edged the poor addict a little closer to the abyss of illiteracy. Froot Loops were contemporary hemlock. I might have gone out and invited death by indulging in a breakfast that my nutritionally correct friends labeled "cholesterol on a plate," but I had never countenanced Froot Loops in the house. And lying around all day could only be justified if one had just spent the week in the Siberian salt mines and had a medical excuse.

"Yo, Ma, what's going on? Thanks for the Tania's invite but it just wasn't going to happen this morning." Having offered that inspiring conversational gambit, my secondborn stretched, yawned, smiled lazily at me, and resumed munching and flicking. Lips compressed, I handed him the container of Tania's cheese pirogi his grandmother had insisted we bring him and moved toward the computer to check my e-mail.

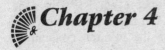# Chapter 4

To: Bbarrett@circle.com
From: Lbarrett@squarepeg.com
Re: Rebecca
Date: Sun, 28 Jun 1998 18:16:14

Bel,

Are you crazy? Why are you encouraging this ridiculous match?
Becky is still in school and that kid, what's his name, the one she
ran away with, is a total fuck-up if you ask me. Did he ever finish
college? I told you, he lives in Seattle and he doesn't even know
what the Sonics are. He parks his bicycle in the kitchen of their
apartment for Chrissake. Next thing you know she'll be telling me
she's pregnant. If she insists on going through with this, I'm not
going to give her one more penny for tuition. And I expect you to
discourage it. Better yet, get Mark to talk some sense into her. And
get back to me ASAP. You know it's allergy season now, and I just
came off tax season. I don't need any more stress.

                                        Leonard Barrett, CPA
                                        Your taxes are my business

My friends Illuminada and Betty were taking turns
reading aloud particularly choice sentences from a
printout of Lenny's e-mail message as they passed it
back and forth over a late lunch at the RIP Diner the
next day. "*Como mierda*, Bel! This is one sick *hombre*," exclaimed Illuminada, flicking the printout contemptu-
ously with the perfect cerise oval nail of her index
finger. I sometimes tease her by asking if her talons get
in the way when she has to pull the trigger because,
believe it or not, this elegantly coifed and manicured
fashion plate is a crack private investigator who packs
heat in more ways than one. I had met her when she
first started teaching part-time in the Criminal Justice
Department at RECC. "I thought we were just getting
together today to figure out who's bringing what to
your house on the Fourth. I didn't expect to have to do
double duty as a family therapist *and* party planner."

"You ain't seen nothin' yet, girl. Just wait until this
doofus hears his daughter is pregnant!" exclaimed
Betty, pushing the printout back in my direction. "Illuminada's right, Bel. I go away for one lousy week and
when I come back, your entire family is rehearsing for
the *Jerry Springer Show*. So what are you going to say
to Rebecca when you talk to her tonight?" Ever practical, Betty was zeroing in on what mattered. Her ability
to cut to the chase was just one of the qualities that
made her indispensable to Ron Woodman, president of
River Edge Community College. The other was her
drive to take charge. Betty was supposed to be Woodman's executive assistant, but everybody at RECC
knew who really called the shots.

"What can I tell her? I love her. I'll try to help them.
I'm dying to ask how she plans to finish school *and*
have a baby. I'm dying to ask if Keith intends to get a
real job or at least a second job. I'd love to know if her

student medical insurance covers prenatal care and delivery expenses, ha ha. Or, for that matter, if his family can help with expenses." Responding to the disapproving glares on both my friends' faces, I raised my hands in a gesture of mock protection. "But relax. I'm not going to hit them with twenty questions tonight. I'll stick to prenatal care and the wedding." Signifying their approval of my strategy, Betty and Illuminada nodded in unison. I paused, picking up the printout on the table. "And I'll tell her to tell Lenny about the baby. She usually plays him like a flute though, so she probably figured he'd need a day or two to calm down before she told him about the coming attractions." Then, my voice crackling with sarcasm, I added, "Maybe I'll have Uncle Mark talk some sense into his father."

"Oh give that poor kid a break, Bel. He'll get it together. Just remember how much you wanted him home." It was Betty again, reminding me of how worried I'd been about Mark when he'd done his postcollegiate trip to Israel during the year when the tiny country became a human minefield. "And remember how he almost married that Israeli woman? The thirty-something ex-army type who was going to follow Mark home and move in with you, but up and married the Australian cricket player instead?"

"*Dios mio*, that had to be hard on Mark. Betty's right, *chiquita*. You expect too much of him. He just needs some time. That's all. And when he gets ready, he'll be up and out and doing something useful with all those languages he speaks. He'll be teaching or interpreting or something. You'll see. He's really a good kid," Illuminada said reasonably.

"Would you like to have him camp on your couch for a year or so while he finds his way?" I asked sweetly, giving Illuminada a poke in the arm as I spoke. "I didn't think so. You two know perfectly well that if Randy or Lourdes vegged out the way Mark is, you'd both be hysterical."

"Yeah. And you'd be the first one to tell us to cool it. Remember how you two practically bound and gagged me after Randy totaled the car?" Betty giggled, recalling a particularly militant stance she had taken in response to news of her son's accident.

"*Caramba!* There are laws about capital punishment for careless minors, you know. You actually said, 'If he's not hurt, I'm going to kill him,' " recalled Illuminada, picking daintily at her tuna salad. "You know, it's interesting, Bel. You and Lenny aren't too far apart on Rebecca's marriage except for his really unfortunate way of expressing himself." Illuminada was too perceptive sometimes.

"Yeah. I know. And that worries me. Whenever I find myself seeing something the way he does, I always rethink my position," I admitted, alternating sips of iced tea with forkfuls of tuna salad. "Sol pointed that out too."

"So now that you're a little calmer, could we talk about something besides your dysfunctional family and your total failure as a mother for a minute?" It was Betty, her fork poised over *her* tuna salad, the air kiss she blew me tempering the bite of her words. "Remember that young man who performed at the Sinatra Park dedication? Gina told me she read in this morning's paper that he was murdered." I could tell from the way she scanned our faces for a reaction that Betty thought her clerk-typist, a legendary font of rumor, gossip, and occasional information, had given her the scoop on this tidbit.

"*Dios mio*, probably somebody who couldn't stand the way he sang," cracked Illuminada. "He should've stuck to acting. Remember I said he looked like Frank and he had Frank's moves and his lingo down pat, but he sure couldn't sing like Frank?" What I remembered was Illuminada holding her nose as Raoul spun her around under the stars and the late Louie Palumbo hammered out a tortured version of "Mack the Knife."

"Vic figured Palumbo should have been able to talk the talk, growing up in Frank's backyard practically, and I agreed with him." Betty still glowed when she talked about Vic, the affable undertaker she'd fallen in love with a couple of years ago when we were looking into the murder of his brother, an adjunct at RECC. Now she had another man besides her son and her boss to push around. She and Vic had been something to see on the dance floor that night. I remember that Sol and I were face to face again after a vigorous Chubby Checker maneuver, all the dancing either of us knew how to do, when Vic and Betty stomped by. Vic was smiling good-naturedly while his lips mouthed the count and Betty literally bopped circles around him, clapping and swaying. "That white boy sings like this one dances," was what she'd snapped as she somehow managed to steer Vic around the floor without touching him. Vic often joked that he just loved the view from under Betty's thumb.

It had been an unexpectedly magical evening for me. Part of the magic came from the realization of how privileged Sol and I were to have found each other, to have made such close and caring friends, and to be in such a truly glorious place with them, having such a good time. The years have taught me to recognize great memories in the making, and that evening was certainly one of them. The rest of the magic came from pure nostalgia. I was transported back to my girlhood in New Jersey in the fifties when hearing The Voice croon the opening lines of "All the Way" had moved me to acts of what passed for abandon then in the backseat of Teddy Lichenstein's father's new T-bird.

I was not alone. With Louie Palumbo as a tour guide, many of us at the Sinatra Park dedication that night had made our way down memory lane. From where Sol and I had stood at the periphery of the crowd, the performer at center stage was Frank. The cocked fedora and the rolled-up sleeves of his white shirt were Frank's. The saunter that had not yet evolved into the signature swagger was the young Frank's. And the lingual dental disasters that turned every *this* to *dis* and every *them* to *dem* were Frank's. And they were all of ours too because most of us singing along and dancing at the river's edge that night were just a generation away from the immigrant's diction that Frank Sinatra had made cool.

I forced myself back to the present to add, "Actually, I did hear about it because guess who nearly tripped over the body while he was strolling with his distraught life partner on Sinatra Drive yesterday?" I have to confess that self-importance had enlivened my voice and straightened my back as I posed this query.

"You're not serious?" Betty slapped the table in disbelief.

"*Caramba*! I would have loved to have seen Sol's face! Did he try to recycle it?" Illuminada joked, referring to Sol's well-known penchant for environmental correctness.

"Well, he was pretty upset, actually. So was I, especially after we figured out who the poor guy was. We had met his folks and everything at the dedication.

Not only that, but I realized that he was involved with a student of mine. She's going to be pretty broken up." Again I thought of Toni Demaio and wondered how she was doing. I took out a Post-it and scrawled on it the words "Condolence note to Toni Demaio." "Later in the day we had to go to police headquarters and sign the report, and the cop on duty there said they were literally clueless about who might have killed him."

"Give them a little time," said Illuminada. "Speaking of time, I'm sorry I can't sit here all afternoon and hear more about your lovely weekend, Bel, but some of us work for a living," Illuminada added, looking at her watch and taking some singles out of her purse. "Here," she said, throwing the ones on the table and getting up.

"I've got to go too. I don't like leaving you-know-who alone in the office too long. He gets everything all confused." Betty's patronizing reference to the president of the college where we both worked was not lost on me. She went on, "But before we go, tell us what you want us to bring to your barbecue on the Fourth." Betty was organizing us as usual. "Vic wants to grill a whole salmon, and I plan to make baked beans," she announced before I could utter a word.

"My mother's making her flan and Raoul is going to do some roast pork," Illuminada said, winking just before she turned and left the diner, clearly delighted that her mom was, as usual, saving her the trouble of doing any cooking at all.

"And then there's my mother," I said, literally throwing up my hands. Illuminada's reference to her mother gave me an excuse to return to what was really on my mind. "My mother thinks it's just wonderful that Rebecca's getting married and having a baby. Can you believe it?" I asked Betty rhetorically. "Rebecca and Mark just plain walk on water as far as she's concerned. And this is the same Sadie Bickoff whose idea of sex ed was to tell me if I ever came home pregnant, life as we know it on this planet would end."

"That's what being a grandmother is all about," Betty said, smiling, as we stood up. "You'll see."

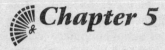

Chapter 5

**SINATRA STAND-IN FOUND STABBED,
LAW STUDENT SUSPECTED**

HOBOKEN—Strollers Sol Hecht and Bel Barrett stumbled across the bloody body of Louis Palumbo on Sinatra Drive yesterday. Palumbo, 32, a Hoboken native, had made a name for himself impersonating Frank Sinatra at events all over the Garden State. "We were just out for a walk, enjoying the day. I bent down to pick a wild flower for Bel and saw a shoe. I thought it was trash. I was angry to think that someone would litter the roadside, so I kicked it. It didn't move, and when we looked closer, we saw him lying there in a pool of his own blood," recalls Hecht. "We called the cops right away."

According to the police, the body appears to have several stab wounds, but no weapon has been found. An autopsy is scheduled for later this week. Officers are questioning Seton Hall law student John Cardino, former fiancé of Mr. Palumbo's girlfriend, Antoinette Demaio. Mr. Palumbo is survived by his parents, Theresa and Joseph Palumbo of Hoboken, and a twin brother, Daniel Palumbo, music teacher at Hoboken High.

Funeral services will be held on Friday, July 3, at 11 a.m. at the Garibaldi Bros. Funeral Home at 422 Willow Avenue in Hoboken. There will be viewings on Thursday, July 2, between 2 p.m. and 5 p.m. and between 7 p.m. and 9 p.m.

Wendy was brandishing the *Jersey City Herald* when I got to my office. She had just finished teaching her late morning children's lit class and was getting ready to leave. Because I was teaching an evening section of speech that summer, I often missed her. But that day I arrived early so as to have a few hours of peace in the office before class. Mark was practicing guitar at home, and the twang of blues blasted through my study. I was trying to complete a paper for grad school that I hoped would evolve into a dissertation proposal. Surely hearing even one more Jimi Hendrix–inspired riff would drive all thoughts on "The Impact of the Personal on the Pedagogy of College Faculty" forever from my mind. The tiny cubicle Wendy and I shared in the English Department at RECC was a sanctuary. "So you and Sol are tripping over dead bodies now," Wendy said, pointing at the paper. I choked up a little when I saw the publicity headshot of Louis Palumbo and skimmed the article.

"Yeah. Can you believe that? Poor guy." I reread the line about how the police were questioning a suspect. They must have latched on to him after we had visited headquarters.

"Sounds like a crime of passion. Jealous lover stabs rival, kind of 'Frankie and Johnny.' Isn't the Demaio girl the same one you're working with on an independent study? The serious one with the dark hair and glasses who's into Dolly Sinatra?" Wendy was gathering her books as she spoke.

"The very same. Poor kid. She must be so unhappy.
Keep reminding me, I want to write her a note or send
her a card or something. She canceled her appointment
with me for today. Small wonder. I guess I won't see
her until after the funeral." I was taking my laptop out
of my book bag. Wendy and I often joked about being
ships that passed in the night as we alternated our hours
in the tiny office. It was a system that had worked for
over two decades. On the rare occasions when we were
both there, we each got less done. Part of that was
because of the small space, but part of it was also
because as old friends, we couldn't resist chatting.

"Blues getting to you again? I thought you *liked* Jimi
Hendrix," Wendy said with a grin, having put up with
my whining about Mark's practice sessions for months.

"I did," I said. "But enough is enough already. Do
you know that sometimes he plays the same thing five
or six times? I just wish he'd get a job and an apartment
and then a nice steady girl, you know, a life." I sighed.

"Bel, he's only twenty-three. And he does temp. Tell
him to practice when you're not home." Wendy was
trying to help. *Her* twenty-six-year-old son Sean had a
job and an apartment and was dating his sister's best
friend.

"Then he'd watch TV and eat Froot Loops all day.
Just the thought of that would drive me nuts." I sighed.
"When we go for our next walk, I'll tell you what his
adorable sister is up to now. I can't wait to hear the
excuses you're going to make for her." Wendy's daughter Ann had always been a poster child for parental
wish fulfillment. And now with another whole year to
go in college, she had already been recruited by the lit-
erary agency she was interning for this summer. They
couldn't wait to hire her full-time. Neither of Wendy's
kids had followed a heartthrob three thousand miles,

was anticipating an unplanned parenthood, needed "direction," whatever that was, or, God forbid, ate Froot Loops. What did she know?

After Wendy left, I was relieved to escape into the world that graduate school had opened to me. Weaving together everything I'd been reading on the relationship between the personal and the pedagogical, I was struggling to express complex ideas in well-crafted, jargon-free sentences when my office phone rang. I picked it up on the first ring. "Professor Barrett," I announced.

"Oh! Professor Barrett! You're there. I was expecting the machine. Oh! I'm so glad. This is Toni Demaio, Professor." I was surprised to hear Toni's slightly breathy voice.

"Why yes. Hello Toni. I'm so sorry about Louis. I've been thinking about you. I was just going to drop you a note." This was not really a lie. I fully intended to send Toni a message of condolence.

"Professor Barrett, I need to talk to you." Toni's voice quavered a little. Then it was steady again. "I shouldn't have canceled our conference."

"Now Toni, don't worry about your project this week. You're way ahead of schedule anyway. Understandably you could use a breather," I advised in what I hoped was a soothing manner. "We can meet next week after the funeral." Some students routinely requested extensions of deadlines to accommodate family and/or work crises while a few others would go to great lengths to turn work in on time. Obviously Toni fell into the latter category.

"It's not about my project," Toni said quickly. "Listen, I'm going to be in Hoboken later today to pay my respects to Louie's family. Can I meet you somewhere? I just need to talk to you." Toni's voice was softer now, as if she feared being overheard.

"I don't get out of class until nine tonight. Is that too late?" I never have learned how to say no to a student in distress. And Toni was an exceptional student going through a difficult time. Before she could answer me, I continued, "You could meet me at my home at 205 Park at about nine-thirty."

"That's fine. I'll go to the Palumbos around eight. Thank you, Professor Barrett."

At first Sol wasn't thrilled that I had invited a student home, but when I told him it was Toni Demaio, his curiosity overcame his resentment at the intrusion. He answered the door when she rang the bell, expressed his condolences, and offered to make iced tea or lemonade. "Lemonade sounds good, nice and cool," said Toni, her eyes red and her voice subdued. I could not help but be amused at how cleverly Sol had found a way to remain in the kitchen, where Toni and I had settled on stools around the counter. She didn't seem perturbed by his presence, and before I had a chance to offer my own condolences or, for that matter, to say much of anything, she blurted out, "Oh, Professor Barrett, I'm so miserable." With that she folded her arms on the counter, lowered her head, and began to bawl. Sol and I looked at each other across the kitchen. The young woman's slender body was heaving with the force of her sobs. With one hand she removed her glasses and shoved them away from her. I began patting her shoulder while Sol busied himself with the juicer. In a few minutes, Toni's sobs became hiccups and she looked up. I pushed a box of Kleenex in front of her at the same time that Sol produced three tall glasses of lemonade over ice.

After a few seconds of swabbing, sniffling, and sipping, Toni reached for her glasses and adjusted them behind her ears as if to say, "Well that's over. Now I'll

talk." And talk she did. "Professor Barrett, I'm so sorry
to bother you, and you too, Mr. Barrett." In the throes of
her misery, Toni had obviously not registered Sol's
name. Neither of us bothered to correct her. We both
made lots of "not a problem" noises, and Toni continued. "Louie and I were going to get married. And now
he's dead." For us, this repetition of the obvious was a
slow start, but I had conferred with enough distraught
students over the years to know that repeating the
unthinkable was a necessary first step toward making it
real and, ultimately, accepting it.

"You met while you were doing your research,
right? In the Sinatra archives?" I knew she was going
to want to tell her tale from the beginning, so I tried to
cue her.

"Yes. It was in the archives. Louie knew everything
about the Sinatras. It was awesome how much he knew.
And he was so helpful." A new teardrop was forming in
the corner of her reddened eye.

At the sight of this harbinger of yet another parox-
ysm of sobs, I quickly interjected a question, "I guess it
was love at first sight, wasn't it?"

Big mistake. I could read Sol's critique of my ill-
chosen line of inquiry when I saw him shaking his head.
We waited for Toni to regain control of herself. "No,
actually, I was engaged to someone else when I met
Louie. A really awesome guy I've known for years, the
boy next door actually." Toni smiled at the absurdity of
this cliche, and a wayward teardrop slipped from her
lash and splattered on the counter. After swiping at the
tiny puddle with a Kleenex, she took a sip of her lemonade and continued. "Well, anyway, my former fiancé—
John is his name—is a law student. One night last
December, he was studying for finals, so he couldn't go
to a concert at city hall in Hoboken that this other Frank

Sinatra impersonator, somebody new in town, was giving. It was to celebrate Frank's eighty-second birthday. Louie wanted to go to check out the competition, you know? He was a little surprised not to be asked to do that gig himself, or at least to share it." Toni shook her head, recalling the logic of the dead man, and forged ahead with her story. "So I invited him to use John's ticket, and we went together. It was there, that night, listening to Luke Jonas singing 'All the Way,' that Louie and I fell in love." For a second my eyes glazed over, and once again I was in the backseat of Teddy Lichenstein's father's new T-bird with Frank crooning over the radio about how glad he was to be near me.

Neither Toni nor Sol had noticed my moment of private tribute to The Voice. When I tuned them in again, Toni was saying, "So right after that I, you know, I broke off my engagement to John. It was only right." For a moment I felt a pang of empathy with the Demaios, who had probably had some difficulty understanding why their bright and lovely twenty-two-year-old daughter would prefer a thirty-something tone-deaf Frank Sinatra wanna-be to a future lawyer. But had the future lawyer been so unhinged by the loss of his ladylove that he had stabbed his rival in the back several times and then pushed him over the palisade? Apparently Toni didn't think so.

"But, look." Toni had reached for the tiny shoulder bag she had hung over the back of the stool and was rooting about in it. "This is terrible. It just makes everything worse." She pulled out a creased copy of a newspaper article, the same one that Wendy had shown me earlier. "Look. They actually think John killed Louie."

"What do you think?" It was Sol's first contribution to what had been a dialogue between Toni and me. I was surprised to hear his deep voice enter the conversation. "It wouldn't be the first time the green-eyed monster got some guy in over his head."

Toni looked at me, puzzlement clouding her tear-blotched features. "Huh? What are you trying to say? John's not a monster."

"It's a metaphor," I offered, "for jealousy. That's the green-eyed monster. Sol's suggesting that maybe jealousy drove John to murder Louie."

"But John would never ever do that. Not in a million years. And that's why I came here tonight. The police questioned him for hours. John's parents look at me like I'm dirt now, and even my own mother says everything's my fault. Louie's parents too. They looked at me tonight like I wasn't really there. And his brother, Danny, too. It's bad enough I lost Louie, but I can't stand to see poor John blamed for something he would never do." Toni's head went down again onto the cradle of her arms, her glasses found their way back onto the counter, and her gulping sobs rasped loud in the quiet kitchen.

When she finally looked up, she said only, "Please help me, Professor Barrett, please. Just help me to prove to them that it wasn't John. I know it was you who really solved the murder of that part-time professor, the undertaker. Everybody at RECC knows that. Please." I glanced quickly at Sol, expecting him to be stone-faced with resistance to the very idea of my getting involved in another murder. But he was gazing down at the young woman's tear-streaked face. When our glances met, I saw in his eyes a look that I read as both resignation and something else, maybe curiosity, maybe kindness.

So I was surprised when I heard myself, notorious bleeding heart of the RECC faculty, saying matter-of-

factly to this extremely upset young woman, "Toni,
I'm going to have to think over what you're suggesting. I don't know how much I could actually help in
this situation. I'll talk it over with Sol and get back to
you."

After Toni left, Sol and I sipped the last of the lemonade and he said, "So what's the deal? You're not rushing
in to rescue this damsel in obvious distress and her ex-
lover? You don't want to play detective anymore? Is
this change of heart attributable to estrogen overload or
what?"

"Actually, I've got enough on my plate this summer,
don't you think? I've got this paper to write for grad
school, one course to teach, and now all the planning to
do for a winter wedding. And for once the cops seem to
be on the right track. So what do I need to get involved
in this mess for? The ex-fiancé is a very logical suspect.
Anyway, if he's innocent, he'll have an alibi and they'll
investigate further and finger somebody else. And
Toni's really very together. She'll get through this. But
what's with you? You sound like you actually want me
to get mixed up in what is clearly a police matter." I
linked arms with Sol as we moved toward the stairs.
"You're not worried?" I asked, looking up at him.

"I guess I feel like we have no choice about this one.
Once we found that poor bastard's body, we were
involved whether we wanted to be or not." Sol spoke
softly.

"Well, thank you very much, but for once I don't
want to be," I retorted, my voice strident in comparison
with his muted tones. Finally I was doing what I had
resolved when I turned fifty, saying no. Like my resolu-
tion to lose ten pounds by cutting back on my M&M's
intake, this promise had been easy to forget. I was still
on too many RECC committees, writing too many

grants, and mentoring too many adjuncts. I squared my shoulders and told my inner Joan of Arc to hush.

"Are you sure your estrogen patch hasn't fallen off again?" quipped Sol, playfully smacking me on the rump as he walked behind me up to bed.

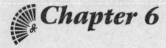

Chapter 6

To: Bbarrett@circle.com
From: Rbarrett@UWash.edu
Re: Awesome wedding site
Date: Wed, 01 Jul 1998 15:23:16

Mom,

Just a quickie 'cause I have to study before work. We are so psyched! We've found the perfect place for our wedding! You know
the catering place where I worked two summers ago, the one
that was in the Petroleum Museum right here in Capitol Hill? You
could almost see it from our old apartment (the one over the
hairdresser's, not the one next to the laundromat). Well, Keith
and I were walking by there a couple of days ago and we both
got the same idea. So we stopped in and talked to the owner. It's
totally cool! Even the ladies' room is done up as if it were in a
fifties gas station. The food is okay. They serve it from an old
train car on dishes just like Grandma Sadie's. And it's really not
that expensive. (Remember? That's why I left. I could get better
tips at that place in Bellevue.) Nobody'd have to get too dressed
up either 'cause the place is so funky. And they have a jukebox
with all the old songs you like. Anyway, it's phat city and I'd like

to give them a deposit 'cause the place is so hot now that it books fast. What do you think? We could use the check Grandma Sadie is sending us for the baby's college education. Daddy hasn't answered my e-mail about the baby yet, but I know you'll talk him through it.

Love,
Rebecca

They've got the whole thing planned already. My pregnant daughter wants to be married amid old gas pumps and ads for Coca-Cola, probably by a grease monkey in overalls. I had not considered who would perform Rebecca and Keith's wedding ceremony before, and the prospects were so chilling I almost drove right into a semi zooming out of the Holland Tunnel. I braked quickly, barely avoiding going to certain death through a red light. Safely stopped, I continued my monologue, a vastly underrated means of working through life's major issues. I didn't care if passing motorists looked at me funny and gave me a wide berth. *I am being consulted only because I'm going to end up paying for at least half of this and browbeating Lenny for his half, so I have to get that through my head too. And furthermore, it doesn't sound like she's even going to wear a wedding dress, so I might as well bag the fantasy of the mother-daughter shopping trip. There would be no dressing room huddles comparing the frock of white organdy with a shawl collar to the creamy chiffon number with the sweetheart neckline . . .* As I drove to work, I realized that adjusting my attitude to Rebecca's engaged/pregnant bride persona was indeed proving to be a challenge.

Pulling into the parking lot at RECC, I was once again grateful that my summer school speech students would soon take my mind off my petty mother-of-the-bride grievances. Sure enough, there was Ndaye Sesay sprinting up to my office door. For a fleeting moment I wondered if she'd like me to take *her* wedding dress shopping. Ndaye was a willowy six feet tall with huge brown eyes and mocha-colored skin. Hailing from Senegal, she spoke with a French accent and dressed with cosmopolitan flair. That day she wore a short brown straight skirt and a matching top made of some clingy material. Her elegant demeanor evaporated, though, when she spoke in winded gasps, "I can't stay for zhee class today eizher, Professeur. I am zho zhorry. I must go to my work. Zhey keep changing my hourz."

Before I could open my mouth to reiterate my customary response to this news, she was gone. Once again I wondered why students thought if they told me about the health, family, work, or transportation crisis that was keeping them from class, their absence would not matter. The fact that something might actually happen in that class that they would miss or that they might influence by virtue of their presence or absence never seemed to occur to them. Even good students like Ndaye sought to talk away their absences as if the act of telling me about them would negate them. I often felt like a priest hearing confessions and expected to provide absolution. Opening the door to the office, I sighed in anticipation of the fact that Ndaye, the most articulate student in the class, would probably fail the six-week summer school course because of excessive absences that she was powerless to prevent.

While some students were rehearsing their first speeches in pairs, I was going over the outlines of those who had been either absent or unprepared the day before. Winston Mack, a great gangling white youth in denim overalls, the ubiquitous baseball cap, and a sleeveless T-shirt that left little about his armpits to the imagination, ambled up to my desk waving his paper.

Wordlessly he placed it in front of me as he sat down on the chair I kept beside my desk for conferences. Yesterday he had been chatty, full of plans for a speech about twins. There were a lot of twins in his family and he himself was a twin. I looked at the outline. It included many relevant facts, indicating considerable research. "You have a lot of good information here. I think we'll all learn from this talk. But how would you feel about putting this part about identical versus fraternal twins after you explain the genetics of twins?" I asked. Winston opened his mouth to reply and then closed it quickly and shoved another piece of paper in front of me. I read: *"Can't talk today. Had my tonge peirrced yesterday. Still bleeding a little. Want to see?"*

"No thanks, Winston. I'll pass on that," I said quickly. "Since you can't talk today, instead of rehearsing with your partner, you'll just have to listen and give her written feedback. I hope you're not in pain," I added, wondering why someone would sign up for a six-week required course and then have the one body part he absolutely needed to pass said course wounded so he couldn't participate. It flashed through my mind that perhaps Winston's ill-timed tongue piercing was really an elaborate avoidance strategy that he subconsciously hoped would exempt him from giving his talk. I dismissed this thought as unworthy. I hoped Winston's tongue would heal in time for him to deliver his speech.

Next came Tomas Oliveri, his slicked-back hair and shining gold earring rendered almost invisible by the high-collared splashy electric blue and bright green sportshirt he wore open over a sleeveless T-shirt and white denim walk shorts. More gold dangled from his neck. Tomas handed me three single-spaced typed pages and opened our session by asking, "Professor Barrett, how much time do we really have? I know you said five minutes, but what if we go over?" I glanced at the outline. His speech was on Y2K, which promised to be a rewarding topic, both timely and practical.

"Great topic, Tomas. Well, let's see. We have about eighteen students in the class but most of them will not go over the five-minute minimum in their first speech, so if you'd like, you could extend your talk to as long as ten minutes. Does that help?"

"Yeah, man. It does. 'Cause this stuff is really important. I mean like we humans are in for a lot of problems . . ." He scratched his head, barely ruffling his slicked back hair, and tugged on one of his earrings. "I got a lot of stuff here." In his hand he clutched a sheaf of paper which he had undoubtedly harvested from the fertile soil of the Web. He reminded me of a wary farmer, stockpiling grain in anticipation of famine. But unlike the prudent farmer, Tomas and many of my other students had a lot of trouble sorting the wheat from the chaff.

Troubled a bit by his use of the word *humans*, I quickly skimmed the rest of the outline. It read like a tract, warning of plots and millennial mayhem. "Tomas, remember that this is supposed to be an informative speech based on facts, not a persuasive one. Why not save some of this for your next talk, which is persuasive, and just give us the facts about the Y2K situation." Tomas's face crinkled with bewilderment. I tried to explain, "Well, you know, like what exactly is the cause of the Y2K problem? What are people doing to solve it? What are some of the country's leaders saying about it? What are computer experts expecting? You'll get a better grade if you stick to that sort of thing and save your fears for later."

By the time class was over, all but Winston had run through their speeches with a partner and so allayed some of their speech anxiety. We had worked out a few positive images of what delivering their speeches might be like. Instead of picturing themselves stammering, forgetting, and failing while their peers laughed at them, I asked them to imagine themselves practicing, speaking clearly from notes, and receiving applause and a good grade. Finally I coached them on tips for practicing at home in front of a mirror or an obliging relative. They were calmer and I was beat. There is no getting around the fact that by the time we get to an evening class like this one, we have all put in long hours at something else and there is a certain eagerness to head for home that, quite frankly, we all share.

I for one was so tired that I almost decided to ignore the flashing red light indicating that there was a voice mail message. But decades ago in the fifties, I learned that my Princess phone was a vital connection to friends and family. Since then I've never been able to resist answering a ringing phone. And now the blinking red signal triggers the same response. I pushed the buttons. "Professor Barrett. It's Toni. You've got to help me. Now the cops think *I* killed Louie."

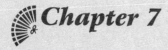 **Chapter 7**

Yo Ma Bel and Sol,

I just want to give you a heads up about Spike. He's Eric's Lab puppy and I'm watching him for a few days while Eric's out of town. But don't worry. Everything's cool. I shut Virginia Woolf in your room until she makes friends with Spike. And I walked him already, so you'll only have to take him out once before you go to bed. Maybe you should put a piece of newspaper down before you go upstairs, just in case, you know. You'll love Spike. He's affectionate and smart too.

We're rehearsing in the East Village again tonight. Don't wait up.

Love,
Mark

P.S. Illuminada called. Said she and Betty could meet you here for breakfast. They'll bring the bagels.

When I got home that night, dog hair blanketed the sofa, an ominous puddle decorated the hardwood kitchen floor, my beloved black cat Virginia Woolf hissed from under the dresser in our bedroom, and Sol held Mark's note. A yipping black puppy with big feet raced in circles around him. Uncharacteristically speechless, Sol handed me the note.

"What the hell is the matter with that kid?" I shrieked as soon as I had scanned Mark's scrawled message. "How could he bring that animal in here without even checking with us? And then he just takes off and expects us to deal with it." Avoiding the sofa and sidestepping the puddle, I sank onto a stool at the kitchen counter. "Mark has always had a soft spot for strays." I sighed, recalling the endless stream of mangy, injured, and starving examples of urban fauna Mark had befriended over the years. "But this is outrageous. He's incredibly immature and narcissistic. What happened to the thoughtful, sensitive, helpful Mark?" I'd so looked forward to having him home again, but now, I just wanted to strangle him.

Sol handed me a beer and said flatly, "He's regressed and so have you." Seeing my eyes widen at his cryptic comment, Sol elaborated. "Christ, Bel. You were so glad he got back from Israel in one piece that you just welcomed him home and started treating him like a kid again. You wait up for him, you nag him all the time about what he eats, what he wears, and what chores he does or, more often, doesn't do." I had risen and headed for the utility closet to get the mop. "And now you're going to clean up after him. I don't believe it. You're turning a perfectly good kid into a slacker prince."

"He's not a slacker. He's just finding himself," I snapped. I had no problem whatsoever criticizing my own kids, but I had a hard time listening to anyone else find them less than perfect. The truth of Sol's words hurt. I wasn't doing Mark any favor by enabling his infuriating lifestyle.

"Sol, I'm not up for this conversation now. You may be right. Damn it, you are right. But I'm exhausted, and as soon as I finish mopping this up and walking that damn mutt, I'm going to bed." I was near tears when Sol disengaged the mop from my hands and, with a few swift strokes, removed the final traces of Spike's "accident" from the floor.

It was late when we got back from walking Spike, whose playful yipping threatened to awaken those neighbors who had already gone to sleep. Actually Sol walked him and I kept Sol company. I'm a sucker for puppies, so I was afraid that once Spike's limpid brown eyes engaged mine, I'd be unable to implement the plan we'd formulated for dealing with Mark's lack of consideration.

As we walked, I told Sol about Toni's phone call. He was shocked to hear that Toni was a suspect. "Gee, they must have serious evidence or something to question her. She's from a family that's done business in this area for two generations. Besides, she seems like such a straight-up kid." Sol paused while Spike critiqued the fire hydrant halfway down our street.

"Well, I'm mad. Toni is a very bright student, a budding feminist, and an all-around good kid. It's bad enough she lost her boyfriend in such a terrible way. Now they're harassing her, probably because they're just too lazy to do the legwork it would take to figure out who really did kill that poor man. I've decided to try to help her if I can." It hadn't been a decision exactly but more like a reflex triggered by Toni's choked-up voice on my message machine. I scanned Sol's face in the glow of the streetlight. He hadn't reacted although I thought I heard a low sigh.

"I'm glad you've called in Betty and Illuminada," he said as we both paused, relieved that Spike had finally found a tree that met his exacting standards. To my surprise Sol added, "I wish I could be around tomorrow morning, but I've got a meeting with Marlene and Jerry about that new development proposed for uptown. We've been trying to get together for two weeks." Sol's priorities were clear. We'd met at a party thrown by the Citizens' Committee to Preserve the Waterfront, a group of diehard environmentalists of which he was a charter member. And since his retirement from the Economics Department at Rutgers, Sol had divided his time between consulting for companies doing business in Eastern Europe and working with CCPW to channel the tidal wave of development threatening to swamp our river city.

Before going to bed, we lined the floor of Mark's room with newspaper, put Spike on it along with a dish of water, and closed the door. I wrote the following note and taped it above the toilet where Mark couldn't miss it.

Mark,

Sol and I did not volunteer to care for Spike and have no interest in doing so. As you know, I have a meeting here first thing in the morning. Please have the couch vacuumed by then. Also I do not plan to confine Virginia Woolf to our bedroom, so I guess Spike will have to stay in yours for the rest of his visit.

Hope your rehearsal went well.

Love,
Mom

He must have seen it because there was no sign of Spike or Mark the next morning when Betty and Illuminada arrived. "How many bagels do you think we're going to eat?" I asked Illuminada, whose dark curls were barely visible behind the bag she carried.

"We thought that Sol and Mark might make a few disappear," Illuminada answered, putting the bag on the kitchen counter and pulling up a stool.

"There's some OJ in there too and cream cheese. We figured you had butter," said Betty, knowing full well that, in spite of the admonitions of the health pundits, I had decided years ago that a life without butter was not really a life. I poured coffee and passed around plates, glasses, and knives while Betty emptied the contents of the bag onto the counter. I handed her a basket for the bagels.

"Let me guess. Your student wants you to help her clear her ex-fiance. And you want us to help you. That's why you called and invited us over here this morning," said Illuminada, helping herself to a poppyseed bagel.

"No. I think Bel just wanted bagels delivered," quipped Betty, pouring three glasses of juice. "And served," she added, passing me the basket.

"You're both right. Sort of. Toni Demaio asked me to help her clear her ex-fiance the other night and I told her I'd think about it. But I was going to tell her no. Actually I thought the cops were on the right track, and, believe it or not, I have other things I want to do this summer." As I spoke, I scratched Virginia Woolf's head where she lay, curled up on a stool of her own. Every now and then her eyes panned the room and her ears and tail stiffened as if in anticipation of an enemy invasion.

"Here comes the bride," hummed Betty, smiling. "You and Rebecca must be making wedding plans."

"Guess again, but that's another story," I answered.

"*Dios mio*, Bel, cut to the chase. I've got to be in Trenton by noon and I have to stop by the office first." Illuminada was nibbling her bagel, on which she had spread a thin veneer of butter. Any minute now she would start checking her watch. The woman had more work than she could handle even with a clerical staff and three full-time field workers. "So now they suspect her, right? And you want us to help clear her, right?"

"Right. She's a really good kid who's supposed to transfer to Rutgers in the fall. There's no way she murdered anyone." I spoke as emphatically as I could around a mouthful of cinnamon raisin bagel slathered with cream cheese.

While Illuminada and I had been talking, Betty had finished her half a bagel. She wiped her hands and reached for her purse, pulling out her Palm Pilot, a device she depended on as if it were another body part. As soon as Betty did that, I knew she and Illuminada would help. "Just tell us first though. Is Sol going to walk out on you again over this? Have you even told him about it? I don't mind trying to figure out who murdered that poor atonal soul, but I'd just as soon avoid you driving Sol into his 'Frankly, my darling, I don't give a damn' mode again."

In spite of her snide reference to a serious misunderstanding between Sol and me the last time I got involved in sniffing out a murderer, I appreciated Betty's question. I was glad I could reassure her. "Yes. He'd be here now if he didn't have a CCPW meeting. Because Sol's the one who actually found Louie Palumbo's body, he feels sort of proprietary about this case. Strange as it may sound, he seemed really disappointed the other night when I wasn't interested in pursuing it. Besides, he's met Toni. She's a very appealing young woman and she was extremely upset."

"It's true. We know Sol has a soft spot in his heart for hysterical women," Illuminada said sweetly. Now she *was* looking at her watch. She put her empty coffee cup down. "I'll talk to the cops here and in North Bergen where she and what's-his-name, her ex-fiancé, live."

"I'll get whatever records RECC has on Toni. That's

about all I'll have time to do this week. But next week . . ." Betty was taking notes with her stylus as she spoke.

"I guess I'll try to find out more about the victim. He seems lost in the shuffle, poor thing. His funeral is going on as we speak. Do you want to talk to Toni? Or her lawyer? I'm sure she must have one now." I knew that Toni's family had the means for private legal representation. And John Cardino was nearly a lawyer himself.

"Find out who's representing each of them for now. Maybe I can talk to their attorneys later on." Illuminada got a fair amount of work from lawyers now and was on a first-name basis with many of them.

"I'll talk to Sarah too. The *Herald*'s already done a couple of stories on this murder. I bet she's planning some profiles and other human-interest articles. She might be interested in the family's reaction. I should call her anyway," I said, thinking out loud and feeling guilty. I had told my old friend Sarah, now managing editor of the *Jersey City Herald*, I'd get in touch with her to arrange a lunch date in May and now June was over and I still hadn't made the call.

Just as I opened the door to let Illuminada and Betty out so they could go to work, Spike raced in dragging Mark, clad only in shorts and sandals, behind him. "Yo! It's Ma Bel's posse," cracked Mark, hugging each of my friends in turn. No wonder they both defended him. He treated them with genuine affection and respect, the way their kids treated me. Well, it was no secret. Other people's kids were like other people's parents and husbands. Easy. Before we could stop him, Spike had circled the room, entangling us in his leash.

"New pet? Super. Your mom didn't even tell us," said Betty. Out of the corner of my eye, I saw a flash of black fur streak up the stairs. Poor Virginia Woolf was once again seeking refuge from this yipping intruder.

"Oh, he's not mine. I'm just watching him for a friend for a couple of days," said Mark as he leaned over to pick up the speeding Spike so we could unsnarl the leash. Once extricated, Illuminada was out the door in a hurry and Betty followed, waving and calling over her shoulder, "He's just precious. Like a furry four-legged two-year-old. Full of energy." I swear I saw her wink at me. I knew they'd be chuckling all the way downtown as Illuminada drove and Betty brushed away the dog hair now trimming their hemlines.

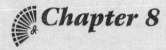# Chapter 8

To: Bbarrett@circle.com
From: Rbarrett@UWash.edu
Re: Psyched again
Date: Fri, 03 Jul 1998 15:35:24

Mom,

Great news! When we realized I was pregnant, Keith applied all over town to be a building manager. You know, live in an apartment building for free and be a super, make sure everything works and sort of manage things. Well, we interviewed in two places (they wanted to meet me and since I'm expecting, that makes us a stable couple) and got two offers probably because Keith's so handy, not to mention cute. Anyway, on August 1 we move to a thirty-unit building right here in Capitol Hill on Bellevue Road! We really love this neighborhood. And we're getting a totally awesome apartment. It's a big one-bedroom with high ceilings, hardwood floors, an eat-in kitchen, and lots of light. The bathroom is really big too. The complex is kind of old, but that's

why the apartments are so big. We're totally psyched! I can't
wait to show it to you.

Love,
Rebecca

P.S. Thanks for the check for the deposit on the Petroleum
Museum. Dad sent one too, but I haven't heard from him since I
e-mailed him about the baby. I guess I'll wait until after the holi-
day and call him.

"You two look stunning!" I exclaimed when I picked
up Ma and Sofia to drive them to the dentist where they
had back-to-back appointments for check-ups. "You
have to be Dr. Dunphy's most glamorous patients." Ma
and Sofia really were dressed up, even for them. Ma
wore a navy linen sheath and her navy and white spec-
tator shoes. Sofia wore a black cotton sheath and her
black patent leather pumps. They both wore pearls and
carried purses that exactly complemented their ensem-
bles. Jackie Kennedy would be proud of her legacy. In
my cut-offs and Hoboken Exterminator T-shirt, I felt
decidedly underdressed. "We went to Louie Palumbo's
funeral this morning," Sofia explained. "We didn't have
time to change."

Before I started the car, I handed Ma a printout of
Rebecca's e-mail. I knew Rebecca's good news would
please her. She read it aloud so Sofia in the backseat
could hear. "I knew that girl would be all right. Isn't she
terrific? My granddaughter always lands on her feet,"
Ma kvelled to Sofia. "Even when she was a kid, she
knew how to make things work out. When she needed
money, she'd bake cookies to sell or she'd shine shoes."
What Ma seemed to be forgetting was that Rebecca's
biggest customers had always been her grandparents,

who, for many years, had enjoyed an endless supply of chocolate chip cookies and sported the shiniest shoes in north Jersey. I knew that the dental hygienist who summoned Ma from the waiting room would have to hear all about Rebecca's latest triumph before Ma would lie silent in the dentist's chair.

"You must be all worn out from the Palumbo funeral," I prompted as Sofia and I sat alone in the waiting room. "It must have been very sad."

"Tragic. It was tragic. Those poor people. Can you imagine *your* son being stabbed to death?" Sofia shook her head. "I heard Tess has to take some kind of tranquilizers now and Joe is pale like a sheet. His hands were shaking all through the ceremony. I saw."

"I bet there were a lot of people there," I said innocently, realizing that, perhaps, I should have gone myself just to check out the scene. It hadn't even occurred to me to attend the funeral of someone I didn't know personally.

"Hundreds," Sofia said. "A lot of them will go straight from the cemetery to the shore. But nobody who knew the family would miss paying their respects. Even if they have to leave a little later for the weekend and get stuck in traffic." Sofia's reference to the fact that many Hobokenites left town for the Jersey shore every summer weekend was not lost on me. One of her daughters had a house on Long Beach Island.

"Are they a big family?" I asked, trying to lead Sofia into telling me something but not quite sure what I expected that something to be. It was like groping in a grab bag.

"They only had two kids, him and his twin brother Danny. Tess has a couple of sisters and a brother. Joe's family is mostly gone. Dead or moved away." Sofia sounded matter-of-fact. I guess for the old, losing family to death or distance becomes commonplace.

"Louie was such a young man, too. Early thirties, I think. He must have had a lot of friends and fans?" I moved my hand about inside the bag.

"More than I thought. There were some bigwigs from Atlantic City there. Louie used to open for name acts at the casinos once in a while. And he grew up here. He knew everybody. Most of Hoboken was that boy's Rat Pack." Sofia sighed, perhaps reflecting on the fact that Louie's popularity had been unable to protect him. "And the girls loved him. Just like Frank. Of course, everybody knew about Nancy. Her and Louie went together for a long time. They planned to marry. Danny married her cousin. Looks just like her. They got a couple a kids."

Jackpot! No wonder the cops were questioning Toni. For a minute I was so mad at Louie for deceiving Toni that I almost forgot that he was dead. Sofia was continuing, clearly engaged by the soap opera quality of Louie Palumbo's lovelife. Her voice deepened and she looked furtively around the waiting room as if to be certain we weren't being overheard. "But then this other girl showed up, one of the Demaios from the old neighborhood, I heard. The one you were talking about Sunday. I didn't pay much attention then. The butcher's girl. But my cousin Anna told me at the viewing that Louie had been two-timing Nancy with some young girl, and sure enough, he must've been 'cause this girl showed up at the funeral. Sweet-looking little thing. Not Louie's type, really."

"Nancy who?" I asked almost sharply. I would have to watch myself. I didn't want Sofia to suspect that my interest in the Palumbos was anything but casual. If she knew I was involving myself in finding Louie's killer, she'd tell Ma, and I was certain that Sadie Bickoff, who still called on rainy mornings to tell me to carry an umbrella, would not want her daughter messing with murder again. During the months when I was trying to figure out who had killed Vic's brother, Ma had been in a Valium- and grief-induced fog. But now that she was herself again, she would make both of us crazy with her worrying. Also, if Sofia knew why I was so interested in Louie's murder, she might tell the Palumbos and blow my cover in their tightly knit community.

Sofia hesitated for a few seconds. Like so many of us, she was no stranger to the short-term memory loss that in later life makes ordinary conversation a guessing game. Then she began thinking aloud, "It was cute the way people always used to tease Louie about his girlfriend's name being Nancy. You know, like Frank's first wife." I nodded, not wanting to interrupt Sofia's effort to dredge up Nancy's surname. "She went to St. Mary's with my granddaughter. Graduated a few years ahead of her, I think. Works in the bank. And I remember Nancy's brother Gio's a mason. He's done a lot of jobs in Hoboken. He patched my stoop steps and made us a new sidewalk. Real hard worker, Gio. The family name was on his truck." Now Sofia's brow was a knotted ridge of concentration. Then a grin flashed across her face, "Deloia! Nancy Deloia," she practically shouted.

"What are you hollering about?" asked Ma, reentering the waiting room. She was reaching in her bag for her lipstick so she could repair the damage the hygienist had done to her makeup. "Stop yelling and go get your teeth cleaned, Sofia."

Our Fourth of July barbecue had been Sol's idea, but I'd readily agreed. Under threat of eviction, Mark had finally planted the annuals I'd bought, so our typical row house patch of backyard was now bordered by a blaze of bright pink impatiens and geraniums, purple pansies and petunias, and saffron marigolds. A pot of bleeding hearts hung from a rung of the fire escape. We were a big group for the small space. Not surprisingly, poor dead Louie Palumbo was the life of the party. Everyone had a theory about his murder.

"I still think it's a classic case of jealous lover turned killer," Sol was saying. "How would you feel if you were a guy and your fiancée suddenly broke your engagement because she was getting it on with some two-bit lounge lizard?"

"I don't know about that, Sol. *Dios mio*, you guys don't exactly have a monopoly on jealousy, you know." Illuminada scowled. "How do you suppose Toni felt when she found out about Nancy? Think about it. Here she's gone and broken off with her fiancé for this new love and she learns he's double dipping?" A few feet away, Betty's son Randy started at Illuminada's choice of words. Kids were always surprised when their parents' generation hinted at even passing familiarity with the less than genteel aspects of sexuality. "She must have felt very betrayed. *Caramba*, she *was* betrayed. I don't know her, but from what you and Bel say, she's very idealistic. Idealists are always shocked when they find out what the world is really like."

"You're right. The Demaio kid is an idealist. But that doesn't make her a killer. Wait until you meet her. You'll see," Sol insisted.

"Did you hear about that Frank Sinatra impersonator? The one who got killed?" Ma was asking Milagros Santos, Illuminada's mom, who lives in Union City with Raoul and Illuminada and therefore might not be expected to know the latest goings-on in Hoboken. Sofia was with her own family at Long Beach Island this weekend, and Ma, although welcome there, had been pleased to get our invitation.

"Illuminada said something the other day. Sol found the body she said." Milagros replied slowly, shaking her head. "*Dios mio*, it is a terrible thing. *Que pena para la familia.*"

"Can you imagine? My friend Sofia, she knows the family. We went to the funeral. They're sick with grief." Mom smoothed back her hair, preening a bit. She was clearly pleased to be privy to the Palumbos' mourning. I sometimes forgot that during her three-decade career as a Brooklyn court stenographer, she had been in on the details of hundreds of murder cases. She must miss the drama and intrigue of the criminal courtroom. I knew I was on target when I heard the animation in her voice as, leaning close to Milagros, Ma announced, "Sofia just told me this morning that Louie Palumbo's girlfriend is pregnant."

I nearly dropped the bowl of potato salad I was ferrying to the buffet table when I overheard Ma's bombshell. "Come and get it!" I called. In spite of the fact that we'd been snacking on cold poached salmon and crudites all afternoon, it was just amazing how fast Mark and Randy lost interest in the grilling process in favor of the grilled product. Betty took over the grill, flipping burgers and moving pieces of chicken closer to the flame with the casual assurance of a pro.

Vic was at her side and Raoul joined them. Holding out the platter so Raoul could fill it with chicken, I said in my best sotto voce, "Ma heard from Sofia this morning that Louie Palumbo's girlfriend is pregnant."

"Which girlfriend?" asked Betty and Vic in unison. The expression on Betty's face was priceless. She was always so surprised when people did things without her telling them to. Even people she didn't know.

"Whichever girlfriend it was," interjected Raoul, "she had a double motive."

"That doesn't make sense though," Betty declared. "If you're carrying someone's baby, what do you want to kill him for? How can he help support the kid if he's

dead? Even a divorced dad is better than none at all,"
Betty went on, knowing that their own experience lent
authority to her words. Her ex was very involved in
Randy's life and Vic lived for the time he spent with his
daughter Maria.

"Sweetheart, not everybody thinks these things
through as rationally as you do. That's why we have
crimes of passion. I suspect murder is often a crime of
passion," Vic added, holding out a platter for the burgers.

I didn't say anything, but I was sure Toni Demaio
wasn't pregnant. She didn't look it. And besides, she
would have mentioned something as important as a
pregnancy to me simply because for unknown reasons,
students routinely confide their most intimate secrets to
their English professors whether or not we want to
know them.

After fixing his grandmother a heaping plate of food
and scarfing down a couple of burgers, a drumstick, and
huge mounds of potato salad, Mark left to take Spike to
the park for a run. The only way he could tolerate keeping the puppy confined was by giving the poor little
thing lots of exercise and attention. Eric was due back
on Monday night. I was counting the minutes. I had a
feeling Mark was too.

When he returned, Mark carried his guitar. Turning
off the CD player and helping himself to a beer from
the cooler, he began tuning up. We all settled into chairs
and listened to the impromptu concert. For once I didn't
mutter to myself about how the last thing the world
needed was another Jewish blues player. I just listened
and enjoyed. And when he turned to me and said, "This
one's for you Ma Bel," and began to strum "Good
Rockin' Mama" in a not bad imitation of John Lee
Hooker, tears filled my eyes. Mark was still my sweetie.
For a few minutes I even forgot about Spike. And Louie
Palumbo.

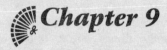

Chapter 9

To: Bbarrett@circle.com
From: Lbarrett@squarepeg.com
Re: Rebecca
Date: Sun, 05 Jul 1998 08:05:00

Bel,

I suppose you think it's just great that Rebecca and that guy are going to have a baby, so finally you can sit around and swap photos of your grandchild with all your friends. But before you start knitting booties, just tell me, how the hell are they going to support a kid? Doesn't she know kids cost money? Not to mention that some people still get married **before** they breed. And now how the hell is Rebecca going to finish school? She only has one more year. You'd think they'd have at least waited until she graduated. But not your daughter. I can't figure out what's wrong with her lately. And Mark either for that matter. Sounds like he needs a good kick in the ass too. He just e-mailed me about how excited he is about becoming an uncle. I'd like to see him get excited about getting a steady paycheck. But why should he? His mother doesn't mind feeding and housing him while he "finds himself." When I was his age, I'd been working for ten years.

And if Mark lived with me, he'd be working by now too. He could look for himself after working hours. Well, don't get too excited about being a grandmother because Seattle is so far away that you'll never get to see the kid anyway. And yes, I sent a check for half the deposit on the place where she wants to be married (don't get me started on that) and I agreed to give her away. What could I say? But you and I have to talk. I'm not a money machine. I'll call you in August when Cissie and I get back from Provence.

L. Barrett, CPA
Your taxes are my business

"Only a month in Provence this year?" Betty smirked. "That's barely enough time to settle into the villa." We were sitting around her dining room table, about to breakfast, this time on some fresh-from-the-oven Hoboken bread I'd brought. Illuminada had said she'd bring juice and melon. Betty was putting jam and butter on the table. We were supposed to be mapping out a strategy for getting the goods on who killed Louie Palumbo, but Illuminada wasn't there yet, and I hadn't been able to resist sharing Lenny's latest message with Betty. She shoved it back across the table in my direction.

When Illuminada came in a few minutes later, she picked it up, scanned it, and then began slicing the cantaloupe she had brought. She said seriously, "*Dios mio*, Bel. This man manages to make even the most natural concerns sound nasty. It's a good thing he's going away. He needs a vacation. Maybe when he gets back, he'll sound more like a father and less like an asshole." She had kicked off her shoes and accepted the cup of coffee that Betty poured her. Betty got out her laptop, a signal that she thought we ought to get started. She had to be at work by nine.

I began, "I'm going to talk to Toni again. I have a conference with her scheduled for this afternoon anyway, and while I still don't think she killed Louie, she just may say something that will lead us to another suspect. And I'm going to figure out a way to meet Nancy Deloia. That leaves John Cardino for you two to fight over." Having said my piece, I turned my attention to tearing off a chunk of bread from the baguette and buttering it.

"Oh, I guess I can check him out. He's sort of a neighbor of mine anyway," volunteered Illuminada, passing the sliced melon to Betty. She considered John Cardino a neighbor because she lived in Union City, and North Bergen where the Cardinos and Demaios now lived was the next town over.

"Oh! Poor me! Nothing to do!" exclaimed Betty. She was feigning regret, but I knew she would really miss being out of the action.

"Actually, I think your front steps here look just a little run down. You should get an estimate for patching and painting them." I articulated this total non sequitur very matter-of-factly, as if it were a logical follow-up to Betty's remark.

Both Betty and Illuminada stared at me. Betty spoke first, her voice tinged with concern. "I've been meaning to get them taken care of, but I didn't know they were that bad. I guess I just got used to them being a little uneven. Did you trip or what?" I could tell she had taken me seriously. She took everything about her perfect condo in her perfect gated community seriously. Illuminada remained silent, waiting.

"Ha! Gotcha!" I exclaimed quickly. I hadn't meant to worry my friend, so I felt a little childish. "Listen up. Sofia mentioned that Nancy Deloia has a brother who's a mason. Not the lodge kind, the cement kind," I added quickly. "If you have him over to give you an estimate on patching those stairs, you can see what he's like. Maybe you can even get him to talk a little."

"God, I'm relieved. I thought for a minute you were hurt or were going to sue me or something." Betty grinned. "Well, girl, I haven't got your magical ability to get people to bare their souls, but I can try. I'm chairing the Facilities Committee here this year anyway, so I really can pitch him the prospect of more work than just those measly little stairs. The wall by the pool needs some attention and so does the patio. The gal who chaired this committee last year didn't do a damn thing." Inefficiency and laziness always bugged Betty, and she spoke disdainfully. Then, as if to restore her good humor, she tore off a small hunk of bread and nibbled on it plain. "God, this stuff is good, Bel. And by the way, Vic and I had a lovely time at your barbecue. I think we ought to make it an annual tradition."

"Yes. Sounds good to me too," echoed Illuminada. "I knew Raoul would enjoy himself, but I wasn't sure about my mother. She gets shy about her English. But she had a great time talking to your mother. She doesn't get out enough. And she loved the live music. It was a real treat for her."

"Yeah. We really lucked out with the weather too. It was a lovely day," I sighed recalling the many pleasures of that afternoon. "But you missed the best part! Spike's owner came by a day early and took his damn mutt home."

"Hallelujah!" exclaimed Betty, raising both hands over her head as if to hail the deity responsible for my deliverance.

"Now maybe you'll get off Mark's case for a while and give the poor kid some space." Illuminada had put her shoes back on and was heading for the door when she continued, "You know, these early morning sessions are interesting, but I can't wait until you finish summer school, Bel. I miss our dinner meetings. I'm not used to dealing with you sober."

Once I got to my quiet office, I was not only sober, but also rested and eager to resume work on my paper. Wendy would be in and out, mostly out, and I had no appointments with students until my meeting with Toni at three. With any luck at all, perhaps I could make some headway on the first draft. I nuked a cup of tea in the department office, checked my mailbox, and got to work. The morning disappeared as the pages multiplied. Ideas were coalescing, relevant examples were leaping out of my notes and underlined texts, and the structure of the thing was gradually emerging.

I had to remind myself to take a lunch break around one-thirty. Actually Wendy reminded me. She breezed in to set up a display of children's books for her afternoon lit class and said, "I'm running over to the RIP to get a sandwich and an iced tea. Want me to bring you something?"

"A container of tuna salad and an iced tea would be great. And a bag of M&M's. It's going to be a long day." While she was gone, I finished the section I was working on. It would be good to talk to Wendy. She'd been away over the weekend and we hadn't seen much of each other since spring semester ended.

"Sorry we couldn't make your barbecue. How did it go?" With our food spread out on our respective desks, we swiveled our chairs around so we could face each other. It was a familiar ritual.

"I think everybody had a good time, especially the older generation, Ma and Illuminada's mother. The food was great, it didn't rain, everybody behaved. How was your weekend?" I asked.

"Pretty good. Lots of family. Lots of food. Everybody behaved. I even had time to read a grown-up book, Jamaica Kincaid's latest. Of course, I can't remember the title," Wendy said, making a face. Her big complaint was that as a professor of children's literature, she had to read so many books written for juveniles that she seldom had a chance to read anything else. "So have you figured out yet who killed that singer?"

"How did you know I was going to work on that? I almost didn't," I said quickly because Wendy always chastises me for taking on too much.

"I just knew you'd be bored only writing a paper, teaching one course, nagging your son, and now, from what you said on the phone, planning a wedding. Speaking of which, congratulations! What's the date, Grandma? I want to write it in," Wendy said, reaching for her date book.

"The wedding date or her due date?" I asked archly.

"The wedding date, dummy." Wendy sounded exasperated. "Jim and I are invited, aren't we?"

"Of course, but you don't want to come. It's in Seattle. In January," I added grimly, convinced that no one would travel three thousand miles in winter to the rainiest place in the world to attend a wedding in a facsimile of a gas station.

"So? What's the date? I've known Rebecca since she was terrorizing the sandbox set with my two hellions. Jim and I wouldn't miss her wedding for anything. Date please?" she repeated, book in hand.

I was too teary-eyed to get my own book out and look up the weekend Rebecca and Keith had chosen. I just muttered, "It's during our January break," and shoved a plastic fork full of tuna salad into my mouth. I had pictured Sol, Mark, Sadie, Lenny, Cissie, and me standing awkwardly among the gas pumps, strangers in a strange land, watching helplessly while Rebecca and

Keith plunged headlong into matrimony 1990s style.

Wendy scribbled something in her book and put it back in her purse. "So what happened? Did your student show up and say, 'I'm so sorry, Professor Barrett. I can't get my paper in on time because my ex-fiancé stabbed my current boyfriend to death and I'm upset?' " After listening to years of student excuses, Wendy had become rather cynical.

"Actually, yes, something like that. Except she's way ahead on her paper. And now the police think she killed him. And she found out he has another girlfriend. And one of them may or may not be pregnant. It's a real soap opera." I sighed. "But Toni Demaio is a bright young woman with an amazing ability to see patterns and relationships in everyday events. And what's more, she writes very well. Her paper's brilliant so far. She has a really promising academic future. And she is not guilty of murdering Louie Palumbo," I stated emphatically. With that I tore open one of the bags of M&M's Wendy had brought, poured a third of them into my hand, and tossed them into my mouth like so many vitamin pills.

"I'm saving mine for later. You'll wish you had," said Wendy, throwing out her sandwich wrapper. "I'll be back after my class."

When she had left, I finished the M&M's and spent an hour rereading my morning's work. I almost didn't hear Toni knock. "Professor Barrett, hi," she said dolefully. She looked even thinner than I remembered, and the skin around her eyes was red and puffy. She was chewing on her lower lip.

"Toni, it's good to see you. I've been worried about you. I *do* want to help you." I gestured toward Wendy's chair, and Toni sat down and stared into the space right in front of her.

"Well, you're the only one who does. My own family thinks I'm some kind of slut because I broke off with John. They never really got to know Louie. And even my lawyer acts like he thinks I'm guilty. He keeps bugging me about an alibi." Her words rushed out, impelled by anger. I thought her anger was a healthy sign. Too bad it wasn't directed at Louie, but that would come when she was ready. It was still too soon.

"Tell me about that. Your lawyer's insistence on an alibi," I prodded gently. I'd keep the lawyer as the interrogator here, let him take the heat for posing an important question that Toni didn't like.

"I told him over and over. That night I was with Louie. We went to a wedding where Louie's band was playing," Toni said these words in the cadence of a child repeating something for the umpteenth time to a not very bright grown-up.

"Oh, I didn't know Louie had a band," I remarked. Come to think of it, he had been backed by a band at the Sinatra Park dedication.

"Yes. The Hoboken Four Plus One. As the singer, Louie was the one. All the guys are from Hoboken. Frank started out in a quartet, the Hoboken Four. That's where Louie got the band's name. But anyway, it's a totally awesome band, and they were booked to play at this wedding reception in Jersey City Heights, and I went along. They were a big hit. Everybody loved them. They got bookings for two more weddings right there. That's how good they were." Toni sighed. She was no longer speaking from rote.

"I believe you," I said for lack of a better response. I was puzzling about how to phrase an inquiry about Toni and Louie's activities during the rest of that evening, the evening that saw Louie dead before it was over.

But I didn't have to worry, because Toni continued her narrative without being prompted. "After the wedding Louie and I stopped at Leo's in Hoboken for some mussels and a bar pie before they closed and then he brought me home. He wasn't feeling so good. He thought it was the mussels maybe." Toni paused, tears welling up in her eyes.

"Your folks must have been relieved to hear you come in," I said. "I still can't sleep until I hear my son come in and he's older than you are."

"They were down the shore," Toni said miserably. "That's the problem. There was no one there to hear me come in."

"I see. So you really don't have an alibi for the rest of the evening," I added, patting her hand as I spoke, hoping the gesture would take some of the sting out of my pronouncement of the obvious. "Did you, perhaps, make any phone calls before you went to sleep? Did you e-mail anyone?" I was prone to sharing my insomnia-inspired ideas electronically, and so were many others. If Toni had made a call or e-mailed someone, there would be at least a bit of evidence to support her contention that she was home in North Bergen when Louie was stabbed in Hoboken.

"No," she answered. "I was tired and I went to sleep."

"Did any neighbors see Louie bring you home?" I asked, unwilling to abandon this line of inquiry until I'd exhausted its possibilities.

"No, Professor Barrett. At least not that I know of. It's a quiet neighborhood. People don't hang out on their stoops like they do in our old neighborhood in Hoboken. These people's idea of nightlife is putting out the trash three times a week. Mostly they watch TV and go to bed early," Toni sighed, bored with both her neighborhood and my questions. "Like you said, Professor Barrett, I don't have an alibi."

"Toni, I've heard that Louie had another girlfriend. Did you know that?" I fired this question at her almost before she had finished speaking.

I could tell my abrupt shift in focus had caught Toni off-guard. She paled and looked straight at me, her eyes filling. "I heard it from the cops. Then my mother told me she heard it from my aunt who still lives in the old neighborhood. I wish I could talk to Louie. I know he could explain. I know Louie loved me." Toni's voice was tremulous, but her hand came down hard on my desk.

"Well Toni, I'm sure he did." She'd have the rest of her life to reflect on the limitations of Louie Palumbo's love. I went on, "I'm going to try to find out a little about her. And I'm going to talk to the band members too. Maybe one of them had a fight with Louie. If you know their names and addresses, I'd like you to jot them down for me."

Diligent student that she was, Toni immediately took a pen out of her purse and began to jot down names on the large Post-it I handed her. "I don't know their addresses, except for Danny's, of course." When I looked puzzled, Toni explained, "Louie's twin brother, Danny. He's the sax player. Here's their card too."

I nodded, and stapled the Post-it to the card and filed them both in my wallet. "Thanks, Toni. And meanwhile, I want you to think real hard about Louie's friends and his family and anybody who might have wanted Louie dead. Because somebody did."

After Toni left, I felt drained. In the few minutes left before my class started, I did serious damage to the reserve bag of M&M's, but even after finishing them, I was still tired. I was glad my students were going to be holding forth so I wouldn't have to. The tension in the classroom was palpable as it always is before the first speech of the semester. Five or six students were

absent, undoubtedly driven away by their terror of
speaking publicly. Ndaye was among them. Damn.

I had my students deliver their inaugural speeches
from their seats in our circle so as to minimize their
dread of "standing in front of the room." To their
amazement, they all spoke. And they didn't do badly
either. Tomas, as he had predicted, talked for ten minutes, explaining the programming snafu that threatened
to make Y2K our most memorable millennium. Every
time Winston opened his mouth, I could see the tiny
diamond twinkling on his tongue. His discourse on
twins literally sparkled. And Ndaye rushed in late, still
wearing her white home health aide uniform, and delivered a talk on the effect of civil strife on children in
Africa. None of their speeches was perfect, but that
wasn't the point. They had done something they
believed they couldn't do. Now they'd be able to do it
again. Likewise, I hoped my earlier successes at sniffing out killers would enable me to determine who really
murdered Louie Palumbo.

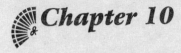

Chapter 10

RIVER EDGE COMMUNITY COLLEGE'S
FRESH START PROGRAM
THE MENTAL MAKEOVER THAT
COMES WITH A COLLEGE DEGREE

Especially designed for women over twenty-five who
would like to experience a college education, RECC's
Fresh Start Program offers the chance to take introductory
classes in the company of like-minded peers. Fresh Start
also provides support services, including tutoring and academic and career counseling as well as a stipend for
books as well as child care . . .

I'd picked up a pile of brochures for the Fresh Start
Program before I left RECC the other day. I called my
friend Sarah Wolf, and while I waited for Sarah to come
to the phone, I stashed the brochures in my purse. They
were going to come in very handy. "Sarah? It's Bel. I
can't believe I got through to you so fast." I was used to
having to browbeat several interns and assistants in
order to get Sarah on the phone at the *Herald*. Right
after Louie's murder, a spate of in-depth stories on the

impersonator had come out. Not realizing that I would have cause to reread these articles, I had scanned and recycled them. Silly me. Now it was faster and more discreet to get Sarah to send me the *Herald*'s file than to sift through old papers at the library or on the Web.

"Yes, and about time too. We're due for dinner. Got your book?" It was always good to hear Sarah's voice. She was the most enduring legacy of a long-ago aerobics class. We had both protested the instructor's choice of motivational music, a percussive piece called "Boom! Boom! Boom! Let's Do It in Your Room" which blasted repeatedly throughout the entire hour-and-fifteen-minute session. Our young classmates had been perfectly content to step and slide to this song, but Sarah and I objected to both the deafening decibel level at which it was broadcast and the misogynistic message of its lyrics. We've been friends ever since. To reduce each other to gales of giggles, all either of us has to do is whisper, "Boom! Boom! Boom!"

Only after we had negotiated a lunch date that wouldn't interfere with my summer school class did Sarah say, "So you and Sol are tripping again, over corpses, that is." She chortled, obviously amused by her retro pun. "Well, I'm not exactly surprised. As Frank put it, Someone's always on site to pick up the pieces . . . or something like that. I figured it wouldn't be long before I got a call. What hapless suspect are you trying to vindicate now, Donna Quixote?"

"It'll keep till we have lunch. Just fax me everything you've got on Louie Palumbo and his women and his Rat Pack, okay?" I said.

"Sure thing, Sherlock. But I hope you've got a strategy. Eating tuna salad as a summer staple is one thing. Sleeping with the fishes is another." Sarah's words were light, but her voice had a warning edge.

My strategy was actually quite simple and, I thought, safe. A quick run-through of the information Sarah sent indicated that Nancy Deloia worked as a bank teller. Sofia was right. I assumed that if Nancy had attended college, she hadn't finished. So I would call on Nancy Deloia in the guise of a RECC Fresh Start recruiter. Like several RECC faculty members, I'd done my share of recruiting at area high schools, so I knew the drill. House-to-house recruiting, which only Fresh Start had the funding to do, couldn't be that different.

If Nancy hadn't murdered Louie, she was still probably in shock over his death. And if she was, indeed, pregnant by Louie, she must be very worried about how she would support her now fatherless child on a teller's take-home pay. If Nancy Deloia hadn't thought about going to college before, I reasoned, she just might be interested in it now as she faced the prospect of a Louie-less life. *And*, my not so inner Jewish mother, who believed education was right up there with chicken soup as a problem solver, added, *if she isn't, she ought to be*. On the other hand, if Nancy had murdered Louie, well, perhaps she'd give herself away somehow.

To make sure Nancy hadn't returned to work yet, I called several local banks asking for her. I soon connected with the one where she was employed and was told that she was on leave and wasn't expected back for at least another week. That meant she'd probably be at home during the day. It could also mean that she was having an understandably hard time accepting the death of her longtime lover.

The articles Sarah sent had not provided an address for Nancy, so next I called all the Deloias listed in the phone book and living in Hoboken. If a machine answered, I hung up. When a human being answered, I asked for Nancy. Two said there was no Nancy at that

address but one party, a child, said, "Oh! She's my
cousin. She doesn't live here. She lives—" and then I
heard, "Gimme that . . ." and the phone slammed down.
The adult in charge there was probably tired of fielding
inquiries about the murder. By the time I finished my
phone calls, I had narrowed the field to two addresses
that looked very promising.

For this outreach effort, I needed no masquerade. I
could be myself. My salt-and-just-a-dash-of-pepper
hair arranged itself in springy curls that I thought were
quite flattering. I was actually grateful for the warm and
humid New Jersey weather that made every summer
day a good hair day for me. I wore flat-heeled sandals
and a plain white short-sleeved shirt tucked into a crisp
khaki skirt gathered ever so slightly at its very forgiving
elastic waist. A wide-brimmed straw hat shaded my
face from the ravages of the bright sun. The huge straw
bag I carried was filled with Fresh Start's promotional
brochures. When I set out, I felt like a cross between a
Jehovah's Witness and an overgrown Girl Scout ped-
dling cookies.

The address I approached first was an apartment in a
large complex between Sixth and Seventh Streets and
Monroe and Jackson. The eight identical beige brick
four-story buildings dated from the fifties, and each
one boasted a garage and access to a common yard
running behind them. Over on the western side of
town, they were a world away from the bar, café, and
condo scene that had made a yuppie heaven out of the
swath of Hoboken closer to the river. I rang the bell
and listened for footsteps. A buzzer sounded. Caught
off-guard, I fumbled with the doorknob, and to my surprise, it opened. I looked for mailboxes, hoping to figure out what floor the Deloias lived on from the
mailbox number. I saw the name just as I heard a shrill

female voice call out, "Come on up, Gio. It's open."

I followed the sound to a door on the third floor that was, indeed, open. "Gio, did you bring the ginger ale?" The voice was a slightly querulous monotone, a little like that of a feverish child or, for that matter, a woman with morning sickness. "Nancy Deloia? Ms. Deloia? Is this the Deloia residence?" I called from the landing, not wanting to startle my unknowing and perhaps homicidal hostess. I stepped through the door to the apartment, stopped, and looked around. I saw him before I saw her. Louie Palumbo stared at me from his pewter-framed public relations photo on the mantel-piece. His eyes bored out at me on either side of a royal blue *X* that had been scrawled over the likeness with what looked like nail polish. "Ms. Deloia," I called again, trying to keep the excitement out of my voice. Getting in had been almost too easy.

"Gio? Who is it?" Even with her pale complexion and red-rimmed eyes, the voluptuous black-haired woman stretched out on the chaise longue like Goya's Maja was beautiful. She didn't move, but she stared at me, her eyes wide with alarm.

I spoke quickly. "Are you Nancy Deloia? I'm Professor Bel Barrett, the recruiter you phoned for an appointment." Her brow contracted, but her eyes resumed their normal shape. "From River Edge Community College. You know, the Fresh Start Program?" I reached in my bag for the brochure, found it, and handed it to her along with my card. While she glanced at the pamphlet, I set my hat down on the low table next to the chaise, pulled a Wash 'n' Dri out of my bag, and began swabbing my face and neck with it. Even though I was practically a poster woman for the estrogen patch, I knew that the right combination of heat, exertion, and stress could still occasionally induce a hot flash from hell. In the summer, the cool squares of alcohol-soaked paper were a godsend. "Quite a climb, those stairs," I said in my most pleasant tone.

"I didn't call no college. I don't know what you're doin' here, but I'm not feelin' good, and I didn't call for anybody. You came all the way up here for nothin'." She flipped the brochure and card to the floor. They lay there next to a heap of what looked like CD containers, all Xed over with blue nail polish.

"Oh dear. There must be some mistake. This is the name and address I got from the Office of Admissions. Look." I approached the chaise longue and thrust forward a list of names including hers that I'd typed up under a RECC letterhead. "Would you mind if I call the office?" Before she could object, I settled into a chair, picked up the phone on the table between us, and dialed my home number. While it rang, I noted the number printed on the phone I was using.

I had expected to talk to my machine. Instead I heard Mark's voice. I ignored his perfectly polite hello and said, "This is Professor Barrett, at one forty-five. I'm at the home of a Nancy Deloia at 644 Jackson Street, the fourth name on my list. She claims she never called the college or requested a visit from a recruiter. Please return this call ASAP and advise. The number is 555-4493." As I read the number, I jotted it down on the list next to Nancy's name."

"Yo, Ma! It's me, Mark. What's up? What are you talking about? Did you dial the wrong number or what?" At the familiar sound of his voice, I started and then frowned. I didn't even have to pretend to look worried. I could picture Mark holding the phone waiting for his mother to say something intelligible to him.

Reluctantly I put down the receiver and, turning to Nancy Deloia, said, "You see, we're expected to make a certain number of contacts each time we go out or—"

"All right, already. Why don't you just say your piece and then you can leave, okay? 'Cause I really don't feel good today. I'm pregnant," she added by way of explanation. "I been sick since the beginning."

"Oh, you poor thing. Is it morning sickness or are you spotting? My daughter's pregnant too." Hearing my hunch confirmed, I responded in my most maternal tone.

My words had the desired effect. Like most women pregnant for the first time and experiencing difficulties, Nancy Deloia was eager to describe her symptoms. A middle-aged mother with a soothing voice was a plausible, even a welcome, audience. "Both." I imagined Rebecca waitressing and going to school, the picture of prenatal health. God, what if she experiences complications? I repressed the thought. Nancy was continuing. "My cousin says I gotta lie here except to go to the bathroom 'cause I'm staining. And I'm sick to my stomach too." The woman's voice was thick with barely repressed fury as she recited the constraints her troubled pregnancy had forced on her. "Anna says I gotta take it easy for a few weeks. I can't even go to work. I'm stuck here."

While Nancy was talking, I glanced around the apartment. On the mantel across from the defaced photo of Louie was a photo of Frank with what looked like an autographed greeting scrawled across the bottom. Between the two photos was a large, framed painting of the crucifixion. White curtains filmed the windows and white carpet covered the floor, both making a stark background for the black leather and chrome furniture. The only colors in the room were a splash of pastel silk flowers on a table near the window, blood dripping from Christ's wounds, and Nancy's royal blue silk robe.

"Oh, I'm so sorry. You certainly are having a very tough pregnancy. I guess your cousin is a doctor?" I asked, somehow knowing she was not.

"No. Anna's not a doctor, but she's had four kids. She knows what to do. I don't need a doctor."

I didn't argue with her, having learned the futility of debating those who reject the help modern medicine sometimes offers. Instead I pursued another line of inquiry. "Oh, I see. Gio, your husband, is he stopping in to check on you? To bring you lunch? You mentioned ginger ale." I paused.

"Gio's my kid brother. He tries to stop by during the day to see how I'm doin'. My fiancé, my baby's father, he died last week." The tears that squeezed out of her eyes were in marked contrast to the sarcasm in her delivery. She stressed the word *died* as if poor Louie had gone and gotten killed on purpose. Silently I cursed Louie Palumbo again, this time for deceiving Nancy Deloia, who clearly had enough on her plate already without being two-timed by the father of the child she was carrying with such difficulty.

Aloud I said, "Oh, I'm so sorry. How awful! He must have been a young man too. Had he been ill? How very sad." I couldn't help reaching out to pat her shoulder.

"It's a long story," she said, petulantly, taking a cigarette from a pack on the table next to her. When Nancy saw the look of horror with which I greeted this gesture, she whined, "Give me a break. Anna says she had a couple a cigarettes a day through all four of her pregnancies and there's nothin' wrong with her kids, believe me." At first I thought she wasn't going to continue to talk, but I was mistaken. Glaring at me almost defiantly, she lit up, took a deep drag, and said, "You probably read about it in the papers. He was Louie Palumbo, the Frank Sinatra impersonator." I stared. "You know, the singer who was stabbed in the back and pushed off the palisade over by Stevens? That's him." She waved her cigarette in the direction of the desecrated photo. Then she reached over and pushed a button on the CD player in the chrome wall unit behind the chaise longue. Louie's voice mechanically mutilating "Love and Marriage" filled the room. Her mouth twisted, Nancy said, "That's him too." She reached over again and, mercifully, lowered the volume.

Recalling that my name had appeared in the paper along with Sol's, I reacted quickly. "Oh no. I know him. I mean, my husband and I found his body. Oh my God, how horrible. I'm so very sorry," I repeated. And I was sorry. The sickly mother-to-be with the tears of grief and rage streaming down her face was truly pitiful. "I thought I recognized that photo on the mantelpiece," I added, hoping to elicit some more information.

Nancy mashed her cigarette stub into an ashtray already holding two butts, glared at the photo of Louie, and hurled her balled-up Kleenex at it. The little wad landed on the floor near the fireplace. "Scumbag. He was a scumbag. He cheated on me. After I got pregnant. I'm planning a weddin' and he's out ballin' some college kid." Nancy's pale cheeks had flushed slightly as she pushed herself up on her elbows and hissed out these words in a sort of feral snarl. As I listened, my face a sympathetic mask, I felt that quick chest contraction I get when my adrenaline output increases suddenly. For a moment or two, Nancy Deloia was truly scary.

But when she spoke next, her tone was different, almost chatty. She took out another cigarette, lit up, and began to speak as if the two of us had been talking girltalk since seventh grade. "I figured somethin' wasn't right when he was always busy, always runnin' somewhere, you know? He wasn't takin' me to gigs so much. I thought maybe he was freaked out about the baby. So finally, I couldn't take it no more. That night he stopped by here after they played a wedding and I just came right out and asked him. He was sitting in that same

chair where you are and I was right there by the window. I said, 'Louie, what's goin' on? Is it the baby? Is it
my brother? Is Gio gettin' on your nerves?' 'Cause
sometimes Gio would crack on Louie, you know? I
said, 'Louie, is it the weddin'?' That's when he told me.
He just said it plain. 'Nan baby, I met somebody else.
I'm in love.' "

Nancy shut her eyes and fell back on the chaise cush-
ions, like a latter-day Mimi or Camille, the smoke from
her cigarette momentarily clouding her face. I was
about to say something when, her eyes still closed, she
continued, "I shoulda listened to my brother. Gio was
right. Gio always said Louie was no good for me. Said I
shoulda married Danny when he asked me. All these
years Gio's been sayin' that." Abruptly her facial features drew together in a grimace, her eyes opened wide,
and she passed one blue-nailed hand over the still small
mound of her belly. "I get these pains sometimes," she
said.

"What the fuck? How'd you get in? I told that other
reporter if she came by here one more time, I'd break
her legs myself." The man's shoulders spanned the
doorway and his arms were long knots of muscle. He
was short, not more than five-five, but very solid. I pre-
sumed that the bag he carried contained ginger ale.
"Leave my sister alone. She got nothin' to say. And you
got exactly one minute to disappear, lady. I'm
countin'." He strode over to the chaise, leaned over his
sister's prone body, and poked a thick finger at the CD
player, cutting Louie off just as he was about to reiterate the inevitable connection between love and baby
carriages.

"Gio, it's all right. She's not a reporter. She's from
the college—" Nancy protested, perhaps embarrassed
by her brother's crudity.

"I don't give a fuck where she's from. I told you to keep the fuckin' door shut." Deliberately abandoning my hat on the table, I was halfway down the stairs before Gio finished his sentence.

Chapter 11

To: Bbarrett@circle.com
From: Rbarrett@UWash.edu
Re: Medical update
Date: Fri, 10 Jul 1998 15:04:31

Dear Mom,

No, I'm not staining, thank you very much. And I told you my morning sickness only lasted a few weeks. I also told you, I went for my regular check-up last week and I (I mean we, Junior and me!) got a clean bill of health. What's with you anyway? My midwife says I just have to watch my weight, and I am. You'd be amazed at what I'm not eating. This baby's going to be born chocolate-deprived! I haven't had candy, beer, or even an ice cream cone since I found out I was pregnant. I don't even drink coffee now.

You sound pretty wired, even for you. Mark thinks you got a little unwrapped over that puppy he was watching. Just the other day he says he got a really strange phone call from you. And today, he e-mailed me that you completely lost it this morning and he can't figure out why. He asked me if menopause had a stage two.

By the way, I hope you'll walk me down the aisle. You and Dad both. Do you think the two of you can hold it together for the time it takes to walk about twenty feet? Come on, Mom. Think about it. Dad has already said yes, but I didn't tell him I was asking you. But he can't back out now. Mark has agreed to play something bluesy for us instead of that corny wedding song.

Love,
Rebecca

"Nice suit, Bel. Rose is a good color for you," Illuminada commented as I lowered myself an inch at a time into the cool water. We were standing in the shallow end of the pool at Betty's condo late Friday afternoon. It was after six, and we had the pool to ourselves except for two boys who were taking turns diving off the board at the other end. I didn't teach on Friday nights, and Betty had suggested we stop by for a swim and then order dinner and compare notes on what each of us had discovered.

"Thanks. I like the color too," I answered. I resisted the impulse to deride my weight by revealing that the front of this swimsuit included a steel panel especially designed to flatten the wearer's tummy or to say that I had bought the suit on sale. Then Illuminada was gone from my side, as she dove obliquely into the water and began to swim.

"At this rate, you and I will never get wet, girl!" exclaimed Betty, splashing me and collapsing onto her butt. "Come on!" She immediately took charge of my submersion by yanking my arm and pulling me down next to her. "The water's great!" She was right.

"This must be where the expression 'chill out' comes from. I feel as if my whole body were just gradually chilling out," I remarked languidly, lying back and making little paddling motions with my hands.

Betty splashed me again. Illuminada swam over to us

and plunked down next to me. "I told you this was a great way to end the day," Betty said.

"*Dios mio*, what we need now is for someone to bring us a gin and tonic each and for Mark to play us a little music." Illuminada sighed with contentment, her hands supporting her head as she floated.

"Don't even mention his name," I said through gritted teeth. "He really got to me this morning."

"I know we're going to have to hear about it, so why not just get it over with. C'mon, Bel. Tell us. What did the poor kid do? Leave the toilet seat up? Or come in after Mama's curfew?" Betty was so smug, I wanted to dunk her. I settled for slapping the water next to her, showering her with spray—a fairly mature reaction, I thought.

"I got up early so I could do yoga, the way I always do. Usually no one is up, and it's peaceful. So there I am, in the bow, a really tight bow, and what do I hear but that overgrown adolescent, that nasal nobody, that cretin Howard Stern talking about nose picking?" I sputtered indignantly. I heard Betty and Illuminada groan in unison. "Every muscle in my body cramped. I wasn't sure I'd be able to get out of the bow. It was awful. I can't stand Howard Stern. It was bad enough that I had to listen to him every morning when Mark was in high school, but now—"

"Why did you have to listen to him then?" Illuminada inquired.

"I figured if I made Howard Stern taboo, Mark would find him even more appealing, but if I just ignored him, Mark would outgrow the show. Although, come to think of it, Lenny never did." I disappeared underwater for a minute, cooling my head and face.

"So what did you say? Tell us how far out of line you got over this," demanded Betty.

"I handled it pretty well at first. I slowly let go of my

ankles, stood up, walked over to the radio, and switched it off," I replied. "Then standing there in his boxers with a carton of Froot Loops in his hand, Mark said something like, 'Hey man, I was listening to that.' And that's when I started screaming about how I wasn't a man, I was his mother and I would not tolerate one more word from Howard Stern in the house ever again and how Howard Stern only appealed to men whose emotional development had been arrested and so on. Finally I shouted something about nose picking being age inappropriate as a topic for humor after nursery school. By the time I finished this tirade, I was sweating and red in the face." I reached for a long plastic tube floating by and hooked my arms over it and let it support me.

"*Dios mio*, I wish you'd taped it," said Illuminada, the traces of a grin threatening to turn her mouth up.

"What did the poor kid say to this?" asked Betty, her mouth not altogether steady either.

"First he said, 'Breathe, Ma, breathe,' like he always says when I go off on him. Then when my breathing had returned to near normal, he got me a glass of water. That's when he said, 'Tell me how you really feel, Ma. Seriously, I didn't know Howard Stern bothered you. I'm sorry.' Then he showered, dressed, and left for a temp job. I've been feeling like a nut case all day." I submerged again, literally soaking my head at the memory of the morning's scene.

"Well girl, don't feel too bad. Last time Randy was home I went off on him big time for leaving half a sandwich in his room until the thing smelled so nasty even the mold left it," added Betty, reassuring me that I was not the only one who occasionally strayed from the path of model motherhood.

"Remember I told you about the night Lourdes came in from Rutgers three hours later than she said she would. And she didn't even have the courtesy or con-

sideration to call. *Caramba*, I met her halfway down the
street and did the whole song and dance about how 'I
don't care what you do in college, but when you're in
my house, you live by my rules.' " Betty and I nodded,
ourselves no strangers to that particular parental chest-
nut. "And I did it loud too, *en español*, so she'd know I
was serious. When I finally wound down, she explained
about how there'd been a train accident and she'd been
stuck on the train for the whole three hours. This was
before cell phones. I felt like a jerk, but hey . . ."

We each swam a few laps just to prove we still could
and then showered at the pool. Later, refreshed and
relaxed, we sat around Betty's table, enjoying the air
conditioning, cold Coronas, and an array of hummus,
stuffed eggplant, stuffed grape leaves, yogurt and garlic
dip, and shepherd's salad from our favorite Turkish
restaurant. Young Frank was singing "Everything Happens to Me" with the Tommy Dorsey Orchestra on a
CD Sofia had lent me.

"Well, I may be a mutant mom, but I scored with
Nancy Deloia. I'm practically a second mother to her
now," I began, eager to tell of my infiltration of Nancy
Deloia's apartment. By the time I finished, Betty was
flexing her fingers, tired from typing so fast, and Illuminada was looking puzzled. "You say she came right out
and called Louie a scumbag? And she made no effort to
hide the CDs and the photo that she's messed up? She's
got them right out in the open?" she asked.

"Right. She actually seemed eager to unload her
anger on another woman. I can't blame her. I think
she's depressed. Actually, I felt terrible leaving her
lying there. She needs a real doctor. Her cousin may
mean well, but I don't think she's any substitute for a
real doctor. And then there's Gio. He seems to be concerned about her, but I suspect that his value as a conversational partner is limited."

"Yes and no," Betty chimed in. "I got him over here and he went on for a while about cement. He's really into his work. But it was hard to get him to talk about anything else. When we went inside so I could give him a cold drink while he wrote up an estimate, he saw Randy's weights and bench. Then he started to talk about strength training. He's a really serious bodybuilder. I had the feeling that he would have gone on for a while, but I was on my lunch hour and had to get back to the office. I think we're going to hire him to do the work here, so maybe I'll get another chance." Betty stopped talking, took a long swig of Corona, and resumed typing.

"Well, as I said, Gio's on the record as having always disliked Louie. And I wouldn't want to make him mad," I added, recalling Gio's menacing manner when he'd found me at his sister's apartment. "He has a short fuse."

"So, *chiquitas*, how do you think brother Gio felt when he found out Louie the Louse betrayed his sister after getting her pregnant?" Illuminada articulated the question that we had each been pondering.

I had another one. "Just tell me one thing. Are the cops questioning these folks? And if not, why not? They're all over Toni Demaio, who had, as far as I can see, no motive. Remember, she didn't even know about Nancy until after Louie was killed. They must be onto these two. I mean, Nancy's got everything but a Louie doll with pins in it, and I wouldn't be surprised if Gio didn't have 'I hate Louie' tattooed on his bicep," I was really thinking out loud.

"And according to what she told you, Nancy was with Louie after he left Toni that night. She may have been the last person to see him alive," Betty added gravely.

"*Si, si,* especially if she killed him," jibed Illuminada.

"Oh shut up," Betty muttered.

"Well, maybe I'm missing something, but I wouldn't talk to a total stranger about how pissed off I was at my dead fiancé if I'd killed him," I persisted. "I wonder if Nancy has an alibi. Fortunately, I left my hat there."

"Oh, you clever thing, you," gushed Illuminada. "So now you're going to call up and arrange to pick up your hat when Gio's not home so you can lean on poor Nancy some more, right?"

"Right," I answered smugly. I was actually rather proud of the hat ploy, a version of the old fifties compact-in-his-car maneuver. When I was in high school, a girl would leave a compact or lipstick in a boy's car so he'd feel obligated to call her to return it, or if he didn't, she'd have an excuse to call him. I lost a lot of makeup that way.

"What did you find out about John Cardino?" asked Betty, turning to look at Illuminada.

"*Dios mio*, the poor boy has no alibi either. He was studying for the New Jersey bar exam, so he stayed home that night. That whole weekend, in fact. And the rest of his family was at the shore, like the Demaios. He didn't talk to anybody or see anybody. He just studied," Illuminada said, shaking her head at the quandary John's diligence had placed him in.

"Well, here's what has to happen," proclaimed Betty, slipping easily into command mode. "I mean as I see it," she added hastily in an effort to create an illusion of free will. "Bel, you need to go back to get your hat and see if she has an alibi for that evening and—"

"—pump her on his other friends and associates too." I finished Betty's sentence just to get her goat. "And I'd like to talk to others in the neighborhood who might have something to say that proves useful," I added, helping myself to a peach from the bowl in the center of the table.

Betty spoke again, now confining her directives to herself. "I'm going to keep pumping Gio. He's supposed to start working here next week, and I'm going to figure out some way to get him talking about Louie. Or

Nancy. I consider getting him to talk about something besides cement or bicep curls as my personal challenge," Betty vowed.

"*Dios mio*, the poor man doesn't know what he's in for," said Illuminada.

"Very funny, but what are you planning to do, Señora Big Mouth?" Betty snapped, passing the bowl of fruit to Illuminada.

"I'm going to find out exactly where the Hoboken police stand on this investigation. Bel's right, they've probably looked into the Deloias. I'd like to know what they think, why no one's been indicted, and, of course, I'll keep on trying to find out more about John Cardino." Illuminada selected a couple of ripe plums before handing the bowl to me.

"I want to talk to Toni again too," I mused aloud. "And I want to walk through that old neighborhood."

"By the way Bel, how is Sol taking all this? How did he feel about your visiting Nancy Deloia alone? Did he give you a hard time?" Betty asked, all too well aware of Sol's unequivocal opposition to my crime-busting activities in the past. "You did tell him, didn't you?"

"Yes, of course I told him," I retorted. "I told him that there was no danger of Nancy finding out who I was from anybody else because I'd tell her myself that I was a recruiter from RECC, period. Sol knows I recruit from time to time, so he really didn't have a problem with my doing it again."

"Praise the Lord for that," Betty said. "We are relieved. Now, enough of this. Tell us about Rebecca's wedding. I've got my book right here. What's the date?"

Chapter 12

To: Motherofthebride@weddings.org
From: Bbarrett@circle.com
Re: Crash course for MOBs in the nineties
Date: Fri, 10 Jul 1998 23:20:17

I need a crash course in how to be a divorced and repartnered MOB (the pregnant bride, yet) in the nineties. First of all, my daughter wants both me and my ex to accompany her down the aisle. (Well, it would be an aisle if they were marrying in a synagogue, but instead they have chosen to exchange vows in a gas station museum in the middle of the winter in Seattle where it rains all the time anyway.) My ex and I don't usually communicate without a certain amount of, shall we say, friction.

Second, as a modern feminist I probably shouldn't care about the whole traditional dress, wedding march, vows thing, but I do. For over a quarter of a century, I've been waiting for my daughter to grow up so I could plan a dream wedding for her. Instead she's making all the arrangements for what sounds like a nightmare.

And third, as a secular humanistic Jew, I don't mind that her fiancé's not Jewish, but I would like at least a trace of Jewishness in the ceremony. And what if they get married by some politically incorrect conservative official or, dare I say it, by a Republican?

Finally, my daughter and I used to be very close, but now it's as if more than just the distance between Seattle and Hoboken has come between us. Help! I'm

Heartbroken in Hoboken

After I found the on-line support group for mothers of the bride and sent off my plea for help, I felt a little calmer about Rebecca's wedding plans. In the past, I'd benefited from advice from my cyber sisters on everything from hot flashes and vaginal dryness to caring for an aging and infirm parent. I was confident that somewhere out there some other MOB would read my words and respond with wisdom and compassion. Just as I logged off, the phone rang. "You want to hear a real Frank impersonator?" asked Ma as soon as I answered. "Sofia says when this guy sings, you close your eyes and it's Frank." I was used to picking up the receiver and hearing Ma's voice. She assumed that I'd recognize her slightly raspy tones, so she seldom bothered to preface her messages with the usual amenities.

"We might be up for that. When? Where?" I knew I'd enjoy it, but I wasn't sure about Sol.

I assumed Sofia had got wind of some local performance, so I was surprised when Ma said, "In New York. At a club, I think, downtown somewhere. A dance place. Maybe we'll go for Sofia's eighty-fourth birthday next week." I quickly translated. Sofia and Ma would like us to drive them into the city to hear this latest incarnation of Frank. "There was a poster Sofia saw. She thought you and Sol might be interested. She's heard the performer. His name's Luke something. He lives in Hoboken now. It's on Wednesday night though,

so I already told her to forget it because you had class."
Ma's voice lowered with disappointment and resignation.

My mother might be getting older, but she hadn't lost
her ability to induce guilt. I had spent years feeling
guilty because I had to leave my children in order to
work, and now that the kids were grown, I felt guilty
because my job might prevent me from taking my octo-
genarian mother and her friend clubbing. What's wrong
with this picture? Clearly I had two choices. I could
ruin Sofia's eighty-fourth birthday, or Sol and I could
take the Odd Couple to New York to hear a Frank Sinatra impersonator.

That's how I ended up heading into Manhattan after
class with Sol, Sofia, and Ma to Swing for Your Supper,
a trendy new club in Chelsea where Luke Jonas was
performing. I was actually curious to hear the singer
whose voice had ignited the spark of love between Toni
Demaio and Louie Palumbo. And I had to admit that it
felt very glamorous to be zipping into the city for a
night out after work. I'd dressed for the occasion in a
flared black skirt and a sleeveless shell of gray silk.
Winston, who with his bejeweled tongue was the epit-
ome of cool, had given me an appraising glance and
then a thumbs-up, and Ndaye had pronounced my outfit
"tres chic." But Ma and Sofia literally outshone me. Ma
wore a black scoop-necked sleeveless dress with a
matching jacket. Earrings of ivory and onyx in the
shape of dice, a fiftieth anniversary present from my
father, glittered in her ears. Sofia was splendid in a
beige-knit ensemble, the scoop neckline outlined with a
rainbow of irridescent beadwork.

Sol had made reservations and mentioned the birthday celebrant, so a hostess escorted us past the young
people thronging the bar to a table on the edge of the
dance floor across from the band. We had arrived

between sets, and I slipped the hostess a twenty and a scrap of paper on which I'd written Sofia's name. I pointed discreetly at Sofia and whispered, "It's her eighty-fourth birthday. Please tell the singer. She came in from Hoboken to hear him."

The timing was perfect. Just as the waiter delivered our four glasses of white wine and four plates of fairly palatable-looking lobster salad, the band struck up the first few chords of "Witchcraft." I closed my eyes. It *was* Frank. The phrasing, the diction, the resonance were pure Frank. I opened my eyes. Frank was gone. From where we sat, I saw a man who was nearly six feet tall, aping the bantam strut of a much shorter man in elevator shoes. He was fumbling with a lit cigarette as if it were his first and sipping delicately from what purported to be a tumbler of Frank's signature Jack Daniels. Traces of a reddish ponytail extended from beneath a brown wig and disappeared under the collar of a white shirt. Quickly I closed my eyes again. When I reopened them, the singer was hidden behind a sea of swirling dancers.

Sofia sat with her eyes half shut, her fingers tapping, and her lips singing silently along. Ma's head was cocked to one side, a dreamy smile on her face. Then the band segued into the lead-in to "One More for the Road." Ma and Sofia looked at each other, sighed, and clicked their glasses, two old women and new friends honoring memories of other times. They ignored their lobster salads until the set ended.

Luke Jonas began the next set by announcing, "Tonight we have with us a very special guest who's come all the way from Frank's hometown across the river to celebrate her birthday. Let's give a very warm welcome to Sofia Dellafemina." There was a burst of applause. Sofia was caught completely off-guard. She looked around her, flustered. In an instant Luke Jonas was at her side, bending down to kiss her lightly on the cheek. He said, "For your birthday, I'd like to sing a song specially for you. What's your favorite Frank Sinatra tune, Sofia?" He held the microphone close to her face.

" 'They Can't Take That Away from Me,' " Sofia replied softly, still a little intimidated to find herself literally in the spotlight. She and Ma clinked glasses again, both pleased with Sofia's selection, both, no doubt, recalling the men who had, until recently, shared their lives. I felt tears welling. I was reaching in my purse for Kleenex when the song ended and Luke Jonas reappeared at our table. "How about a tune for your friend? Your choice, little lady." He leaned over to catch Ma's response, cued the band with a gesture, and performed a scorn- and sin-filled rendition of "Luck Be a Lady" that was pure Sinatra. Ma was beaming. I knew she'd be a winner at the casino this week.

When the set was over this time, Luke Jonas approached our table again, signaled a waiter, and ordered a bottle of champagne. "Let's really celebrate. This is a very special occasion." He pulled over a chair and seated himself between Ma and Sofia. Up close he could have been anyone's son but Dolly Sinatra's. His makeup barely coated the freckles at his hairline. In fact, his hairline, a hybrid border where his Frank wig battled for supremacy with his ponytail, fascinated me. I just couldn't keep my eyes off the fugitive tendrils of reddish hair tunneling under his shirt collar. Looking at each of us, he said simply, "I'm Luke Jonas," initiating introductions all around the table. The champagne arrived, the waiter uncorked it, and Luke poured, saying with more than a hint of the gallant, "Again, a very happy birthday to you, Sofia. And many more." We all drank.

"So how do you like the show?" he asked, his eyes panning all our faces before they settled on Sofia and Ma.

"It's sensational. Absolutely sensational. You sound just like Frank. And I heard him live, too," gushed Sofia, sipping her champagne. "Plenty of times."

"Well, thank you. Coming from you, that's high praise. Believe me, I work hard to get his phrasing and his pitch." Luke was leaning back in his chair, enjoying the moment. "And to get that sense of chatty intimacy too," he added. I wondered if he were quoting from his own reviews.

"One of my students says she and her boyfriend fell in love listening to you sing 'All the Way' at the birthday party for Frank last winter at Hoboken City Hall," I interjected, eager to pass on Toni's compliment. "Now I can understand that."

Luke smiled and said, "That was a good show too, if I do say so myself." He lowered his eyes modestly. "We were celebrating another very special person's birthday that night. Jeez, folks in Hoboken sure do get into the whole Sinatra thing," he exclaimed, almost to himself. "It's like he still lives there, like he never left."

Not liking to be out of the conversational loop, Ma put in her two cents. "I never saw Frank perform live, but I saw all of his movies. Every single one." She straightened her back and patted her mouth delicately with her napkin.

"Did you see the film Tina made?" Sofia asked. Many Born-and-Raised Hobokenites were on a first name basis with the entire Sinatra family. Ma looked blank, so Sofia went on, "Tina Sinatra, his daughter. She made a film about his life. It was on television."

"Interesting movie," said Luke, his eyes casting about the room now as if looking for someone. "Philip Casnoff did a great job as Frank. What a break that part was for him." He craned his neck a little, and the motion pulled an auburn tress out from beneath his collar. "This thing's a damn nuisance," he said irritably, stuffing the wayward curl back under his shirt and patting the wig with an almost automatic gesture. The artery in his neck pulsed, an index of his annoyance with his clumsy disguise. But in a minute he was smiling again.

"No. I meant I saw only the movies Frank was actually in. The *real* Frank," said Ma, still trying to stake out a place in the conversation.

"Oh! There's my agent. Sorry, gotta go make nice. He's the one who can make it all happen." Planting quick kisses on Ma and Sofia's star-struck cheeks and waving goodbye to Sol and me, Luke left the table and joined a large bearded man across the room. The two shook hands and exchanged bear hugs.

Later after we dropped off Ma and Sofia, I said to Sol, "Thanks for going with us tonight, and for driving and making the reservations. I owe you one. You were so quiet. Did you hate the whole thing?"

"No. I got off on what a good time the Odd Couple were having, and that was the point, wasn't it? Besides, I was glad you didn't make me dance. And you seemed to be enjoying the show too, so that was a bonus." Sol reached over and squeezed my thigh.

"Well, it just amazes me that anyone would want to earn a living impersonating someone else," I mused. "What a fascinating concept."

"It's called acting, my love, that's all. Just another kind of theater." Sol parked the car in the vest pocket lot where we rent a space and, hand in hand, we walked across the street to our house.

"This is different from regular acting. In theater, the play's the thing. In impersonation, it's the personality, the looks, the voice, a character in a vacuum without a play to be in. I think it's weird. I want to know more about it," I said from within a big yawn. "But not tonight."

The impersonator I really wanted to know more about was the late Louie Palumbo, so the next morning I dialed Nancy Deloia's number. She answered on the first ring, and without giving her time to argue, I told her that I was stopping by to pick up my hat. When I got there, she buzzed me in and opened the door for me herself. Her long black hair was dull and matted, her eyes sunken, and her skin gray. "C'mon in. I'm real sorry about my brother, how he acted the other time when you were here. Sometimes Gio runs his mouth too fast for his brain." This ashen-faced Miss Manners in jeans and a T-shirt was a far cry from the barely civil siren in royal blue silk who had greeted me last week. Today she looked older than her thirty-something years.

I spoke quickly, ignoring her apology for the moment. "Are you supposed to be up? Please don't get up on my account." Alarm rushed my words and made them sharp.

"No problem. Not anymore," she said. No sooner had she spoken than her lip began to quiver and her eyes filled. Abruptly squaring her shoulders and literally swallowing her tears, she looked up and said, "I lost Louie's baby. First I lost Louie and then I lost our baby." Her voice was expressionless, but in her trembling hands and rapid breathing I could read the effort she was making to contain her feelings.

"Oh, I'm so sorry. I really am. Two losses, one right after the other like that, have to be pretty hard to handle," I murmured, reaching out to pat her shoulder. "I guess the shock and sadness of your fiancé's death was just too much."

Nancy moved away from me and motioned for me to follow her into the kitchen. Walking behind her, I noticed that the defaced photo of Louie no longer graced the mantelpiece. She poured herself a Coke and said, "Coffee?"

"Tea, please," I answered, hoping this second foray into hospitality meant that she was again in need of a sympathetic listener. It did. In a moment she had nuked a cup of hot water and handed it to me along with a surprisingly respectable choice of tea bags. As if we had been exchanging confidences for years, we automatically settled at the tiny kitchen table.

Nancy's next words shocked me. "It's the goddamn cops' fault I lost that baby. I know it." My face must have registered my surprise, because she rushed on to explain. "First they came round bothering me about that night when Louie was here. They wanted to know what happened between us. Like it's their business. Like I'm going to tell that stupid Al Montegna my business. Excuse me, *Captain* Montegna. I've known that creep since seventh grade. He thought he was so smart. Wouldn't let nobody cheat off him in math. And that's not enough, he's got a mouth bigger than the Atlantic Ocean. Think I'm gonna tell that SOB that Louie fell in love with somebody else and wanted to dump me? He can see I'm pregnant. He'll think I'm some kind of fool. Everybody will. I already done enough to my family."

When she slowed down to breathe, I asked, "What do you mean?"

"Well, thank God my parents never lived to see me in this mess." She crossed herself and looked up quickly. Following her eyes, I noticed a framed collection of family photos over the table. In the center was an old wedding portrait of a bride smiling happily at the groom by her side. Like her daughter, the bride had been a voluptuous beauty. Like his son, the groom had been short and sturdy.

"Oh no! Are they both dead?" I asked.

"My father dropped dead of a heart attack at the plant one day. And a few years later, my mother had headaches, real bad headaches. One day she got dizzy right outside here." Nancy gestured toward the street. "One of the neighbors took her to the emergency room. Turns out it was a brain tumor. She died on the table. They both been gone for years now. There's just me and Gio left." Nancy lowered her head. Now I understood why she was so vulnerable to even the slightest show of solicitude. She was an orphan, no stranger to loss. Louie and the baby were just the latest in a string of losses. When she spoke again, her voice was hard. "It's just as well they're gone 'cause, like Gio says, this shit with me and Louie woulda killed them."

I was beginning to wonder if Gio ever said anything positive when Nancy spoke again. "So anyway, like I was saying, this cop is around here buggin' me about that night, and I don't tell him that after Louie left, I was just here by myself markin' up Louie's picture. Some alibi, huh?" She flashed me a twisted smile that made a grotesque mask out of her pale, hollow-eyed face. The stiffening hairs on my neck reminded me once again that she was a pretty disturbing lady.

"Well, I can deal with that. I don't much care about myself now. But when they came back last week, not long after you left really, there were two cops. And they were asking me questions about Gio. Like how did Gio feel about Louie? Where was Gio that night? They kept buggin' me. That's what got me upset. That's why I lost Louie's baby. Everybody knows I practically raised Gio. He never made a secret how he felt about Louie. Thought Louie shoulda had a real job like Danny, not just spend his time tryin' to be Frank. Thought Louie wasn't good enough for me."

Nancy turned to me and said, "Do you mind?" Without waiting for a reply, she lit up a cigarette from a pack on the table, took a long drag, and said, "The cops think Gio might be the one who stabbed Louie." Nancy's face was grave. "And you know what gets me, Professor? Really gets me?" I shook my head, but her question had been purely rhetorical. She barely paused to let the smoke out before she said, "Maybe he did. That's the sad part. Maybe he did. I'm so scared because maybe he just fuckin' did. And right after those two cops left here, that's when I lost the baby."

Chapter 13

To: Blbarrett@circle.com
From: Llyons@juno.com
Re: Nineties MOBs
Date: Thurs, 16 Jul 1998 10:02:45

Dear Heartbroken in Hoboken,

I've married off four daughters, and I've come up with some rules I share with first-time MOBs:

1. *It's not your wedding*. If you've been fantasizing over twenty-five years about planning your daughter's wedding, she's probably over twenty-five herself and can plan her own wedding, and you need to seriously upgrade your fantasy life.

2. *Your ex-husband is your new best friend*. Show me a mother who cannot put aside differences with an ex for the duration of a wedding weekend and I'll show you an immature and short-sighted woman. Be polite and don't let him get to you. I was so nice to my ex at my second daughter's wedding that my sister started taking my pulse. I was even nicer to his date, a twenty-two-year-old secretary. He may be my ex-husband, but that SOB is still my daughter's father.

3. **Suggest your ideas to the bride and groom—once**. If you have a suggestion for who might officiate or how the ceremony might reflect your Jewish background, then make it, ONCE. They are not mind readers. I wanted my little nephew to have a role in the festivities, and when I suggested this, my daughter thanked me for giving her such a good idea. She hadn't thought of it. That's because she was worried about how to get the guests assembled at the hang glider landing site for the reception after the private airborne ceremony. Their baby was born two days later. Yes, you got it. Don't ask.

My speech class went pretty well that night even though I was disappointed when Ndaye didn't show up again. This time she'd left a breathless run-on sentence on my voice mail explaining that she had to work. Winston, still enthralled by the new babies in his family, was preparing photos and diagrams illustrating the various factors influencing the life of twins in the womb such as the time the fertilized egg splits, the number of placentas and amniotic sacs, the position of the umbilical cord. He had practiced using an overhead projector. And Tomas was planning props to dramatize his speech admonishing us to stockpile food, water, and medicine along with a battery-operated radio, a flashlight and an Uzi in preparation for a millennial takeover by the Forces of Evil. I ix-nayed the Uzi as a visual aid.

After class I rushed home to greet Illuminada and Betty, who were coming over to compare notes and try to figure out who might have killed Louie Palumbo. When I arrived, I was surprised to find both Illuminada and Betty sitting on my stoop. "Sorry to keep you waiting. Didn't Mark or Sol let you in? I think they're both home," I said, catching my breath and getting out my key.

"Nobody answered the door," said Betty. "Sounds as

if Mark's home though." She was right. I could hear the music as I inserted my key in the lock. When I swung open the door, a deafening sound blasted through it, nearly knocking me over. Mark was so intent on his fingering that he didn't see me at first. The other guitarist and the bass player had their backs to me. A can of beer sat on the floor next to each musician.

I walked over to Mark and positioned myself in front of him. I was livid. When he finally looked up, he smiled and said, "Yo, Ma Bel." Still strumming but more softly now, he leaned over and planted a kiss on my cheek. "When Sol booked this afternoon, I invited these dudes over to jam till you got home," he said amiably. The music had stopped and I heard Eric and Carl behind me putting away their instruments.

"Where did Sol go?" I asked through clenched teeth.

"Alexis called. She needed him up there for a few days to baby-sit or something. He left about six. He'll call you tonight or tomorrow," Mark explained. Sol thought nothing of driving to Peekskill where his daughter and her family lived to help out in a baby-sitting crisis. Mark was heading for the front door with his friends. "These dudes are leaving their instruments here just for tonight. That's cool with you, isn't it? We're going to Maxwell's to hear some music. Don't wait up." And planting another kiss on my cheek, my son and his partners in pandemonium were out the door calling good night as they left. I heard them greet Betty and Illuminada who, for lack of earplugs, had waited outside until the decibel level decreased.

"Thank God Randy just took a few piano lessons and gave it up." Betty sighed.

"*Dios mio*, Bel," he plays so well, but . . ." Illuminada seated herself at a stool around the kitchen counter, and Betty and I followed her.

"Does this place smell of beer or is that just my over-wrought imagination?" I asked, automatically counting the cans in the trash.

"No, but what else do you have to drink that's cold?" asked Betty. We settled for some cranberry juice. "So what've you found out? Vic says you sounded pretty excited on the phone."

"Well, Nancy Deloia had a miscarriage." I paused for a moment, remembering Nancy's sad eyes. "She blames the cops." When Betty cast me a puzzled look, I explained. "The cops have been on her case after all," I recounted, as Illuminada nodded her head. Apparently what I was saying jibed with her findings. "Nancy has no alibi for later that night because after she and Louie fought, she claims he left, and she stayed home alone and messed up his photo." Betty had begun to type into her laptop. "She knows she's a suspect, but she seems much more worried about the fact that the cops also suspect her brother. She's very close to Gio. She took care of him after their parents died. The cops questioned him and they questioned her about him. Nancy knows they suspect him of killing Louie. And she's worried that Gio might actually have done it." I hesitated, as much to give Betty a chance to catch up as to let them react to my words.

"He very well might have," said Betty, pushing her laptop out of the way and sipping her juice. "That's one weird dude. Definitely the strong silent type. If he talks at all, like I said the other night, it's about his work or his weights. I spent twenty minutes in the hot sun the other day trying to get him to open up about his family. I asked him straight out if he came from a big family or not. He just grunted no and kept on working." I made a mental note to give Betty a little lesson in interviewing strategy. Yes-or-no questions guarantee dead-end re-sponses. "Then I brought him a cold drink and asked him if he'd heard about the singer who was murdered in Hoboken." Betty paused, letting the audacity of her question sink in. "You know what he said?"

Illuminada began tapping her fingernails on the countertop. I yawned audibly. Betty got the idea and resumed her story. "He said, and I quote, 'If Louie Palumbo was a singer then I'm a fuckin' ballet dancer. That sonovabitch couldn't sing worth shit.' All the while he just kept on smoothing the cement. Didn't even look up." Betty smiled a little and continued, "I laughed and said I agreed with him. I told him I'd heard Louie Palumbo sing once and it had been a near-death experience. I thought he'd say more, but he didn't. He just kept moving that trowel back and forth. He's creepy."

"His sister's pretty creepy at times too," I added, recalling Nancy's twisted smile. "But I don't know if she killed Louie. I just don't know," I added, thinking out loud.

"*Caramba*, Bel," said Illuminada. "It's so annoying that not one of the suspects has an alibi. The Hoboken cops think one of the North Bergen duo did it. They'd like to see John Cardino nailed for this one or Toni Demaio. Of course the North Bergen cops want to pin it on the Deloia siblings of Hoboken. But there's no evidence and no witnesses. Until someone walks in with a knife covered with fingerprints and dripping with Louie's blood, they won't indict anyone for Louie's murder."

"I still want to talk to more people, cast a wider net," I said. "You know, there's something too symmetrical about this. I mean, Louie betrayed both Toni and Nancy. They are both logical suspects, especially Nancy. And they're both trying to protect men who also had strong motives. That's so odd."

"I don't think you can compare Louie's betrayal of

Toni whom he knew for only a few months to cheating on Nancy. *Dios mio*, he went with Nancy for years and she was carrying his baby," said Illuminada. "Those two are not apples and oranges."

"I know you're right," I said, sighing, "because I'm positive Toni didn't kill him. We have to remember she didn't even know she had anything to be jealous about until after Louie died."

"That's what she told you, *chiquita*. And we know you believe her, but . . ." Illuminada's voice was filled with skepticism. She had earned the right to question. That's why she was a PI. But I was an English prof, and I thought I knew something about students. I believed Toni Demaio. For now at least, I decided to ignore Illuminada's well-intended warning.

"I'm going to look into other aspects of Louie's life too," I added. "I just haven't had a chance yet." I pulled out my date book and scanned the month. "I'm having lunch with Sarah this week, and maybe she'll have more background material. And I'll talk to the Palumbos. Maybe one of Louie's relatives had it in for him. I remember Louie had a twin brother. Could have been a little sibling rivalry or something. And I haven't talked to the band members yet. Maybe there was something there."

"Go, girl, go," said Betty, heading wearily for the door. "Just remember, I'm going to be at a Board of Trustees retreat with President Woodman part of next week, so stay out of trouble. Come on Illuminada, I fell asleep half an hour ago."

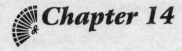

Chapter 14

To: Bbarrett@circle.com
From: Jfarley@msn.com
Re: MOB advice
Date: Fri, 17 Jul 1998 14:25:19

Listen up Heartbroken,

I bet back in the sixties you and your ex had one of those hippie weddings in Central Park or on a mountaintop someplace, right? Probably married by an Ethical Culture type or a pro-choice judge with all your Peace Corps and food co-op friends zonked out in a circle singing "Blowin' in the Wind" and "Cumbaya." You were barefoot in a tie-dyed mini-dress and wore "flowers in your hair." I can just see it. You must have been a very groovy person back then. What happened?

If you ever decide to get remarried (instead of—what did you say you were now—*repartnered*?), this time around you could have a traditional wedding in a synagogue, wear a long white gown, walk down the aisle to "Here Comes the Bride," and see what you missed. But your daughter's wedding is her show, not yours, and she's got the right idea. I live in Seattle, and I've been to two weddings in the Petroleum Museum. It's a trip, that place. Funky as hell and very hip. You'll all have a great time.

So I say, put those flowers back in your hair, be civil to your ex, and focus on becoming a groovy grandma.

Peace. Love.
Jasmine

It was cloudy when I set out on my fact-finding mission. Once again, I didn't need to pretend to be other than what I was, a middle-aged Sinatra fan, one of the hundreds of pilgrims from all over the world paying homage to her idol by visiting his birthplace and early stomping grounds. I recall reading a magazine article whose author dubbed Frank Sinatra the "Proust of Hoboken." It's certainly true that a few bars of "I'm a Fool to Want You" or "Violets for Her Furs" are the musical madeleines that draw his fans here. But unlike the others who worship at the familiar shrines, this time I was not seeking the aura of the deity himself. Rather I sought to get in touch with an acolyte, one who'd made a lifestyle and a living out of playing the god.

An early draft of Toni's paper was going to serve me as both map and passport on my quest. Winded and sweating, I climbed to the second floor of the charming but unair-conditioned Hoboken Public Library, where the Sinatra archives are housed, only to find a reference librarian whom I didn't recognize busy on the phone. When the graying, bespectacled woman hung up and turned to me, I hid my real purpose behind a version of the truth. "I'm just checking a few references. A student of mine at River Edge Community College has done some research on Dolly Sinatra here, and I want to verify a few of her sources." The librarian nodded and escorted me over to an oak cabinet where I could see numerous books about Frank displayed behind ornate curlicues of decorative metal over glass. She unlocked the door and gestured for me to help myself. Then she unlocked a nearby file cabinet and took out three folders filled with newspaper clippings and letters. "This is pretty much what we have on the family. Help yourself. Of course, none of this stuff goes out. But we do have a copier." She pointed to the Xerox machine in the corner. "You need change though. We don't provide change. Let me know when you're finished."

She was about to return to her desk when I said, "Thanks. Before you go, though, I do have a question. My student cites interviews with a Louis Palumbo. You know, the Frank Sinatra impersonator who died?" A shadow momentarily darkened the librarian's face. "She cites him frequently and describes meeting him here. You must have known him. Was he really the authority she seems to think he was? Would you consider him a reputable source?"

"Louie Palumbo's one of the first people I met when I started to work here. Frank Sinatra was his whole life. That man interviewed anybody in town who ever breathed in the same room with Frank or any of the Sinatra family. Louie was born and raised here, so other native Hobokenites trusted him. He spent hours and hours talking with people who had known the Sinatras. And he understood what these folks had to tell him. Some of it's probably true. Some of it," she said, shrugging her shoulders. "Some of it's probably, shall we say, embellished. That's the way it is with oral history. You know some people like to put in their two cents even if they don't have it." She smiled at the thought of our human tendency to fabricate. "Let's put it this way, if it happened to Sinatra or his family in Hoboken, Louie probably knew about it. I'd say he was a pretty reliable source on the Hoboken years. I referred a lot of reporters to him and even one or two academics. Biog-

raphers too. Especially right after Sinatra's death. Louie
Palumbo was very generous with his time and his information. He'd talk to anybody." Then she surprised me
by adding almost sheepishly, "I'm going to miss him."

"Thank you," I said as she turned and headed back to
her desk without further comment. I was relieved at not
having to listen to yet another woman lament the loss of
Louie Palumbo. I made a pretense of rifling through the
folders and then Xeroxed a couple of articles. Next I
thumbed through one or two of the books. When a
decent interval had elapsed, I returned the files to the
librarian and left.

Toni's paper referred to Sinatra's birthplace, which
seemed a logical place to go next, especially since I
knew there was a little shop next door where, for the
price of a T-shirt, I might learn something new about
Louie. The proprietor who makes a living hawking
Sinatra memorabilia to tourists had once sold me a
poster-sized reproduction of a sheet music cover photo
of the young Frank leaning on his folded arms and staring at the camera. To this day it quickens my pulse
every time I look at it. I hoped the same chatty guy was
still there.

Walking west, I was struck as always by how little
that side of Hoboken has been affected by the influx of
yuppie newcomers. This neighborhood manages to get
along without the cafés, bars, gyms, and shops that
have sprung up to supply the lattes and grilled veggies,
designer beer and loud music, and personal trainers and
trendy duds the latest immigrants require. Here the
streets are still quiet, the few pedestrians are older, and
most row houses boast carefully tended planters, American flags, or both. From some windows, a statue of
Mary or Jesus surveys the streetscape. Here lattes are
harder to come by, but you can still buy fresh mozzarella at Fiore's as Dolly Sinatra used to, and coal

oven baked bread at Dom's on Grand Street, the place that shipped it to "The King" himself after he defected to Hollywood. But even here, far from the waterfront now dubbed the Gold Coast by real estate mavens, there are signs of change. Men filling Dumpsters, operating bulldozers and cranes and rigging scaffolds were transforming even the west side of Hoboken in preparation for its future role as a stop on the new light rail. In five years, Dolly would barely recognize the place.

By the time I got to Monroe Street, the morning's clouds had given way to a sudden hard rain. Sprinting from the corner, I took refuge in the souvenir shop, where I quickly discovered I was not alone. The weather had driven several other pilgrims inside too. "I've come all the way from Melbourne to visit Frank's birthplace and it's raining! What a nuisance! Really!" huffed a tall ruddy-cheeked woman in her fifties with very short graying hair. She wore a Burberry trench coat and sensible shoes. A camera hung from a strap around her neck and a bouquet of bright orange tiger lilies seemed to sprout from an opening at the top right corner of her backpack.

"We've come from Iowa. We could sure use this rain out there," commented a tall big-boned forty-ish man with the rough hands and weathered skin of a farmer.

"Now, Gavin, don't you be thinkin' about home. We're here finally, right next to where Frank Sinatra was born. Don't you go spoilin' my visit now. I waited a long time to get here. I want to enjoy it." The tiny old woman at his side reached up and gave her son a playful poke in the ribs. Then she turned to the proprietor of the store, the thin chatty man I remembered, who smiled broadly, clearly delighted that the rain had filled his small shop with potential customers. "You say the house was destroyed by a fire?" she inquired.

"Yes, that's what happened. It was a wood frame

house, and it just burned. In '67. The city tore the shell down the next year. The guys who bought the property during the seventies, they're the ones who put up the arch there. It's like a marker. Now they grow corn and park cars out back," he said, jerking his head in the direction of the former house as he recited the familiar explanation.

"You say they grow corn here?" asked the farmer, obviously intrigued by the thought of city folks growing anything.

"Yes. Some. We got lots of people grow their own vegetables here," the shopkeeper explained, a little miffed. "Not for nothin' they call Jersey the Garden State."

"Excuse me, but why do they want to go and park their cars in the cornfield then?" Perplexed, the farmer persisted.

"Well, here parking's pretty tough to come by. People here'd park in their living rooms if they could figure out how," replied our host.

The Australian woman held up a familiar-looking CD. "This one has all my favorite Sinatra tunes, but the recording artist is somebody named Louis Palumbo, not Frank. Is that some sort of joke?" Her clipped Australian accent made her query sound more indignant than perhaps she intended.

"Louis Palumbo was a Frank Sinatra impersonator. One of the best. But two weeks ago he was murdered. That CD will probably become a collector's item now," answered the shopkeeper. I had a hard time repressing a giggle as I ferreted through a pile of T-shirts emblazoned with Frank's face smiling over the words "Hoboken Original." Louie Palumbo's CD would become a collector's item when the proverbial pigs took to the air. I was just going to ask about the T-shirts when the shopkeeper continued. "Louis Palumbo was a very talented young man. He sang in Atlantic City at the casinos. I seen him there once. He coulda been a movie star." A picture of Marlon Brando saying "I coulda been a contenda" a few blocks away in *On the Waterfront* flashed before me. Marlon Brando *had been* a movie star. Frank Sinatra *had been* a movie star. Louie Palumbo had *never* been a contender for stardom on the silver screen. I wondered how many of the late Louie's CDs this guy was stuck with.

"Do you have this T-shirt in an extra large?" I asked. I was still a bit disconcerted by the Marlon Brando movie playing in my mind, but I managed to hold up a medium for the shopkeeper to see.

"Just what's there. But lemme check in the back." He disappeared and I continued to flip through the T-shirts. I came across a tiny one, "0-3 months" its little label read. I held it up. Suddenly Brando disappeared from my mental movie screen, replaced by a dimpled and succulent baby wearing this wee T-shirt. It was there in that cluttered souvenir shop that I felt like a grandmother-to-be for the first time. As if to mark my epiphany, a rainbow, visible through the open door, suddenly framed the baby garment I was holding. The summer storm had ended.

"Sorry ma'am, no extra larges." The proprietor apologized, emerging from the back of the shop in time to ring up the purchases we were all making.

"Never mind. I'll take this one instead," I said, handing him the wee T. "My daughter's expecting my first grandchild." I made this announcement to the general delight of my fellow shoppers, who were most congratulatory. I was so filled with goodwill that I offered to take a picture of the Australian visitor adding her bouquet of tiger lilies to the flowers, candles, hand-lettered

signs, and envelopes that had made a shrine out of the
bronze plaque in the sidewalk commemorating Frank's
birthplace.

Still somewhat euphoric, I decided to stop at Fiore's
on Adams Street. When I got to the deli, I ordered a
mozzarella and garlic roasted red pepper sandwich to
take to the office with me. The rain had cooled the air
and taken the edge off the humidity for a while at least.
As I strolled east, I tried to picture the area as it had
been in Sinatra's day. According to Sol and Toni, these
quiet blocks, the bastion of working-class Italian immigrants, had teemed with street life. There had been bars,
social clubs, gyms, and shops. Kids had played stick-
ball in the streets, teens like Frank had harmonized on
street corners, and grown-ups had congregated on
stoops. As I approached Willow Avenue, I tried to picture it as the dangerous border crossing Sol had
described, the Rio Grande of Hoboken, separating the
Italians to the west from the Irish and Germans to the
east.

Enjoying my time travel, I was not aware of the black
pickup truck that had slowed to keep pace with me on
the deserted street. When I got to the intersection, the
driver pulled in front of me, blocking me. He rolled
down his window. He was so close the cold air from
inside the truck chilled my arms. Coming out of my
reverie, I looked up, expecting him to ask directions. It
was Gio Deloia. Even in broad daylight only a half a
block from Fiore's, I felt a knot in my stomach at the
sight of his glowering face just inches from mine. I
could see the hairs in his nose as he barked, "Listen,
Professor, leave my sister alone, unnerstan'? I ain't
gonna tell you again. Stay away from her."

Having delivered this rather classic warning, Gio
rolled up the window and peeled out. Starting to sweat
and breathing rapidly, I resumed walking, but now I

moved as fast as I could without breaking into a run. I knew I could no longer run for more than a block or two. I was also aware that my heartbeat had accelerated dangerously. Whenever I heard a vehicle approach, I turned to look over my shoulder, stumbling several times on irregularities in the sidewalk. Gio had made his point. I didn't want to see Nancy Deloia ever again.

Chapter 15

To: Bbarrett@circle.com
From: Shoppinmama@juno.com
Re: MOB mishegas
Date: Sun, 19 Jul 1998 09:56:02

Dear Heartbroken,

Shopping is the solution to your MOB problems. First go to a Judaica shop and buy one of those new wineglasses that comes in a cloth bag and is specially designed to break on contact. Have it gift-wrapped and send it to the bride and groom in a care package with some other wedding-related *tchotchkes* like a blue garter and, in this case, books on parenting.

Then e-mail your daughter that you want *her* to help you shop for an appropriate outfit for *you* to wear to the wedding. Finally, buy an airline ticket to Seattle and spend a little time shopping with your daughter for your outfit, for her outfit, for the baby, for whatever. It really doesn't matter what and it shouldn't matter how much, a lot or a little. In the familiar atmosphere of crowded dressing rooms, lines at the cash register, department store ladies' rooms, and, of course, over lunch, you two will soon reestablish your mother-daughter bond.

Remember, Heartbroken, a day at the mall costs less than family therapy and is a lot more fun. Trust me. My daughter and I were not speaking after she insisted on dropping out of college to marry a professional juggler. The ceremony took place in a tent after a circus performance and included a lot of ring tosses and an elephant. The best man wore a clown costume. But I agreed to shop with her for appropriate gifts for the wedding party (what do you give a man with a big red nose who wears a size twenty shoe?). My daughter and I made up in the ladies' room at Bloomies.

Judy

"Please tell me why you insisted on lunch here? I've spent nearly half an hour trying to find a damn parking space. And why did you want me to take the whole afternoon off anyway? And bring a camera? I haven't carried around a camera since I was a rookie reporter in Trenton. What are you getting me into that I don't really have time for?" Sarah didn't look nearly as out of sorts as she sounded. After we hugged, she sat down opposite me at a small table in the middle room of Leo's Grandez-Vous, an old Italian restaurant on the west side of Hoboken. The jukebox had almost every song The Voice ever recorded, and I had just paid a quarter to hear his 1959 version of "I'll Never Smile Again," which I had selected in memory of Louie. Pictures of Frank, performing or posing with celebrities and locals alike at all stages of his career, hung on the walls.

"I thought maybe we'd get inspired here," I said. Sarah gave me a puzzled look, so I added, "Supposedly Frank used to drop in here late at night when he came back to town to see Dolly. So Louie Palumbo hung out here a lot. He was actually here the night he was murdered."

"I get it. But before you tell me what you've found

out and what you want from me, let's order. I'm starving." One of the things I like best about Sarah is that her priorities are very clear. Food first. "What's good here? What do you usually order?"

"Mussels with sweet sauce and a bar pie," I answered promptly, my mouth watering at the thought of the savory little pizzas with the perfect thin crust that Leo's does so well. "Let's each get a bar pie and share some mussels. That ought to hold us for a while."

After lunch Sarah and I were both feeling the way you feel after you have eaten just a little too much on a hot summer day, stuffed, logy, and guilty. I had filled her in on Nancy and Gio Deloia and Toni Demaio and John Cardino. She leaned back and signaled the waiter for some coffee and a check. "So what do you want *me* to do? That's the part I'm still not clear on," she said patiently. It struck me that since Sarah became a grandmother, she's a lot more patient, even with me.

By the time we had paid the check and left Leo's, Sarah not only knew what I wanted her to do, but she seemed to be looking forward to the assignment. "Actually I was going to send someone out to get this story in a day or two. We need a follow-up to fill in some dead space this weekend when all the politicians are at the shore and there's nothing to cover but festivals, a few drug busts, and, of course, that new urban sport, pioneered in Hoboken, public urination." Sarah smirked.

I stuck my tongue out at her reference to the unfortunate truth that every weekend throngs of young New Jerseyites drawn by bars and bands pour into Hoboken to drink, brawl, roll garbage cans down the street, and pee in public. Publicizing the names and employers of those young men and women caught with their pants down, so to speak, fining them, and forcing them to appear in court has done little to curb their enthusiasm for relieving themselves behind cars and in doorways.

"Sol calls them the 'whiz kids,' " I said, "for the obvious reason. They drive him nuts."

"I can imagine," said Sarah. "Anyway, I'm glad he's not upset by your involvement in this whole Palumbo thing."

"Me too. But I've been very cautious. Nobody who might be involved even knows I'm snooping except for Toni. So I don't understand why Gio Deloia's on my case. I don't even pretend I'm anybody else, so I always have a good reason for going wherever I go and for talking to people. That's why I'm really glad to have you with me on this call. Now I don't have to pretend to be you." I smiled at Sarah as we approached the Palumbo home.

"I'm only the photographer, remember. I just take pictures. You do the interviewing. And, Bel, don't take no for an answer. We've got to get in and get them talking to us no matter what. Forget that they're old people mourning the violent death of their son and probably still in shock. Just leave your bleeding heart at home on this one. Pretend that if you get this story, you get not only a byline, but also a raise, a promotion, and maybe even a prize." Listening to Sarah, I envisioned the many plaques on the wall of her office and I recalled why, in just a few short years, she had been promoted to managing editor of the *Herald*.

The house was one of four identical one-family attached brick homes built at the end of long driveways. This set them apart from most Hoboken dwellings, which were built just a few feet from the sidewalk and lacked driveways. In the Palumbos' driveway there was a fairly old-looking maroon Chevy. In a neighbor's driveway sat a tarp-covered boat, undoubtedly awaiting a tow to the shore. The driveway next door accommodated two motorcycles and a small truck. Sarah and I walked up the Palumbos' driveway, which doubled as a front walk and which, like the others, was flanked with blossoming rose bushes, shrubs, and beds of geraniums and petunias. We climbed the stairs to the front door and rang the bell.

I heard a vaguely familiar voice call out, "Don't get up. I'll get it." Before I connected that voice with a face, the door opened and Nancy Deloia stood in the Palumbos' living room staring openmouthed at me. "Professor Barrett, what are you doin' here?" she asked. And then she smiled. It wasn't a big smile. Nobody would accuse this Nancy of having a "laughin' face," but neither was it the twisted grimace that had so distorted her features last week. Rather it was a small guileless smile telling me she was not sorry our paths were crossing again, she didn't know her baby brother had made wise-guy noises at me, and that she was feeling a little better. The aroma of oregano and tomatoes wafted in from the back of the house. Nancy was feeling better enough, I surmised, to comfort and cook for Louie's parents, whom she had known for years and who might have been her in-laws had things gone differently.

I said, "I freelance for the *Jersey City Herald*. I'd like to talk to Mr. and Mrs. Palumbo about their memories of Louie and how they're getting on now. This is Sarah Wolf, a *Herald* photographer. Let's close this door so that heat doesn't get in here," I suggested. As I spoke, I stepped inside with Sarah at my back. Obediently Nancy closed the door behind us. In my most professorial tone I went on, "Nancy, please tell Mr. and Mrs. Palumbo that we're here to see them." Sarah had to be impressed by my tactics so far. Nancy turned to leave the room but not before I noted that her hair was glossy and pulled neatly back from her face and her color, even without makeup, was good. She was wearing black slacks and a modish white jersey partly covered by an apron. I heard voices.

Nancy returned after a minute. "Mrs. P's lyin' down.

She still don' feel like talkin' to nobody, but Mr. P, he says he'll talk to you for a few minutes. Come in the kitchen." We followed her and entered a bright sunny room looking out on a tiny yard where I glimpsed a few staked tomato plants already heavy with green fruit. Louie's dad had aged. In fact, the frail little man seated at the table looked like the father of the hearty man I'd shaken hands with at the party the previous summer. As Nancy introduced us, I reached out to take his trembling hand and express my condolences. I could feel my own hand begin to tremble. Louie Palumbo's father was living every parent's worst nightmare. The fact that Louie couldn't sing worth shit and that he had betrayed two women even as one of them carried his child paled in the presence of this grief-wizened man. Louie had been his baby, his boy. I felt tears fill my eyes. Suddenly I was nearly immobilzed by a sharp pain in my ankle. Before I could cry out, I realized that Sarah had kicked me. Hard.

"Thank you for agreeing to this interview, Mr. Palumbo," I said, blinking my tears away and taking a microphone out of my purse. "Will this bother you? If so, I can take notes. This is faster though," I said.

"It don' matter," he said, brushing away the question with his hand. "My wife, she can't talk about Louie. Me, I can't stop. She won't go in his room. Me, I like to go in there. Come. I'll show you. It's a nice room. And he kept it nice. He never wanted to move away like some kids. He was going to stay with us until he and Nancy here got married." Sarah and I followed Mr. Palumbo as he slowly walked toward the stairwell and even more slowly climbed the steps. On the top step, he paused and then turned to the right and paused again at the first door. "See. Louie had a nice room. Look." He turned the knob and pushed open the door.

The room was the oddest I'd ever seen outside a Red

Grooms exhibit. Photos of Sinatra vied with posters
from his movies and sheet music covers to create
crowded collages on every inch of three walls and part
of the ceiling. On the fourth wall a shelving unit held
books on Sinatra, some of which I could see were the
same as those at the library. There was also a rack of
CDs and a collection of LPs and tapes and a stereo set.
On a dresser sat three faceless mannequin heads, each
topped by a different wig. I recognized the Bryl-
creemed bad boy curl of the young Frank, the shorter
flattop of the middle years, and the silver cap of Frank's
old age. I was willing to bet that in the closet there were
not clothes but costumes, the signature trench coat, the
tuxes, the silk suits, and, of course, the fedoras and elevator shoes.

There were only two signs that someone named
Louie Palumbo had actually lived in that room himself.
One was the layered heap of newspaper clippings, sheet
music, letters, and bills littering the desk in the corner
opposite the bed. The other was a snapshot of a much
younger Nancy Deloia stuck in the corner of the mirror.
The room was half museum, half crypt. It gave me the
creeps.

"You're right, this is a remarkable room," I gushed to
Mr. Palumbo. "Sarah please. Some photos. Take a few
different perspectives. Be sure to get a shot of those
wigs, and the desktop, and the walls, Sarah, all the
walls." Now it was my turn to galvanize Sarah who,
upon entering Louie's room, had stood transfixed in the
doorway, gaping at the walls and the wigs. I was
relieved to see her start snapping away all the while
repeating, "Remarkable room. Truly remarkable."

"Excuse me, Mr. Palumbo, could I use the bathroom
for a moment?" Sarah would be impressed with that
move. Not only would I get to check out the Palumbo
family medicine cabinet, but I'd buy her a few more

minutes to document poor Louie's lair. Our host pointed down the hall to an open door. I locked myself in and began to inspect the contents of the medicine chest. Nothing unusual there except for two bottles of Xanax prescribed recently, one for each Palumbo. Otherwise their medicine stash was not too different from my mother's and Sofia's, a collection of baby aspirin, Mylanta, Tylenol, sunblock, tooth whitener, and hemorrhoid cures. The linen closet next to the tub contained the usual sheets and towels, but also a whole shelf of stage makeup, presumably what Louie had worn when impersonating his idol. I had not used a bathroom since we'd left Leo's at least half an hour ago, so I was only too glad to avail myself of the Palumbos' facilities. I checked out their choice of reading material and found only a few old issues of *People* and a copy of this month's *Movieline*.

By the time I rejoined Sarah and Mr. Palumbo, they were making their way slowly down the stairs. "My Louie, he was always a fan of Frankie's. Other kids got into trouble, but not Louie. And not Danny either." While Mr. Palumbo paused, I tried to picture Louie's twin brother, the Hoboken High music teacher with the little girl. I got as far as recalling a bearded face when I tuned in again to Mr. Palumbo saying, "Louie was always practicin' with the band or talkin' to the old people about Frankie. Or readin' about him. Or he was with Nancy here." Saying this, Mr. Palumbo took Nancy's hand and held it for a minute. Her eyes filled. I wondered if he knew about Louie's relationship with Toni Demaio. Or had he managed to deny his son's one major blooper?

Nancy turned away and began to fill a kettle. "I'm fixin' some coffee and tea now for you. That's what Mrs. P would do if she was up to it."

"Tell me about Louie's band," I asked.

"It was Louie and Danny and a couple a boys from the neighborhood," Mr. Palumbo said simply. "They were gettin' a lotta gigs lately. People started dancin' swing again. They got even more calls after Frankie died. Lately the band was real busy."

You bet he was busy, I thought. *Getting involved with my student and cheating on the mother of his unborn child. That's pretty busy, all right.*

"They're gonna have a tough time without Louie." Mr. Palumbo looked down and his shoulders slumped. He seemed to shrink even further as he contemplated the band's future and faced yet again his own agony.

"You mentioned Louie's twin brother. How's he takin' the fact that his brother was murdered? They must have been very close. Is he out for revenge?" I asked, piling on the questions in the hope that at least one of them would engage him.

"Danny," Mr. Palumbo exhaled the name so it came out as a protracted sigh. "He's like my wife. He's taking pills too. My wife, she never even took an aspirin before this. Depression, the doctors say. Give her time. Give her medicine. Not like me. I'm not takin' no pills." I thought of the bottle of Xanax with his name on it I'd seen in the medicine closet, but I didn't argue with Mr. Palumbo.

Instead I tried to refocus him on Louie's brother. "I guess they were very close, the twins." I persisted, hoping my designation of the over-thirty Palumbo brothers as "the twins" would trigger a revealing response. It did.

"Yeah. They was close. They liked the same things, the same people. Even the same girl once, remember, Nan?" Nancy blushed and lowered her eyes as she got up from the table. "Danny wanted to marry Nan here, but she was always Louie's girl." The old man sighed again. So Danny married her cousin Anna, a good girl too, right, Nan?" Mr. Palumbo looked across the table at Nancy who, having served us tea and coffee, had taken a seat opposite him.

"Yeah, for sure. Me and Anna are like sisters." Nancy looked up and managed a slight smile.

"Danny and Louie was very close. They always liked music. They spent a lotta time together. Louie was the godfather to Danny's kids. They talked a lot. The way my wife says it is, they was always like this," Mr. Palumbo, held up two thin trembling fingers and crossed one over the other.

We were interrupted by the ring of the telephone, and after Nancy answered it, she returned to the table saying, "Gio's comin' to pick me up, so I'm gonna put the water on the stove for the pasta. When Danny and Anna get here, all they gotta to do is put the noodles in. The gravy's ready. There's salad in the fridge. Gio's bringin' bread. You gotta eat."

I felt my chest constrict at the mention of Gio's name. I had to get out of there. What if Nancy mentioned my appearance at the Palumbos' to Gio? How could I be sure she didn't? "Uh, Sarah and I would like to keep this interview secret until the article comes out. So please don't mention our visit here today to anybody, even close relatives like Danny and Gio. It's important that nobody scoop us." It was lame, but it was the best I could do. Nancy and Mr. Palumbo nodded as Nancy took a large pot out of a cabinet and brought it to the sink.

"You're a good girl, Nancy," said Mr. Palumbo, his eyes following her. "You always been a good girl. Maybe tonight she'll eat somethin'." He seemed to be referring to his wife again, and as he spoke, his head fell to his chest. I felt for him. It was bad enough to lose a son to murder, but to lose a wife and maybe a son to depression at the same time must be almost unbearable.

I took Sarah's arm firmly and said, "Well, we'll not

tire you anymore. Thank you so much for your cooperation." I pulled Sarah out the door and hurried her up the driveway to the sidewalk. I didn't stop for breath until we were around the corner. I had no interest in running into Gio Deloia again.

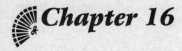 *Chapter 16*

To: Rbarrett@UWash.edu
From: Bbarrett@circle.com
Re: Wedding bells
Date: Mon, 20 Jul 1998 08:10:37

Dear Rebecca,

Of course I can "hold it together" walking you down the aisle with your father. Let me remind you that after Mark's graduation we all shared a very pleasant lunch. Even though your father and I are no longer married, we are still both part of your family. Thanks for asking me.

I'd really like to get out there to see you in August after summer school is over for both of us. I don't want to wait until Thanksgiving and miss the whole first half of your pregnancy. I want to come and watch you gestate! And I'd love to check out your new apartment too. Also if I could visit the Petroleum Museum, it might give me an idea of what to wear to the big event. What does the modern mother of the bride wear? Any ideas? I need guidance. Maybe we could do a little exploratory shopping out there. If this visit sounds like a good idea to you and Keith, give me some dates that work for you.

Love,
Mom

After e-mailing Rebecca I felt so good that I rocketed through my evening class. Winston gave a fascinating speech on the prenatal life of twins, dazzling us with his photos and graphs as well as with how smoothly he coordinated their appearance on the board with his presentation. He had mastered the overhead. Tomas's talk went well also, although we all felt a little anxious about our prospects for coping in the year 2000 after he showed off his "millennium survival kit." Ndaye was not in class.

After the students had all given their speeches, I introduced our unit on strategies for a successful job search with a mini-lecture outlining the underlying reasons why employers bother to interview job applicants and a film on interviewing. Ndaye entered the room halfway through the film. Later when Winston asked, "What about, you know, jewelry? Can I wear my tongue stud and my nose ring?" I didn't lose patience. Instead I reminded myself that whatever Winston knew about the white-collar workplace he probably learned from television or the movies. I repeated the point made in the film about dressing neatly and conservatively. When Tomas queried, "Why can't we ask about pay and benefits, man?" I suggested that candidates hold those questions until they receive an offer of a position. I planned to invite a few people who worked in different fields to come to class to speak on how to look for work in their particular area of expertise.

I left class with Ndaye and took advantage of the walk down the stairs to say sternly, "Ndaye, you've already missed too many classes and been very late to most of the ones you do attend. I sent you a midterm advisory notice. I want to remind you that you really can't miss any more classes if you expect to pass the course. Can you explain to your employer that you need to have evenings off on class nights for another three weeks?"

"I weel zpeak to zhem again. But it don't do no good. When zhey short of 'elp, zhey call me and zhey let me know zhat if I say no, zhey fire me." Her eyes widened at the prospect of being fired, and then she lowered them. "I try hard not to miss ze class no more, Professor."

We had reached the curb in front of the building and there we parted. My eyes followed Ndaye's lithe figure as she turned, ran across the street, and jumped on the bus. Just as I stepped off the curb myself, I heard an engine and felt a rush of air and a thump. The next thing I knew I was in a heap on the ground, pain searing my chest when I breathed. My books and bag lay strewn in the gutter. I had been sideswiped by a car. "You okay, Professor? Let me help you. Damn! That truck was really movin'. You coulda been killed." The twinkle above my head as much as the familiar voice told me that the good Samaritan gathering my books and purse was Winston.

"Don' move. Maybe somethin's broke. I'll call 911." Piling my belongings neatly beside me, Winston pulled a cell phone out of his book bag and began to dial.

"Wait a minute. Please." I spoke as strongly as I could while flat on my back in the gutter trying not to breathe. "Maybe I'm okay." That was my inner denial queen expressing herself. I was not okay. There was a knife in my chest that sliced through me unless I held my breath. Tentatively I wiggled my hands and feet. I bent my legs and arms every which way. At least they seemed all right. Even as I lay there, my estrogen patch was pumping that bone-friendly hormone into my body. I tried to focus my attention on this infusion. "Just give me a hand," I directed. Winston grabbed my outstretched arm and pulled. I screamed. I must have freaked out poor Winston because he froze and then lowered me gently to the ground. I was sure I was having a heart attack. I tried to remember the latest excuse Sol and I had given each other for not redoing our outdated wills.

I heard Winston giving the operator our location. When he pocketed his phone and said the emergency medical people were on the way, I muttered through clenched teeth, "Winston, please check to see if my grade book is there." Losing that is every professor's recurring nightmare. If this was the Big One, I was going to expire with my grade book in my hand. I was relieved when he held up the dog-eared record book for me to see. I tried to reach for it. Winston handed it to me.

"Winston, did you notice what kind of car hit me?" I spoke without taking any deep breaths. I thought I had heard him say something about a truck. I had to check.

"It was a truck, a small black pickup. Had some letters on the door, but I couldn't read 'em. He was movin' too fast." My stomach contracted at hearing my suspicion confirmed. That didn't seem to hurt. "Man, he booked. I couldn't catch the plates either. Had to be a DWI." Winston shook his head. It was then I heard the sirens.

By the time Sol called later that night, I was home and feeling a lot better. I could talk with only mild discomfort. I forced myself to tell him that once again I was a moving target for some loony tune who made homicide a hobby. Just as I was learning to be candid in the name of intimacy, Sol was learning to accept the fact that occasionally I put myself at risk. ". . . so I wasn't having a heart attack. No. Just some bruised ribs, that's all, and a few scrapes. They gave me some pills to take for a few days. It really only hurts when I laugh or sneeze now. But I'm glad you're coming home tomorrow anyway and I'm even gladder that you're not angry."

"Bel, I'm not angry, but I am worried and upset. Are you okay there tonight? Please don't go out. I'll go to class with you tomorrow night. Don't you think you ought to report this to the cops? After all, if, as you say, this Gio doesn't know you're investigating the murder, what's the harm in reporting what happened to the police? He's a hit-and-run driver. You could have been dead." Concern had lent a rasp to Sol's normally deep voice.

"Maybe, but I'm not sure it was Gio, so there's not much to report. Don't worry, though. I'm not going anywhere. And I'm not alone, remember? Mark's here. He went to RECC and got my car and picked me up at the ER. I really gave him a scare. In fact, he's putting together a late supper for the two of us as I speak. Maybe I can sound him out a little about his life plan tonight." I hoped I sounded reassuring.

"I'd feel better if you told Betty about this too. You said this guy was doing some work out at her place, right? You ought to let her know what kind of creep she's got patching her retaining wall," he advised. "This guy's definitely not your ordinary run-of-the-mill mason."

"Good idea. She's away, but I'll tell Vic. I'll call him before Mark and I eat. Good night love." I didn't even put down the phone but just pushed the button that would automatically dial Betty's number.

Vic answered on the first ring. "You mean to tell me Gio Deloia tried to run you over? Wait a minute, Betty just came in." I waited while Vic greeted Betty with what I clocked as a ninety-second smooch and then repeated my news to her. She was just getting back from the RECC Board retreat. "You should sleep here tonight," Betty said, skipping pleasantries in favor of taking charge. "Or do you want us to sleep over there?"

"Betty, get a grip. Vic too. Mark's home and he's staying in tonight. I'm fine here. And Sol will be back tomorrow. The only reason I'm calling is that Sol thought I should let you know just who you've got playing with cement at your gated condo paradise." I couldn't resist teasing Betty about living in a gated community. "So don't try to stiff him on his bill. Talk to you soon. Give my love to Vic." I wrapped a seersucker robe of Sol's around me and joined Mark in the kitchen.

"Yo, Ma. Sit down and chill. I'm making you the best homemade pizza you ever tasted. I spent half the afternoon shopping. I'm using Fiore's mozz, fresh New Jersey plum tomatoes from the Farmers' Market, and basil from your garden. I got the dough for the crust at Marie's. Just help yourself to a glass of vino and give me a minute or two." Mark's floury tomato-splotched T-shirt looked as if he had engaged in a bloody battle with the big whitish blob on the counter, which had then crawled away to die in agony, knocking every pot and pan we own into the sink. "I'll skip the wine, thanks. They gave me some kind of pill, so I'm already feeling no pain."

"You sure look a lot better than when I got to the ER," said Mark, picking up the amorphous corpse in one hand and attempting to pound it into the shape of our baking sheet with a floury fist. Even from the other side of the room where I sat, I could see flour dust settling on every surface in the kitchen. I ignored it, focusing instead on how glad I was to be alive. Having forced the dough into submission, Mark was slathering it with chopped tomatoes.

"Remember when you taught me to make pizza the first time, Ma?" he asked slicing a coil of mozzarella.

I recalled a long ago winter day when five-year-old Mark was home recovering from a bout of strep. Wearing his jammies and still dragging his ratty old blanket around, he was bored. We had made pizza for lunch. "Yes, I remember."

"That was BD, right?" Events in our family would be forever dated Before the Divorce or After the Divorce. I nodded.

"I made it all the time in college. It was awesome. And I didn't even have fresh ingredients like we get here." He opened the oven and carefully lowered the pizza into it. "Now that's going to take about ten minutes to bake, so let me see if I can make some of this stuff disappear before you lose it over the mess I've made. You're controlling yourself very well, Ma. Keep breathing. But not hard enough to hurt," he added quickly, grinning the same dimpled grin he'd flashed at five when, also covered with tomatoes and flour, he'd watched me put the pizza into the oven. Mark could almost always make me smile. He was tackling the sink full of dishes and by the time the smell of oregano and tomatoes permeated the room, he had filled the dishwasher and scrubbed down the counter.

"Speaking of Dad," he began, removing the pizza from the oven and placing it on the stovetop. "He called me today." Mark began chopping basil leaves.

"I thought he and Cissie were in Provence," I said.

"They are. They got there last week." Mark was sprinkling the pizza with chopped basil. He had inherited the family tendency to draw out a story. I knew there was a story because my ex-husband did not make long distance calls lightly. Also Mark and his father had not been on easy terms since Lenny had e-mailed Mark inquiring about the earning potential of "second-rate blues guitarists." Mark got out two plates, knives, forks, and napkins. Mark's creation looked like a pizza that would defy picking up.

"Their house-sitter's father was in a car accident. She has to go take care of him. They can't get anybody else they trust on such short notice, so Dad and Cissie want me to house-sit for them. They'll pay me. I'm driving up first thing in the morning."

"Will you call me when you get there?" I asked, immediately picturing Mark's old Toyota breaking down somewhere between Hoboken and Newton, Massachusetts.

"Say no more, Ma," Mark said. "I've got it on tape," he added with a sigh referring to the fact that he had certain of my more predictable maternal riffs committed to memory so there was no need for me to repeat them.

"Do you know the house well enough to take care of it?" I persisted, feeling stupid as soon as the words were out. After all, Mark was not an idiot and Lenny and Cissie's fancy digs were not my problem anyway.

"Yeah. I'll water the house plants and the garden, bring in the mail and the papers, feed the fish, and fend off burglars with my bare hands, Ma. That's going to be the tricky part." Then sighing again, Mark said, "Chill, Ma Bel. It's an easy gig. I can practice guitar twenty-four-seven and not bother anybody, watch TV all night, blast Howard Stern every morning from all the radios in the house and log on to porno chat rooms while I'm gorging on Froot Loops. And if I kill the fish, I'll just fry them and buy more." Mark's eyes were twinkling, and I had to laugh with him.

That was a mistake. "Don't make me laugh," I said, holding my aching ribs. "Wow! This is just what the doctor ordered. You make terrific pizza!" I added. I helped myself to another slice from the rapidly diminishing pie on the counter between us.

"I had a good teacher," Mark replied, raising his glass in a toast.

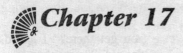# Chapter 17

To: Bbarrett@circle.com
From: Lbarrett@squarepeg.com
Re: Mark
Date: Tues, 21 Jul 1998 07:52:16

Bel:

As you know, Cissie and I have had to hire Mark to take over house-sitting for us. Please keep tabs on him. Remind him to read the instructions for the other house-sitter we left on the kitchen table. If those fish aren't fed regularly, they die, and if they're overfed, they die. Also, we don't want our mail sitting outside for days on end. Do you think he realizes how fragile the white slip-covers in the living room are? They're Cissie's pride and joy. I really need a break this month and I don't want to have to worry about the house and neither does Cissie.

Lbarrett@squarepeg.com
Your taxes are my business

It's too bad I didn't murder that narcissistic cretin in his sleep when I had the chance, I thought for the

umpteenth time as I clicked away Lenny's latest cyber
salvo. I didn't have time to even think about him. I was
rushing to keep an appointment with Toni Demaio at
RECC. About a half an hour after I took my first pain
killer the day after my "accident" I could almost
breathe without wincing. That's why I didn't even consider canceling my class or the meeting with Toni,
which I had initiated. Lately I hadn't seen much of her.
It seemed as if after getting me involved, Toni herself
had lost interest in Louie and who killed him. She
entered my office and sat down, her lovely face pale
and her eyes dull behind her glasses. I welcomed her
with a smile and said, "Toni, I'm worried about you.
We've been out of touch. I guess you're still pretty broken up over losing Louie."

"Yes and no. I just don't know anymore. I never
wanted to get involved in anything like this. I heard that
other woman Louie had been seeing was having a baby
and she lost it. My aunt says she lost it because she
found out about Louie and me. I feel really bad about
that. I mean as a feminist . . ." She sighed the sigh of
one facing for the first time the messy mesh between
theory and reality. "I didn't expect to wind up as 'the
other woman' and break up a longtime relationship.
'Specially one with a baby coming. Louie should never
have gotten involved with me while he was still with
her. And he shouldn't have even thought of leaving her
if she was having a baby. I feel like I'm living in one of
those soap operas my mom watches."

Toni had been thinking. As usual I was impressed by
her smarts. At the same time her litany of *shoulds* and
shouldn'ts proclaimed her youthful faith in absolutes.
She still believed there are simple rules for living. Toni
didn't know it yet, but she was going to be okay. She
sighed again. "And John is so miserable. You know,
he's wanted to be a lawyer since forever. But now he's

so wrecked that he even stopped studying for the bar, so they decided he's clinically depressed. And the doctor put him on this medication. He . . ." Her voice was getting lower and lower.

"He what, Toni? I can hardly hear you," I said gently.

"They put him on this medication and he . . . he took all of it at once." Tears coursed down Toni's cheeks as she forced herself to tell me that her ex-fiancé had tried to kill himself. "They had to take him to the hospital and pump his stomach. And now the cops . . . They think he did that because he feels guilty about stabbing Louie. John's parents won't speak to me or to my parents. Of course they won't let me visit him. Even my own parents are still hardly talking to me."

"Well, Toni, when we do find out who really killed Louie, people will see that you and John had nothing to do with it. That should help some." I spoke with more confidence than I felt. "It would help me to figure out who Louie's murderer is if I could meet the members of Louie's band. Is there some easy way to do that without giving away why I'm interested?"

"Well, you could pretend you're having a wedding or a party and ask to sit in on a rehearsal maybe," Toni said softly, her voice muted and monotone. "That's what a lot of people do who want to audition the band for an event."

Toni was right. When Joe Vecchio, a member of the Hoboken Four Plus One, returned my call, I told him Sol and I were looking for a band to play at the fiftieth anniversary party of a relative. He immediately invited us to sit in on a rehearsal the very next night. Sol had insisted on driving me to work and picking me up. He was parked right outside the door waiting for me when I emerged from the building. We drove to the western edge of Hoboken, where the band rehearsed in a cav-

ernous former factory that had been converted to studio
spaces. After circling the block twice, we lucked into a
parking spot, a miracle only possible on the outskirts of
town. The high-ceilinged practice space dwarfed the
two musicians, their chairs, music stands, a microphone, a battered piano, and a jumble of what looked
like electrical equipment piled on the floor along one
wall. A headshot of Frank had been blown up and wall-
papered one entire side of the room. Frank smiled
engagingly at us, a larger-than-life muse. I recognized
the aesthetic sensibility of Louie Palumbo at work in
this decorative statement. Martha Stewart had nothing
to worry about for the moment.

"Joe Vecchio, here," said one of them, shaking hands
with each of us. He was a short, wiry man in his early
thirties dressed in shorts and a blue sport shirt. Joe's
dimpled baby face framed by curly brown hair seemed
at odds with his sinewy physique. "We're gettin' a late
start. Danny and Nick haven't showed yet. Have a seat."
Joe waved vaguely in the direction of the piano bench.
Then, almost as an afterthought, he said, "This here's
Ralphie. Ralphie D'Onofrio. He plays the clarinet." He
pointed to the other man, also short, but quite portly.
His aquiline nose and the angular lines of his face were
set off by the fact that his long dark hair was pulled
back into a ponytail. It suddenly occurred to me that
Ralphie's face would have made a lot more sense on
Joe's body and vice versa. While I was imagining the
switch, Ralphie walked over and shook Sol's hand. He
nodded to me. His expression was not unfriendly, but
he was clearly a man of few words and fewer smiles
and he wasn't about to waste any of them on us. "I'm
the trumpet player." Joe held out his trumpet as if to
prove his statement.

Just as we seated ourselves, the studio door opened
and a slender disheveled man with shoulder-length

brown hair ran in. He appeared a few years younger than the other two. Before he noticed us, he rushed to the piano, ran his spidery fingers down the keyboard in a glissando, and then, skipping one hand over the other, he worked his way back up the scales finishing with a showy fanfare of crashing chords. Turning to face all of us, he announced, "I called him. He said maybe. Maybe he'll be here tomorrow night. Where's Danny?"

"Danny's late for rehearsal for a change," said Joe. Half to himself he added, "Who knows if he'll even show?" Then turning to us he said, "This here's Nick. As you could see, he's our pianist. Nick, these people— Sol and Bel, is it? They're lookin' to book a band to play a fiftieth anniversary party this fall. They wanna hear us rehearse."

Nick shook hands perfunctorily first with me and then with Sol. His duty done, he turned to Ralphie and Joe. "Well? I just told you Luke Jonas might come hear us too. Isn't that great? We gotta get a singer. And a drummer. And we gotta get 'em fast if we wanna keep all the bookings we got for the rest of the season. Especially the feast gig." Nick was staring from Ralphie to Joe, waiting for a reaction to his announcement.

"I can't believe you really wanna replace Louie with that asshole," said Ralphie, obviously deciding that the time had come to speak.

"I can't believe you asked him to come here without sayin' nothin' to the rest of us," said Joe. "Considerin' you know how Ralphie here feels about him. And considerin' you don't know how Danny'll take it."

"Ralphie doesn't even know him," protested Nick. "Ralphie, you never even talked to the guy. You just don't like the way he looks." Nick ran his fingers down the keyboard again. Sol winced.

"You bet your ass I don't like the way he looks. He don't look like Frank. He don't talk like Frank. Louie looked like Frankie, he dressed like him, he talked like him. Louie could *do* Frank." This was a long speech for Ralphie.

"Yeah, Ralphie, but this guy can sing like Frank. He sings better than Louie." Suddenly Nick put his hands up as Ralphie, his face darkening into a scowl, moved toward the piano. Nick started talking faster. "Listen, Ralphie. I know you and Louie and Danny came up together. I know how you felt about Louie. We all felt that way." The closer Ralphie got, the faster Nick talked. "C'mon, Ralphie, for Chrissake, man. I'm gettin' tired of takin' your shit . . ."

"See what you done, Ralphie," Joe said, separating Nick and Ralphie by standing between them and placing a hand on each of their chests. "You just got to use those hands, don't you? And you," he said, turning to Nick, "since Louie died, you act like you think you're some kind a goddamn honcho around here. Besides, maybe Danny—"

" 'Maybe Danny nothin.' No way is Danny gonna do Louie doin' Frank and you know it." Nick dismissed that idea with a wave of his hand.

Imitating him, Joe growled, "Well, get this through that thick skull of yours once and for all. We don't do nothin' unless we all agree, you hear?"

"And if we don't get it together, that's just what we're gonna do, man, nothin'." Nick spoke fast and his face was red. Because his hairline was slightly receding, the flush extended to the exposed part of his scalp. "Listen, Ralphie. You're right, man. Louie *could* do Frank. But he could only do Frank here, in Hoboken or Jersey City or maybe Bayonne. I mean, it was like a big deal for us to open for a name in Atlantic City. Or even to play a feast in Garfield. But Christ, Frank didn't stay here. Don't you get it? Frank left here and Louie couldn't leave here, and he couldn't do Frank after

Frank left and really learned how to sing." Nick paused, turning up his palms in a classic plea for understanding.

"What's a matter? You go to Montclair State for two years and study a little music and now you wanna go big-time? Maybe you think we should play the Garden? Or Hollywood Bowl?" Joe asked, his voice heavy with sarcasm.

"So what's wrong with that? You think I wanna work at Top's the rest of my life sellin' dishwashers and air conditioners? Do you two really wanna climb around on construction jobs when you're old? Danny, he don't care, man. He's got a day job he can live with. He likes bein' a teacher." Nick paused for a moment and when he resumed speaking, his tone had softened slightly. "Listen, Louie was a great guy. With him we got a lot of steady gigs around here. But he's DEAD!" Nick shouted the last word. His dramatics had the desired effect. Ralphie flinched and Joe paled visibly.

Then Nick continued in a lower voice, now speaking slowly. "It sounds cold, but that's the way it is, man. We carried his coffin, right? Louie is dead. Now if you think people are gonna hire us without a singer, you're dumber than I think you are. Bands are a dime a dozen. Every kid in high school with a keyboard is a band now. Some people just use DJs. They don't even bother with live music. You need a hook, man. Louie and Frank, they were our hook, our gimmick. Now we lost Louie. We either get another singer or we get another gimmick or . . . both."

"What the hell's that supposed to mean?" Joe suddenly remembered that we were there. Holding up his hand to stifle the others, he walked over to where we sat mesmerized on the piano bench. "Hey! Listen, you guys. I'm sorry. I dunno what's with Danny. But this ain't such a good night. As you can see, we're havin' a little family feud right now. Maybe you wanna come back when we've had a chance to shake down a little after losin' Louie." He was walking with us to the door of the studio that was still ajar after Nick's entrance. "Here take our card. Your event's not until October, right? We still got a little time. Call us in a week or two. Stay in touch."

On the way home I was unusually quiet. "Bel, are you hurting? I thought you'd have a lot to say after that little scene."

"I'm thinking, that's all. I'm not hurting. Those pills are dynamite," I answered. I remained silent, lost in thought, until we got home.

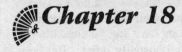

Chapter 18

**SLAIN SINATRA IMPERSONATOR'S ROOM
SHRINE TO HOBOKEN'S HERO**

The late Louis Palumbo, slain Sinatra impersonator whose killer remains at large, had made his bedroom into a shrine memorializing the star whose life and work Palumbo had studied extensively. The *Herald's* own managing editor Sarah Wolf took the pictures for the photo essay that follows. Captions are by free-lance reporter Bel Barrett . . .

The day the photo essay came out began with Sol's voice murmuring, "Bel! Beautiful! Wake up! It's okay! You're dreaming." He was stroking my forehead, trying to interrupt my dream without provoking a sharp movement that might hurt my rib cage. I was down to only two painkillers a day, but until I took one, sneezing, laughing, and sudden moves could still induce acute discomfort. "Now tell me what that was all about?" Sol leaned over me and smoothed a lock of hair out of my face. The clock beside our bed read 7:32. The sunlight pouring in between the slats of the blinds read morning.

"What was I saying?" I asked, ignoring his question for the time being.

"Sounded like you were trying to sing the words to '*Frere Jacques.*' You know, the part that goes '*son y le matine.*'" Sol's bass voice sounded close to my ear. "You kept saying it over and over, but you had the tune all wrong."

"Actually it was 'My Funny Valentine.' I dreamed I was walking along a street that looked a lot like Washington Street right here in Hoboken. It was lined with restaurants, cafés, pizzerias and bars just like the ones on Washington Street. Everything was very quiet, and then suddenly all the doors of all these different eateries started opening one at a time. From each one I could hear Frank singing 'My Funny Valentine.' It was like he was singing a one-man round all up and down the street." I thought better of stretching and just wiggled my toes and bent my knees.

"That's not far from the reality of life in our Mile Square City," said Sol, rolling out of bed. "It used to be they just played Frank at Leo's and Piccolo's but since he died, I hear him everywhere."

"Except at Johnny Rockets," I said, trying not to giggle at the thought of the local franchise that blasted fifties and sixties pop onto the sidewalk nonstop. Sol called this noise pollution, but I noticed that every time I passed the place, my fingers snapped and my pace quickened. "That place is committed to playing 'Down on the Boardwalk,' even in my dreams."

I lost the race for the bathroom, but I knew I had to hurry because I had promised to take my mother to the doctor for her annual checkup. I scheduled her routine doctor's appointments during the summer when my teaching load was lighter. And I knew Ma and Sofia would like to go out for lunch. Sofia's daughter was at Long Beach Island for the month, so she hadn't been around lately to take them anywhere. They were probably a little stir-crazy since it was too hot for them to venture out much on foot. My Post-it list of things to do also included making plane reservations for Seattle, working on my paper, and calling Sarah to congratulate her on her first photo essay. I wanted to ask her something too. It was just a hunch, but . . .

Fortunately Ma's checkup was uneventful. Ma had beaten breast cancer twice, and leaving the doctor's office, she looked visibly relieved the way that all cancer survivors do each time the doctor pronounces them free and clear, in effect granting them a reprieve for another six months or a year. I knew she would feel buoyant for the rest of the day. I was pretty relieved too. Not only was her cancer gone, but her arthritis continued to respond to the shots she was getting and her mind was clear. Once again, my mother had beaten the odds.

Just as I was about to suggest that we pick up Sofia and go out for a celebratory lunch, Ma announced, "Sybil, Sofia's making lunch for you. You can't say no. You know how she gets. And, remember, I have to live with her." I was very familiar with the games Ma and Sofia played to get their way. Masters of manipulation, but bored with only each other to manipulate, they honed their skills on their hapless daughters, who went along with their usually harmless ploys. Fairy godmother–wicked witch was one of the Odd Couple's favorite strategies.

"I never turn down a free meal, Ma. You two know that. Let me find a parking space or put the car away and walk back," I said, scanning the sides of the street for a space. No luck. I let Ma off in front of their house and continued my search. The closest parking space was four blocks away at a meter on Washington Street, but I was grateful for it.

Walking back, I passed a poster advertising the Feast of St. Ann, an annual week-long orgy of food, live music, and games sponsored by a local church. The feast brought thousands of people to Hoboken. Former townspeople returned to see family and friends and enjoy the familiar food and festivities. Feast freaks made St. Ann's a stop on their circuit. Present-day Hobokeners came out of curiosity or religious fervor, eager to follow the statue of the saint borne through the streets on the shoulders of six women on the final day of the event. I had my own reason for wanting to go. At the feast I'd be able to buy a paper bag of twelve freshly made zeppoles and gorge on the warm powdered sugar–coated fried dough balls till I burst.

In the meantime I had resigned myself to being manipulated into a lunch of ripe figs and prosciutto drizzled with balsamic vinegar that Sofia served with wedges of perfect cantaloupe. I allowed myself an extra helping of this new-to-me delicacy in honor of Ma's clean bill of health. "You know what we're having for dessert, Bel dear?" Sofia asked.

"Dessert?" I squawked. "You can't be serious. I can't eat another thing."

"They're very tiny. Look. I walked all the way over to Lepore's myself to get these for you because your mama says they're your favorite." Sofia produced a small plate in the center of which, displayed like jewels, sat six, count them, hand-dipped, dark chocolate–covered marshmallows. "See, only two each," she added quickly lest I get too predatory. "No harm can come from only two."

I hoped Sofia didn't know that I used to walk to Lepore's and buy these by the quarter-pound and gobble them all up before I'd walked the four blocks back home. Lepore's chocolate-covered marshmallows were gourmet Mallomars for grown-ups. I'd put Lepore's off-limits except for special occasions after Wendy had suggested that the place wasn't exactly a health food store.

"Sybil, I changed my appointment with Dr. Frazier. The new one is a week from Tuesday. Will that be okay for you?" Ma asked sweetly. I repressed a twinge of irritation. I'd gone to such trouble to choreograph Ma's medical appointments around her weekly trips to the casino and my classes and now she'd changed one of them without even mentioning it to me first. "Sofia needs me to help her with the food for the feast."

"Yes. Poor Tess Palumbo won't be chopping onions this year. That's for sure. Your mama offered to take her place," said Sofia. She had finished both her chocolates too.

"You mean to tell me that you two are actually planning to sit outside in the sun and chop vegetables next week? Are you crazy? It's too hot! You'll chop and then you'll drop!" I exclaimed, picturing the two of them succumbing to heat exhaustion. Then I tried to visualize Sadie Bickoff, charter member of the Passaic chapter of Hadassah and president of the local B'nai Brith, chopping onions for St. Ann's or any other church.

As if she could read my mind, Ma said, "Sybil, what's the difference if I chop onions for St. Ann's or for the shul? You think God cares?"

"I didn't know you were still into chopping onions for anybody," I answered, smiling. Since my dad's death, Ma had embraced dialing for dinner with the fervor of a convert, a fervor matched only by my own. Sofia still cooked, but when it was Ma's turn at the stove, she often made a beeline for the phone.

"Sofia and I are chopping onions for Jesus," Ma giggled.

Sofia grinned and said, "Yeah and for Tess Palumbo, too. Don't worry, we can chop in the church basement if it gets too hot out. And we get to be at the feast and we get seats." Most people at the feast stood in the crowd that milled around the platform where the entertainers performed and thronged the closed-off streets where the food and souvenir vendors plied their wares.

"Yeah. We get to sit with the onions!" Ma was still laughing. "But a seat is a seat, no?"

"And guess what? I heard from Dom Gennaro at Lepore's that they got Luke Jonas to sing Saturday night. That's when they have the Frank Sinatra Memorial Evening. Maybe he'll sing 'One More for the Road' again," sighed Sofia.

"He better. 'Cause we're giving up our day in Atlantic City to chop onions, so he just better. Here, Sybil. Here's when my new appointment with Dr. Frazier is," Ma said, handing me a piece of paper. "If that's not convenient, dear, change it for some day the week after next when I'm not chopping." I slipped the scrap of paper into my date book and finished my last bite of marshmallow just as Ma said, "I hope at the feast they have those delicious—what do you call them? Zeppelins?"

When I got home Sol was out. I called Sarah and asked her to send the photos she took of Louie Palumbo's bedroom by messenger to Illuminada's house before evening. I called Toni Demaio and chatted with her for a few moments. Finally I called Daniel Palumbo at home and at Hoboken High School, told him I was calling about Nancy Deloia, and left messages asking him to return my call. There was still a little time to sit in the backyard and edit my paper.

But once I was settled in my lawn chair, I found myself instead flipping through the copy of *Movieline* that I'd picked up on the way back to the car from Sofia's. Flipping through the pages of gossip and glossy photos of glamorous and mostly young people, I felt decidedly unglamorous and unyoung. I briefly entertained another makeover fantasy. I could have various pads and pouches nipped and tucked, new lines erased, old veins removed, and offensive cellulite and collagen vacuumed out. Next somebody would snip and style my unruly frizz and a makeup artist would smear my skin with elixirs that would make it glow. This familiar fantasy always had a strangely numbing effect, and I felt myself dozing off. I was half asleep when I read about the indie film company named Back Room Productions that was casting a low-budget musical film based on the story of Frank Sinatra's early years.

Chapter 19

To: Bbarrett@circle.com
From: Rbarrett@UWash.edu
Re: Stuff
Date: Thurs, 23 Jul 1998 08:00:04

Dear Mom,

Keith and I are both totally psyched about your coming in August! We're going to have a party so you can meet a few of our friends, especially Karen and Hillary and Louise and Kenny. Karen and Hillary are in my study group, remember? They're planning a bachelorette party for me! And Louise and Kenny are having a baby shower for us. Kenny trains with Keith, and Louise and I hang out during races together. I'm not sure of the dates yet, but maybe you could come out a little early for the wedding and be there for the bp and the shower. That'd be awesome.

Speaking of the wedding, it will be fun to help you pick out something to wear. Remember, nothing with fringe (the sixties are old, Mom), and none of that flowing stuff you're always draped in. Bag the baggy look. And please, Mom, no black. Black may be chic as hell, especially back East, but you wear too much of it. You need a new, nineties fashion statement, something Seattle-ish.

Did I tell you that they're going to let me work front-of-the-house the last couple of months of my pregnancy? That means I can tend bar or seat people and I won't have to carry trays. Gotta run. I work tonight. Exam tomorrow. Did Mark e-mail you about the girl he met in the pet store when he was replacing Dad's fish? Don't tell him I said anything about the girl or the fish.

Love,
Rebecca

Betty and I pulled into Illuminada's driveway in Union City on Friday night during one of those annoying summer downpours that soaks everything and cools nothing. We ran up the few steps to the front door, but got drenched anyway. Answering the doorbell, Illuminada quipped, "Well, *chiquitas*, at least you have enough sense to come in out of the rain. Here," she said, herding us into her chilled kitchen where we could drip on the linoleum rather than on the wood floors.

Entering Illuminada's kitchen was always like traveling back in time for me. It reminded me so much of my mother's kitchen in Passaic. Raoul was an inveterate haunter of flea markets and scavenger of other people's throwaways, and he had outfitted their kitchen with a Waring Blender, a Sunbeam mix-master, and Fiestaware. Whenever Illuminada's mother, who lived upstairs, came down and served *tres leches* or some other Cuban delicacy, I was always surprised to see her instead of my own mother presiding there.

"Where's your mom?" I asked.

"Upstairs vegging out in front of Spanish TV. She's tired. She had her hair done this afternoon, and I think the heat got to her a little on the way home. Of course, she insisted on walking back here." Illuminada made disapproving clucking sounds, clearly annoyed with her mom's stubbornness and knowing I would understand.

Lord knows, I was no stranger to the will and pride of elderly moms. "And Raoul's at the Meadowlands. They're having a big antiques and collectibles expo this weekend. *Dios mio*, I hope that man doesn't come home with anything else. We don't have room for one more of Raoul's finds in this house."

"I'll take it if you don't want it," said Betty. We both admired the way Raoul made stunning one-of-a-kind art objects out of other people's trash. Illuminada did too, even though she always complained about his collecting.

"I ordered Cuban sandwiches for dinner. I figured it was a beer-and-sandwiches night. That okay?" Illuminada's query was purely rhetorical. She had long ago hooked Betty and me on the tender slices of roast pork, ham, cheese, and pickle pressed between two pieces of Cuban bread by a special hot iron.

"Twist my arm," I said, sitting down at the table and taking the bottle of Corona she passed me.

"Ya gotta do what ya gotta do," said Betty, grinning as she sat down in the chrome-legged chair on the other side of the table. "So Bel, did you update Illuminada on your little run-in with Gio the other night?" Betty asked, not even waiting until she got the cap off her beer bottle to start directing the conversation. I smiled. Sometimes it was hard to remember that Betty's penchant for control used to drive me nuts. To tell the truth, every once in a while, I still bridle when her inner dominatrix surfaces.

"What happened?" asked Illuminada, sitting down between us at the head of the table and kicking off her sandals.

"Leaving work the other night, I got swiped by a black truck. Knocked me down. Bruised a few ribs. Before you even ask, no, I didn't see the plates and neither did the student who was with me." Illuminada's raised eyebrows were the only indication of her concern. I knew she would want the details and I didn't have any.

"She had to go to the emergency room," said Betty. "She could have been killed." Illuminada's eyebrows went up another half an inch.

"Well, I wasn't seriously hurt. But I was knocked down and my chest hurt when I breathed, so I thought I was having a heart attack," I explained somewhat sheepishly. "Now Sol's so worried he follows me practically everywhere. But I'm fine. The problem is I can't swear the driver of the truck was Gio Deloia. And if it was, I can't imagine what his motive is. Even if he did kill Louie, he doesn't know I'm looking into the murder. All he knows about me is that I teach at RECC."

"And you tried to get his sister to go to college," chimed in Betty.

"*Dios mio,* people don't usually go around threatening and running down college recruiters," retorted Illuminada. "That's kind of extreme, don't you think?"

Betty pushed away her laptop and took a swig of beer. I could tell she had something to add. Her eyes were glittering. She was like a teapot just before it starts to whistle. When Betty did speak, her voice was serious. "Well, I think Gio Deloia is one extreme dude. He probably did try to intimidate you, Bel, by knocking you down the other night. But I don't think he did it because he killed Louie and he's afraid you'll figure that out. I think he did it to keep you away from his sister. He doesn't want her to go to college." Betty sat back and waited for the barrage of questions she knew her enigmatic statement was bound to elicit.

"*Caramba!* Why on earth not?" sputtered Illuminada.

"Whoa!" I said stretching out my arms and raising my hands to stifle Betty's presentation of her conclusions about Gio Deloia. "Start at the beginning, please.

I want to know how you got enough out of him to even begin to speculate on his motivation for doing *anything,* let alone for trying to run me over."

Just then the doorbell rang. It was the delivery person with our supper. After we had unwrapped our sandwiches, Betty spoke in between bites. "Well, actually this was Vic's idea. Vic said I should ask Gio to teach weightlifting to kids at the Saturday school Father Santos is starting at our church."

"Let me get this straight," I gasped, my eyes wide with disbelief. "Vic wanted you to ask this murder suspect to work with kids? At a church, yet?" I noticed that Betty had taken advantage of my question to make further inroads on her sandwich.

"You better believe it, girl. And it was a right-on suggestion too." To hear Betty tell it, every word out of Vic's mouth was the essence of wisdom and truth, so I was a little skeptical until she went on. "He got me to thinking that what Gio and I have in common is our Catholicism. He wears two crosses and has a cross tattoo. I figured maybe if I tapped into his Catholic guilt, I could get him to open up. Besides"—Betty paused to grin widely and wink—"as a good Catholic, you know I can lie myself silly and then go to confession, right?"

"So there is no Saturday school?" asked Illuminada. She tossed her question over her shoulder as she pulled three more beers out of the fridge.

"Right, but Gio won't find that out for a while and when he does, it won't matter," said Betty. "Anyway, I told him all about the school and how it was to help kids whose parents had to work Saturdays and who had no adults to hang out with, kind of like a Big Brother/Big Sister program." Betty took a swig of her Corona. "And when I said 'Big Sister,' he just gave it away. He just started to talk." Betty took a big bite of her sandwich now, clearly pleased that she had gotten through to Gio.

Illuminada, not known for her patience, broke in, "Take your time. We've got plenty of beer. You can take all night to tell us what he said."

The acid in our friend's tone did not escape Betty's notice. She continued. "He practically began to cry. He started talking about how after his folks died his sister Nancy raised him. He said how on Saturdays she would take him to work with her rather than leave him to hang out with the wrong people. And how the two of them stayed on in the family apartment and how Nancy redecorated it . . ." Betty paused.

I took advantage of the break in her story to ask, "You mean to say he lives there with her? In the same apartment?" I had seen no trace of Gio at Nancy's, but I had not been farther than the living room and kitchen.

"Yes. You know, she still cooks dinner for him every single night? And packs a lunch for him? In his own messed-up way, he adores her. He's so proud of the fact that he's made enough money lately so she could get new carpet and drapes and some new furniture for the living room."

Recalling the chrome and white room, the chaise longue, and the built-in furniture, I said, "But . . ."

"Yes, there was a *but*," Betty cut me off to resume her story. "Louie Palumbo was the *but*. Louie didn't make enough for him and Nancy to get another place in Hoboken, but they could have managed at Nancy's, which is rent-controlled. So after he married Nancy, he was going to move in with her and Gio was going to have to get his own place. Nancy told Gio it was time for him to find a girl and start his own family. Gio never liked Louie, probably because Nancy did. But Gio realized that someday, Nancy and Louie would marry.

What kept Gio cool was that Louie hadn't been in any hurry to marry. Then when Nancy got pregnant, probably on purpose, the timetable accelerated and Gio went a little nuts."

"*Caramba!* He really has a double motive for murdering Louie," muttered Illuminada, wiping her mouth and washing down her last bite of sandwich with a quick swig of Corona. "He feared that Louie was going to displace him, not only in his sister's heart but also in his home, the family home. He'd be out on the street. Who knows? In Hoboken now, even Gio might never be able to find another place he can afford." She shrugged her shoulders, a silent summary of Hoboken's much-publicized shortage of reasonably priced housing. Affordable apartments and parking spaces in the Mile Square City had become hot items over which otherwise cool-headed people regularly came to blows. An affordable apartment *with* a parking space was an oxymoron.

"Especially an apartment like that one with a driveway and a garage. He can keep his truck there. To get another place like that, he might have to move out of Hoboken, out of the old neighborhood," I elaborated. "Did he have this all figured out?"

"Yes. Gio actually said he was so relieved to have things 'back to normal,' as he put it, that he went to church to say Hail Marys in gratitude to the Blessed Virgin for seeing to it that Louie disappeared from the picture. No wonder the cops are after him." Betty paused, shaking her head. "And if you ask me, that messed-up dude is also glad his sister lost the baby. Now he can be her baby again."

"So why the hell wouldn't he want her to go to college? That wouldn't cause her to evict him or stop cooking for him." I had many students who cooked and cleaned for families while studying.

"He just wants everything to stay the same." Betty's measured tone almost made Gio's wish seem reasonable. "Plus he knows people from the neighborhood who've gone to college and then moved away, dropped old friends, even lost touch with their families. He once had a friend who went to Rutgers on scholarship, and suddenly he didn't have time for Gio anymore." Betty spoke quietly. "I don't know if he killed Louie. Maybe Gio's only sin is that he's glad somebody did."

"I do know that he threatened me and maybe even tried to run me over, thank you very much," I added, helping myself to a bunch of grapes. "If you ask me, Gio Deloia's pretty messed-up. But I don't think he killed Louie." Both Betty and I turned our heads toward Illuminada to see where she would weigh in.

"It's hard to imagine that he would go around telling people how glad he was Louie was out of the picture if he killed him," admitted Illuminada. She continued speaking, her voice steady and her words clipped. This sort of talk was all in a day's work for her. "But I won't write him off yet. That could be just a ploy to throw us off. Remember, even his sister is afraid he might have done it—and he has no alibi. Like poor John Cardino." Illuminada's voice trailed off as she contemplated the plight of the hapless, alibiless, and Toni-less John Cardino.

"Yes. Toni says he tried to commit suicide. Now the cops are even more convinced that he killed Louie. They think he's feeling guilty and that's why he overdosed on his antidepressants," I reported, recapping Toni's latest bulletin from North Bergen.

Illuminada nodded. "Yes. I've been keeping tabs on him. He couldn't even kill himself though, so I doubt if he had enough *cojones* to inflict multiple fatal stab wounds on Louie Palumbo."

I had to admire her logic. "What do you think, Betty?" I asked.

"I think that was one good sandwich!" exclaimed
Betty, finally swallowing her last mouthful. "I'm with
the señora over there. I think he's just miserable over
losing Toni. Remember, when you're young, a broken
heart is the end of the world." Having shared that pearl
of midlife wisdom, Betty opened her laptop and sat
poised beside her empty Corona bottle, ready to record
someone else's findings. Then, thinking better of it, she
stood and said, "The help here has gone off-duty, I
guess. Anybody want another beer?" I took advantage
of her run on the fridge to visit the bathroom, recalling
with a burp the days when I could drink four or five
beers before nature called me to account and when a
broken heart was more than an illness to be cured with
a pill.

We had each knocked back our third beer before I
finished recapping the story of how Sol and I had tried
to get Louie's band to audition for us. Illuminada was
the first to speak. "So what do you think? Do you think
Nick did Louie in? Or Joe for that matter? Or what
about the other one, the twin brother who wasn't there?
Danny?"

"We figure Nick will sooner or later get work with
another band that's more upwardly mobile. At least
that's how Sol put it. Joe just seemed to be a peace-
maker trying to hold things together now that Louie's
gone. We don't know anything about Danny except that
his dad says he's broken up over Louie and that he was
once in love with Nancy D. I'm going to try to get him
to speak to my class. That way I'll finally get to talk to
him."

Illuminada nodded. "You might as well give me all
their last names while you're at it. I can run them
through the computer just to see what comes up."

"But what about Ralphie? He sounded a little freaky.
Think he's kind of a Gio type, maybe?" Betty was ask-

ing this with her head down as she continued to type my words into her laptop. She was a multitasker extraordinaire. At the ceremony at which he presented her with the coveted award for the Most Valuable Staff Member, RECC President Ron Woodman commented that Betty Ramsey, his executive assistant, could do five things at once, all perfectly, in the time it took him to tie one shoe. I loved watching Betty in action.

"Sol wondered about Ralphie too," I said. "But I agree with Nick. Ralphie seems paralyzed by his memory of Louie just like Louie seemed kind of stuck doing the young Frank. It's like they're cases of arrested development."

"Well, the same is true for Gio, isn't it?" Betty wasn't going to give in easily. "Gio lives in the past too and he wants to hold on to it."

"Maybe Ralphie's like Gio in that sense," I mused. "I got the impression that Ralphie, Louie, and Danny grew up together, and I asked Toni. She says they've known each other for years and that the three of them started the band. They were really tight."

"*Como mierda!*" Illuminada was grinning. "You two are off the beer. It's got you both talking psychobabble instead of your regular babble. You sound like wanna-be psychologists. I'm getting some coffee for both of you before you start analyzing me!" She stood and flounced over to the counter.

"I'd never tell Illuminada this, but I think she does have a point," I said, speaking loudly enough so Illuminada could hear me on the other side of the kitchen. "I think that just like the cops, we've been too distracted by the love triangle and the human interest angles in this case. I think it's possible Louie was murdered for a different reason . . ."

"What's this? Another speculation? Are you solving a murder or reading the tea leaves, *Profesora*?" Illumi-

nada was back with a tray holding three mugs, sugar
and cream, a few tea bags, and a bag of Pepperidge
Farm Mint Milanos. "We try to determine motive,
method, and opportunity in this business. I keep telling
you, solving a crime is not like interpreting a novel . . ."
Illuminada left the table again mid-lecture, returning
with a pot of coffee for herself and Betty and a kettle of
hot water for my tea. I was trying not to salivate over
the prospect of Mint Milanos.

"Illuminada, where is the package that was delivered
here today?" I asked, choosing a chamomile tea bag
and finally helping myself to a cookie. For a fleeting
moment I allowed myself the doomed and unworthy
hope that neither Betty nor Illuminada cared for Mint
Milanos. I am one of those people who sometimes has
reservations about the advantages of sharing. This was
one of those times.

"My mother left it here for you. The messenger
delivered it around four," Illuminada said, reaching for
a large manila envelope on the counter and handing it to
me. "What the hell is in it?" When I told her, she agreed
to have one of the photos blown up by a lab she dealt
with whose work she said was flawless. Meanwhile
Betty was removing all the little pleated paper cups of
cookies from the bag. She divided the cookies three
ways and placed a pleated cup of cookies in front of
each of us. Damn.

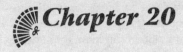

Chapter 20

To: Bbarrett@circle.com
From: HedySalter@MSU.edu
Re: Bachelorette parties
Date: Fri, 24 Jul 1998 16:18:23

Dear MOB,

You want to know what a bachelorette party is? It's the gal version of the bachelor or stag party. Get this. Twelve of my daughter Dot's girlfriends chipped in to take her to dinner at a lovely Italian restaurant where they had reserved a large table in an alcove. They invited me because I'd just flown in that afternoon and I hadn't seen Dot in months. They gave Dot a white T-shirt on which they'd written in big letters a list of things for her to do later in the evening when they hit the local bars. I remember it said for Dot to get three colored and three ribbed condoms and a pair of men's boxers and to fake an orgasm in public! They'd also made her a veil of toilet paper. While we sipped wine and nibbled hors d'oeuvres, Dot, wearing that way-out T-shirt and her toilet paper veil, mind you, opened her other gifts: a small leather whip, satin handcuffs, a book called *10001 Ways to Have Sex*, a penis-shaped straw that she sipped her Soave from, and a penis-shaped dog toy (she hasn't got a dog). On the table big as life sat the cake they had brought, a sugary confection topped by a life-sized marzipan you-know-what.

Remember when we'd write down the bride's comments when she opened her shower gifts and read them back as a preview of what she'd say on her wedding night? Pretty tame, huh? I took a cab home after dinner, leaving Dot and her friends and their designated drivers to hit the bars without Mom. I figured Dot would have a better chance at getting some strange guy in a bar out of his boxers without me tagging along shouting instructions.

Sol was driving me crazy. He was afraid that Gio would try to hurt me again. And I must admit the thought of running into Gio *was* terrifying. I decided to confront the situation head-on. I assumed that Nancy would be back at work by now since when I'd last seen her, she'd appeared quite recovered from her miscarriage if not her grief. I left the house on the pretext of running the usual errands at the produce shop, the post office, and the bank. But instead of heading for my regular bank, I went straight to the one where Nancy worked. I noticed her immediately and short-circuited the line to stand directly behind the elderly woman she was helping. I waited there until the woman had counted the bills Nancy gave her and carefully folded them into a change purse. When she finally turned away from the counter, I stepped forward and said, "Nancy, I need to talk to you privately. Now. It will just take a moment."

Nancy's initial smile of welcome faded. Her eyes widened and the hand she raised to her cheek trembled. "Yeah sure, Professor Barrett. Give me a minute." She reached under the counter and grabbed her purse. Then she stepped over to a woman at a desk in the enclosure and whispered something to her, jerking her head in my direction. A minute later Nancy Deloia and I stood under the shade of the awning of the café next to the bank. She immediately lit a cigarette. "What is it? What do you want? I can't take a lot of time off. Yesterday was my first day back." She looked around her, obviously worried about how this unscheduled break would sit with her manager.

I talked fast. "Nancy, two weeks ago your brother Gio threatened to hurt me if I attempted to visit you again." She raised a hand to brush her long hair back out of her eyes and then held her head with it. "Then one night last week, after I ran into you at the Palumbos', someone in a black pickup truck ran me down in the street when I got out of class." I paused to let my words sink in. When she put her hand over her face as if to shield herself from my message, I continued. "I think it was your brother. There was a witness." I didn't mention that the witness hadn't seen much. "I bruised several ribs and had to go to the emergency room in an ambulance. I could have been killed." Her eyes were enormous now and the hand holding the cigarette shook. "If you don't call him off, I'm going to report him to the police and accuse him of trying to kill me. They already suspect him of killing Louie, so—"

"Holy Mother of God, please don't report him. I'll talk to him. I swear . . ." Nancy put her hand on my arm as if to physically restrain me from ratting on Gio.

"I think he's come unhinged at the thought of you going to college. But that's not the point. You've got to make sure he leaves me alone." My voice was harsh, threatening.

"Oh, I will. Gio'll do what I tell him. He don't mean to hurt nobody." Nancy dropped her cigarette butt to the ground and stepped on it.

I said, "Running down pedestrians is hurtful, Nancy. You can kill somebody that way. Call him off or I'll turn him over to the cops." I walked away, leaving her holding her head in both hands. I felt confident that Nancy would be spending her lunch hour laying down the law to her baby brother. I was glad I'd talked to her because I didn't want to have to be concerned with Gio trying to make me into roadkill anymore. I had enough to worry about besides that.

That afternoon I visited the Frank Sinatra archives again, and chatted with the same reference librarian who'd been there during my earlier visit. "Still getting lots of inquiries about Frank?" I asked casually.

"Yes. It's just amazing how many people find their way up here." She shook her head. "And now I've got no Louie Palumbo to fob them off on, so I have to talk to them myself. Takes a lot of time." She adjusted her glasses, smiled a martyr's smile, and unlocked the cabinet.

"Are they mostly local folks or out-of-towners, would you say?" I reached for Pete Hamill's book, *Why Sinatra Matters*, and took it off the shelf.

"Mostly locals. There's another tribute bard, you know, Luke Jonas. He'll be singing at the St. Ann's Festival, I heard. He comes in every now and then to look up something. Nice enough young man, but not like Louie. Not really local." She reached for a copy of *Sinatra, the Artist and the Man* by John Lahr and handed it to me. "This one's good too," she said helpfully.

It took me a minute or two to process *tribute bard*, and once I had, I stifled a giggle and managed a reply. "I've heard Luke Jonas sing. He's excellent." I took the book from her. "I wish he'd make a CD of Frank's songs."

"He's got a CD out. I know that. He showed it to me. It's not just Sinatra songs though. It has a lot of show tunes too. In fact, I think the only Sinatra song on it is 'Blues in the Night.' He studies voice and acting in New

York. Wants to be in musical theater or cabaret work. In fact, he told me he was auditioning for an understudy role in *Cabaret*. I guess he didn't get it." The librarian paused and then continued with a slight smile. "Says he's not much of a dancer. That may have been his problem."

"I'm surprised he doesn't want to be in films. So many young people today want to be in movies." I had begun leafing through Lahr's book, admiring the vibrant photos and trying not to let them distract me from finding out what I wanted to know.

"You're right. In fact, there was a guy in here a couple of months ago. Young fella. Said he was writing a screenplay on the young Sinatra for one of the studios. Lucky he got to talk to Louie." She sighed. "He wanted to read and hear everything about Frank." We both looked up suddenly, distracted by the sound of someone taking the marble steps two at a time. Luke Jonas rushed into the room, smoothing his long reddish hair back from his flushed face. At the head of the stairs, he paused and glanced around the room until he spotted the librarian. He didn't notice me at first.

"Why, Luke Jonas, speak of the devil," she remarked by way of a greeting. Her rather serious demeanor was transformed into that of a coy schoolgirl. "I was just telling the professor about you. Your ears must be burning. What can I do for you today?"

"I hope you were saying something good," the young man said, smiling down at the woman. He turned to me. "Don't I know you from somewhere?" His brown eyes scanned my face. It occurred to me that this tribute bard must wear blue contact lenses when he impersonates Frank. Come to think of it, I bet Louie did too.

"Bel Barrett." I automatically extended my hand. "I caught your act at Swing for Your Supper a couple of weeks ago. We were celebrating the eighty-fourth birthday of my mother's friend, Sofia Dellafemina, remember? You were terrific." I assumed the compliment would jog his memory, and I was right.

"Yeah, of course. The table from Hoboken with those two wonderful ladies. Oops. I mean three wonderful ladies." The abashed grin he shot my way more than made up for his near blooper. I returned a grin of my own.

"Do you need any help?" repeated the librarian, offended, perhaps, that Luke and I had established a tie that excluded her.

"I just wanted to leaf through those photos in the Lahr book again," Luke said.

"Here, I've got it, but I'm through with it. You can have it." I handed him the book. "Those photos are really splendid, aren't they?"

"Thanks," he said. "Yeah, man. I depend on them to get the details right. I'm doing a Frank impersonation in acting class tonight and then at the feast this weekend. I hope you'll both be there?" He looked from one of us to the other.

"I'll have to see," said the librarian. "Maybe my sister will go with me."

"We wouldn't miss it for the world. Sofia and Sadie and I are becoming Luke Jonas groupies," I said, grinning at him once more as I turned and headed for the stairs. Then I quickly retraced my steps and positioned myself in front of Luke again. "Luke, I'm a prof at River Edge Community College. Would you consider talking to my speech students for say twenty minutes one evening in the next week or so? I can't pay you, but you could think of it as service to the community."

He smiled an easy smile, clearly flattered by my invitation. Then his brow furrowed. "Sure, I'd be happy to, but what would I talk about?"

"Oh, the class covers strategies and skills for speaking in public and for conducting a successful job search. I'd like you to talk about looking for work in show business. Of course, you'll be modeling good speaking skills."

"Of course." He grinned with the assurance of the young and good-looking. "And man, do I know a lot about pounding the pavement. Here's my card. Give me a call and we'll set up a date."

I took the card, but got out my book. "Let's set it up now. Summer school ends almost before it starts." Before I left the library, Luke Jonas had agreed to speak to my class the following Monday evening on the ordeal of finding a job in show business.

When I got to my office at RECC, Illuminada was waiting for me at the door with a tubular package in her hand. She kept looking at her watch as she paced back and forth. "Oh stop fussing and have lunch with me," I said, giving her a hug. "We can get a sandwich delivered or go to the RIP."

"*Caramba!* Bel, I work for a living, remember? This is America. Time is money." But she was already pushing buttons on her cell phone and I knew she was juggling her schedule and letting her staff know where she was. "Let's stay here. I want to look at this photo with you. Since you're the only one who knows what you're looking for, you're the only one who'll know when we've found it. Give Betty a call and see if she wants to get cozy here with us." I tried Betty's extension but she was at a meeting. At RECC many administrators do not work. They meet. As executive assistant to the president, Betty often attended meetings whose sole agenda was whether to schedule other meetings.

While I called the RIP Diner and ordered two tuna salads and two iced teas, Illuminada removed a large rolled-up photo from the tube and smoothed it out on Wendy's desk. We both stood over it, looking at the blown-up image of whatever was on Louie Palumbo's desk the day Sarah took the photo. The left-hand side was a mishmash of dry cleaning receipts, Visa bills, wedding programs, newspaper clippings, an uncashed check for $650 signed by a Giovanni Gerino, a package of Breath Mints, and the sheet music for "I'm a Fool to Want You." Part of a bill from somebody named Jack Dawson was in the top right corner over what looked like a couple of blank band contracts. The bottom right-hand corner of the desk was obscured by a calendar turned to the month of July. There were notations under some of the weekend dates and *P*'s written under some of the weekdays. July 28 was circled and "FFBRAUD" scrawled across the circle.

"For starters, I'd like to know who Jack Dawson is. And I'd give anything to know what FFBRAUD stands for," I explained, continuing to scrutinize the photo. I think P means practice as in band practice and see . . . the names on these weekend nights must be the names of people who hired the band to play gigs.

"Well, I can probably find out about Jack Dawson, but as for breaking the poor man's code, I don't know." Illuminada opened the door to the delivery person who had brought our lunch and paid for it before I had even begun to fumble for my purse.

"A run-down on Jack Dawson would help. I'll try to figure out what that other stuff means. I just think we have to keep looking for more people who have motives for getting rid of Louie." I opened my tuna salad and attacked it. I hadn't realized how late it was. While we ate, I told Illuminada about how I had handled Nancy Deloia.

"*Dios mio*, Bel. I don't know whether to be worried or impressed. I sure hope Nancy has the kind of influence over that brother of hers that you and Betty seem to think she does. And I also hope that she hadn't borrowed her brother's truck and decided to run you down herself." Illuminada sighed. "Well, I can worry about you this week because I don't have to worry about my mother. Raoul has some business in Miami, and he took her with him so she can see her sister. I told them both it was too hot for her there, but did they listen?"

"I know the answer to that one. Guess whose mother is chopping onions to raise money for a Catholic church as we speak? Last night I called to see if she was all right and she sounded great. Go figure." Illuminada and I toasted our willful mothers by raising our bottles of iced tea.

Class was stressful that night. We were reviewing the fifty questions most commonly asked at job interviews in an effort to understand corporate culture. It was so hard to get across the idea that *how* one answered was as important as *what* one said since the interview serves primarily as a means of assessing one's communication skills, presence, and suitability for a particular work-place. Leave it to Winston to get to the heart of the issue. "So someone like me who don't always express myself so good, even if I say what they wanna hear, I ain't gonna get the job, right? That's what this means, right, Professor?"

"Well, that's one way of looking at it, I suppose. I prefer to think that if someone as smart as you are knows what's expected of him, he can learn how to do it. I won't say it's easy, but people do what they have to to get what they want." As I answered, I wondered if Winston would ever want a position badly enough to abandon his jewelry and learn standard English. It might take a while, but I suspected he would.

"What about if you got an accent?" asked Tomas. Lots of shy students with accents nodded their heads as he articulated their fears.

"Today some people in powerful positions do have

foreign accents. But there are accents and accents. Upper-class British and French accents often have more status here than other accents, including Brooklyn and New Jersey accents. Can the person with the accent be easily understood? Is her grammar standard? Those are important questions to think about." Tomas did not look reassured.

Once again I walked downstairs after class with Ndaye. "Ndaye, you've missed two more classes since I last talked to you. I don't see how you can pass this course. You've only delivered one speech out of three so far." Hearing myself, I felt tired.

"I zpeak to zhem at work again. I try. You know, Professor, I try. But I cannot loze *zhees* position. I have to pay zee rent to my seezster's husband each week and I have, of course, zee otzhar expenses. But I try to come more often. I promeezse."

It was good to get home and enjoy a simple late supper with Sol, who had prepared a few ears of Jersey corn, a couple of filets of fish, and a salad. He poured me a glass of white wine and said, "There's a message on your machine from Danny Palumbo."

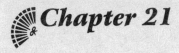

Chapter 21

To: Bbarrett@circle.com
From: Mbarrett@hotmail.com
Re: Phat City
Date: Thu, 30 Jul 1998 18:10:26

Yo Ma Bel!

Great news! Eric just e-mailed me that the dude who manages his cousin's band liked our demo tape and is getting us a gig at a bar in Hoboken over Labor Day weekend. I know Hoboken's pretty dead over Labor Day, but it's a start, right? We don't even have to audition. Eric said he really went for our song "White Boy Blues." (I wrote the lyrics for that one.) We had to think of a name for the band real fast, so we came up with Nomen. It's Latin for *name*. Get it? Watch for posters around town. Awesome, huh?

More great news. Just when I was getting pretty bored up here with only Howard Stern for company, I met this neat girl Aveda one day when I was out doing a little shopping. Her brother works in a sound studio in Cambridge, and he got me a job filling in for him while he's on vacation. I'm really learning a lot. Between what I'm making at the studio and what Dad and Cissie are paying me plus what I've saved living at home, I may have enough cash in hand to take off for someplace interesting this fall. Maybe Aveda will come with me.

Stay cool. Hi to Sol.

Love,
Mark

As I scanned Mark's e-mail, I smiled to myself. Maybe Sol was right. Without me standing over him monitoring his every breath, Mark was doing fine. He'd already acquired a girl and a day job not to mention a gig. I felt good when I set off the next morning to walk over to Hoboken High to meet Danny Palumbo.

I knew he had only agreed to meet me because I'd said I wanted to see him about Nancy, but I didn't care. I had assumed, apparently correctly, that he would be interested in anything related to the woman who had been his dead twin's girlfriend, his wife's cousin, and perhaps most important, his own first love. I had arranged to meet Danny Palumbo at Hoboken High where, according to Illuminada's sources, he ran a summer music program for the kids in the school's brass band. I called him when I was outside the building and he came to the entrance to escort me through the security now commonplace at urban high schools all year round. Summer school classes and band practice had ended for the day. Apart from the security guard and a few clerical people in the office, the building looked empty.

Like his dad, Danny Palumbo had aged. The bearded and ponytailed young man I recalled meeting at the Sinatra Park dedication had looked lean and fit. This man with the shaggy shoulder-length hair and the wild unkempt beard was wraithlike. As we shook hands, I noted that his eyes were glazed, not wild, and it crossed my mind that perhaps, like his parents, he too was on medication. "Come into my office. We can talk there," he said politely after greeting me with a perfunctory handshake.

His office, a cubbyhole in the basement of the building, seemed oddly familiar. Pictures of John Philip Sousa conducting, composing, and marching with the U.S. Marine Band were plastered all over the walls of the tiny room. Photos of the Hoboken High band filled the bulletin board. Papers and newspaper articles and concert programs littered the desk. It seemed that Louie and Danny had used the same decorator. I stared at him, looking for other traces of the dead singer.

"You said you wanted to talk to me about Nancy Deloia. Is anything wrong?" He looked genuinely bewildered. While I'd been sizing him up, he'd been looking me over too and was probably wondering how I came to be connected with Nancy.

I handed him my card. To my amazement, I found myself speaking the truth. Or mostly the truth. What I said was, "Thanks for agreeing to see me today. I know this is a difficult time for you and I'm so sorry about your loss. I don't know if you were aware, but my husband and I were the ones who found your brother's body." He nodded and lowered his head in a wordless acknowledgment of my condolences and of my revelation. Then he looked up, which I took to be an invitation to continue speaking. "I really wanted to talk to you about Nancy. You see, I met Nancy when I was recruiting students for RECC's Fresh Start Program. I came upon her at a bad time, but—"

Just then there was a knock on the door and a young woman entered. "Oh! I'm sorry. I didn't know you were busy." With her straight dark hair and glasses, she bore a striking resemblance to Toni Demaio. She had that same angelic beauty. "I'll talk to you later, Mr.

Palumbo." Blushing a deep rose, she left as quickly as she had come, closing the door behind her.

"That's Eileen Farrelly, a student teacher from State. She came in to help out when I had to miss some classes," he explained. I recalled Winston's talk on twins and how identical twins tended to go through the same stages and experiences at the same time in similar ways and with similar people. Sitting there in the nearly deserted school in the eerily familiar office, I realized that Danny Palumbo was probably betraying his wife with Eileen Farrelly, who would eventually have her heart broken just as Toni Demaio had. It was more than a little scary. I tried to control my suspicions and the animosity they engendered in me.

"Anyway, as I was saying, I tried to recruit Nancy to RECC's Fresh Start Program. It's especially designed for women who've been out of school for a while. She impressed me on the two or three occasions I've talked with her. Now that her plans have changed, I'd like to see her try college and I thought you might put in a word with her. She spoke so highly of you." All right, so I wasn't telling the whole truth, but I *would* like Nancy to go to college. "She could attend classes in the evening, so she'd be able to keep her position at the bank." I paused. Was Danny Palumbo counting the seconds until I left so he could join Ms. Farrelly somewhere? Or was he thinking about what I said? Or was he just too miserable for either Ms. Farrelly or me right now? When he didn't reply, I said, "Perhaps I was wrong to come today. My timing is poor, I know. But I just feel so strongly about this. I'm sorry." I stood.

"Don't go just yet, Professor Barrett. I'll talk to Nancy. Sure I'll talk to her. And I'll get my folks to talk to her. She listens to them. Especially now. But I'd like to hear about how you found my brother's body. If you don't mind talking about it, that is." Now it was his turn to pause. I seated myself again.

"No, I don't mind, but there's not much to tell. It happened pretty much the way it was written up in the paper. My friend Sol Hecht and I were out for a walk. Sol bent down to pick a flower for me and he saw this shoe in the weeds. It was a man's oxford. Sol thought it was trash or litter and he gets nuts over the way people throw trash all over the place. Then he . . ." I looked up to be sure he wanted me to continue.

"Go on," he urged. "I really want to hear about how he looked. I wasn't the one who identified the body at the morgue. I didn't see him until the viewing. By then the autopsy had been performed and the undertakers had given him his last makeup job." He turned his head away, perhaps so I wouldn't see the tears glittering like tiny jewels in the corners of his eyes.

"Well, when Sol realized the shoe was not empty, he walked around the big boulder in front of the body and pushed aside the shrubs and the weeds and there he was." I looked up.

My listener nodded and said, "Yes . . . go on."

"We were shocked. You see, he looked just like Frank Sinatra as a young man." I was totally unprepared for the grin that spread over Danny Palumbo's gaunt features. It somehow made me feel better, so I continued. "His eyes were open and they were bright blue. He wore a white dress shirt. There was no blood on the front, but . . ." Danny nodded again, so I continued. Either he was a really ghoulish type or he was just a grieving relative looking for closure anywhere he could find it. "He was lying in a pool of blood." I decided to omit from my narrative the presence of the flies attracted by Louie's blood. Instead I said, "He had on the wig with the curl in front and his shirt collar was

open. That's all I remember. We called the police right
away and they came pretty fast. They recognized your
brother by name. They took our names and started to
rope off the area and that's when we left." I shrugged
my shoulders and cocked my head to one side to indi-
cate that my story was over and that I knew it was not
much of a story to offer him in his anguish.

Danny didn't reply for a minute. He leaned back in
his chair until its two front legs were in the air in that
infuriating way that men and boys do and said, "Louie
lived for his act and the band. It's kind of stupid of me,
I guess, but Louie would've liked knowing that you
bought his last act. You two were his last audience." His
voice was somber.

"We saw him perform at the dedication to Sinatra
Park. We loved his act then. He was very good." I
waited.

"For a guy who couldn't sing his way out of the
shower, he was terrific," Danny Palumbo said with
another grin. "And he worked so hard to be more like
Frank than Frank. I think he started imitating Frank just
to do something I wasn't doing, because we were so
much alike we used to get mixed up ourselves sometimes. But then he really got into it like I really got into
this music teacher thing. Louie and me, we were very
close. That's how I know he had something on his mind
in the last few weeks. He said he was looking at a big
break. The break he'd been waiting for all his life."

"I guess that makes his death even harder to bear," I
speculated, hoping to elicit more information about the
nature of the break that Louie was anticipating.

"Yeah, for me and the folks and poor Nancy too. But
it probably makes it real nice for the chickenshit SOB
who stabbed him in the back. Real nice." Danny hissed
these words out between his teeth. "You see, Louie was
closer to me than my parents, my wife or even my kids.

I feel like part of me has been killed too." He lowered his head to his chest and I saw his fists clench. Raising his head, he said quietly, "And I'm gonna find out who did this to us."

"Do you have any idea who might have wanted Louie dead? Did Louie have any enemies? Do the police have any leads?" I tried to keep my tone conversational, gossipy.

At the mention of the police, his lips formed a sneer. "The cops! They've been watching too much daytime TV. They think Nancy mighta killed Louie 'cause she found out about some girl he met in the library. They think Nancy's brother Gio mighta done it 'cause he just plain hated Louie's guts. They think the library girl mighta done it 'cause she found out about Nancy and the baby. And they even think her boyfriend, some guy in North Bergen, mighta done it because Louie stole his girl. They even thought I mighta done it because I was jealous that Louie was the leader of our band. Next thing you know, they'll be askin' my mother and father questions. Jesus!" He stood up, looking at his watch. "I'll walk out with you. I don't mean to rush you, but I have to pick up my daughter at her day camp in twenty minutes. She gets out early today. I'll talk to Nancy."

I was a block and a half from Hoboken High nearing the corner of Willow Avenue when I heard Frank singing "I'm Walking Behind You." The next thing I knew something hard and heavy caromed out of the sky and, grazing my back, crashed at my heels on the sidewalk. I screamed.

Chapter 22

To: Bbarrett@circle.com
From: Rbarrett@UWash.edu
Re: Grandma Sadie's latest
Date: Fri, 31 Jul 1998 15:58:39

Dear Mom,

In my last letter to Grandma Sadie, I told her Keith and I
expected her to be here for the baby's birth along with you, Sol,
Mark, Keith's mom, and Keith's friend Jeremy (he's the sports
photographer) who's going to video it. Jeremy's also letting us
use his deck so I can have one of those little pools to sit in during
labor. My midwife says it's so relaxing. Anyway, Grandma
should be there. So we just got a letter back from her with a
check in it for fifteen hundred dollars. She says it's half the money
she's won at the casino in the last two years and it's for the baby's
college fund. She's saving the other half for when Mark has a
baby. She already sent us a check when I told her about the wedding. Can she afford this? Should we send it back to her? If we
do, will she be insulted? HELP!

Love,
Rebecca

Would I even be around to participate in my grand-child's on-camera birth-in was the question that flashed through my mind as I looked down at the cinder block on the sidewalk behind me and then up at the scaffold that, presumably, it had fallen from. I felt like Chicken Little on estrogen. And my patch must have been really pumping that day because instead of feeling scared I got mad. These construction crews all over the place had turned my town into a minefield where a law-abiding citizen couldn't even walk the streets in broad daylight without getting beaned by falling debris. Jesus! I looked up and saw two faces staring out at me from the flat roof of 429 Sixth Street. One was Ralphie D'Onofrio's and the other belonged to Joe Vecchio. Ralphie appeared to be holding a cell phone to his ear. "Are you okay, lady?" Joe yelled.

One head disappeared and in a second Joe stood beside me on the sidewalk, concern etching lines in his thin face. He stared at the cinder block. "I don't know how this got loose." He looked up at the side of the building where the scaffold dangled near the fire escape. "You're the lady from the other night. Jesus, you could have been killed." He bent down and picked up a chunk of the block with both hands and put it down next to a tarp-covered mound beside the curb. Then he yelled, "Ralphie! Haul up that fuckin' scaffold." Ralph-ie's head disappeared and then I saw the scaffold slowly moving up the wall of the building. Ralphie reappeared and pulled it onto the roof. Joe stood there next to me, scratching his head. "You sure you're okay?" he asked again, probably worried because I'd not responded to his initial inquiries.

My brain was slowly checking in. *Who had been walking behind me?* I wondered, remembering the frag-ment of Frank I'd heard just before the sky fell. "I'm okay," I finally said. "Just a little shaky. I wasn't expect-ing that," I added stupidly. Suddenly I wanted badly to be somewhere else. "I'm going home now before something else happens to me." I turned and took a few steps, but not before I'd noticed the black pickup truck double-parked in the street. *How long had that been there? Whose was it?* I wondered. There was no name on the side. And I began to walk swiftly, leaving Joe shaking his head and staring at the place where the scaffold had been. When enough time had passed for him to retreat inside the building, I doubled back, hid behind an SUV, and jotted down the license plate number, make, and model of the black truck. Then I hightailed it for home.

It wasn't hard to spot Sofia and Ma at the feast the next night. They stood with a few other hard-core types on the top steps of the church, their webbed lawn chairs propped against the church door behind them in case they needed to sit. They seemed oblivious to the heat and humidity that combined with the smoke from the many grills and fry vats to make the sweat sizzle on your skin. From their vantage point, they had a clear view of the stage rigged up across the street.

Sol and I joined the line for zeppoles that snaked through the throng for about a hundred yards. "You owe me for this, Bel," Sol said, swabbing the sweat from his face and neck with a handkerchief. "If there was ever a night to stay home and watch a movie with Mark in air-conditioned comfort, it's tonight."

"I told you you didn't have to come," I said petulantly. "The worst thing that could happen to me here is that I'll put on a few pounds, and you're no protection against that, God knows." When I told Sol how close I'd come to getting brained by a cinder block he'd insisted on walking over to the feast with me even though the event's mix of religious fervor, junk food, second-rate popular music, and crowds was anathema to him. I reached into my purse and pulled out my fan. I'd gotten into the fan habit a few years ago when I had measured my life in hot flashes. And now when I ventured outside for any length of time on summer evenings, I tried to remember to bring a fan along. I moved the air around in front of Sol and me as we inched forward. By the time the lady with the too-frizzy perm and the voice of a circus barker handed me the bag of piping hot zeppoles, the sun had set and the musicians were warming up.

We elbowed our way up the stairs to where Ma and Sofia stood and shared our goodies with them. "Look! There he is! Look!" Sofia was carrying on like one of those teenagers who swooned over Frank during his now legendary performance at the Paramount in 1942. I was so taken by her enthusiasm, that I didn't immediately notice that the backup band was not the Hoboken Four Plus One.

When this fact finally did register, I nudged Sol and said, "Look, it's a different band."

"They probably didn't have the heart to play the feast without their leader. Talk about tasteless. That would have been a real slap in the face to the family," Sol said, reaching into the hot bag and withdrawing his hand quickly. "Ouch. Those things are hot, too hot to eat."

"More for me then," I gloated. "You just have to eat them fast. Look! Check him out!" A bewigged, tuxedoed, and probably contact-lensed Luke Jonas was doing his best to swagger onto the stage. Once there, he took off his jacket and tossed it over one shoulder, hooking his index finger under the collar. Thus positioned, he began to sing the opening bars of "I've Got a Crush on You." I closed my eyes. It was Frank. Next he sang "It Was a Very Good Year" and I saw Ma squeeze Sofia's arm. When he shifted the tempo and swung into "I've Got You Under My Skin," Sofia and Ma, arm in arm, began swaying to the rhythm.

"Look! Isn't that the man Luke met at Swing for

Your Supper? The one Luke went over to and hugged? His agent, he said it was." Ma squealed and pointed at a bearded and ponytailed man whom I too recognized as the person Luke had identified as his agent, "the one who makes it all happen." He stood at the periphery of the crowd, below the steps, talking animatedly to a shorter man who was beardless and totally bald. Every so often the agent would look up at Luke, point to him, and then turn back to face the bald man.

"You know who that is?" Sofia didn't wait for any of us to respond to her question before bursting out with, "That bald guy is the person Mary talked to about renting her house for a movie. From Hollywood, I think. They want to shoot some scenes for a movie in her house. She's going to make a fortune."

"Mary Garibaldi or Mary Cantone?" asked Ma. Sometimes she had trouble keeping the names of Sofia's many friends and family members straight.

I didn't catch Sofia's reply, though, because as soon as I had heard Sofia utter the word *Hollywood*, standing there in the crowd in the heat I had my own version of an epiphany. It was one of those marvelous moments when something triggers my mind into synthesizing seemingly unrelated scraps of data. Mark's latest e-mail flashed through my brain and resonated there with Louie Palumbo's bathroom reading, his desktop scribblings, and the fragment of "I'm Walking Behind You" I'd heard the day before. Grinning, I squeezed Sol's hand so hard he pulled it away. "What's the matter?" His voice was sharp.

"Nothing. Don't worry. Be right back. It's okay. You can see me from here. Don't follow me." I shoved the bag of zeppoles into his hands saying, "Save me some." Then I elbowed my way down the stairs, pulling a pad and pen out of my purse as I moved. In the time it took Luke to finally divest himself of the jacket, roll up his shirtsleeves, and loosen his tie, I was beside the two men. I was willing to bet they wouldn't notice me if I stood next to them for a moment or two. Women my age are not even part of the landscape for some men. We just don't register on their radar. So I stood beside them and eavesdropped as best I could with Luke Jonas bragging into the mike about how he had the world on a string just twenty feet away. There was a lot to be said for being invisible sometimes.

"Go with me on this one J. J. Close your eyes. I mean, you gotta admit, the kid's pure Sinatra, right? Are we talkin' Sinatra here or what? When my cousin asked me to take the kid on, I was, like not enthusiastic. But then I caught his act . . ." The agent smiled ingratiatingly at J. J.

"Yeah, Al. He's got the voice down. He sounds like Frank." J. J. was looking around at the church, the crowd, the food stands, and the makeshift stage.

Al gushed, "You know I appreciate you comin' alla way out here tonight, J. J. Ya see why I didn't want you to miss this?"

"Well, since I was out here anyway to nail down the set rental . . ." J. J. was mid-sentence when I made my move.

"Al, Wolf here. Sarah Wolf." Placing my substantial self squarely between the men, I faced the agent and stuck out my hand. "I write for the *Jersey City Herald*."

"Uh, yeah. J. J. Meyers here," said Al, like a good boy, introducing me to his companion while at the same time trying to place me.

Taking advantage of the element of surprise, I pressed on. "Your client sounds so much like Sinatra and since he's actually living here in Sinatra's town, we want to do an in-depth piece on him. Is it true he's being considered for the lead in a new film on Frank's early years?"

Al was caught. He couldn't in good conscience spurn

the press, even the local press. And yet he didn't want to miss the chance to chat up the suit from the studio. His dilemma resolved itself when J. J. stuck out his own hand to Al, saying, "Bye, Al, baby. Got a plane to catch. Let's stay in touch." He disappeared into the crowd.

"Yeah. Yeah. In fact, J. J.'s one of the honchos from the studio. I think Luke's got a good shot at the part." With the departure of J. J., Al's features smoothed out and his antsy animated speech eased into an easy flow.

"He sure sounds just like Sinatra. I've never heard an impersonator who captured Sinatra's pitch and phrasing so exactly," I said ingenuously. "I can't imagine there was any serious competition for the part."

"In this business there's always competition." Al sighed. He sounded resigned rather than bitter. "But Luke Jonas has a trained voice and he's a good-looking, personable kid. He's done a lot of cabaret work and theatrical stuff too. They're thinking of using him to understudy a singer in *Ragtime*."

"But a movie about Sinatra would really make Luke's career, wouldn't it?" I persisted, writing furiously on my pad, trying to look as if I was actually taking notes.

"That's what he thinks, even though he got into this whole Frank Sinatra impersonator thing only after he moved here to go to acting school. That's a cute story actually. Straight human interest." Al looked at me for the first time and asked, "Wanna hear it?"

"I'm all ears. Don't go too fast," I replied. "I don't want to miss a word of it."

"Luke was jokin' around with his roommate one night last summer. You know they share a terrific apartment in a renovated building here. On Sixth Street, I think it is." Al gestured vaguely east. "Only fifteen hundred bucks a month. Two bedrooms, hardwood floors, new appliances, a working fireplace . . . everything. Nothin' like it in Manhattan for that price, let me tell you . . ." I sighed. Once again, real estate was upstaging other realities in Hoboken. "So they were out on the deck. Can you believe a deck too for fifteen hundred a month?" I nodded, praying he'd go on. "Anyway, like I was sayin', he was tellin' a story about how he was in some spaghetti joint here where they got all these Sinatra songs on the jukebox, and he imitated the way the locals would play those tunes one after another for hours. Like he did this whole medley of Sinatra songs right there in the apartment. His roommate was so blown away he submitted Luke's name to be in this show they were havin' here for Sinatra's birthday. Luke didn't even know about it till he got invited to audition. And he went to the tryout, kind of as a joke, ya know? And he got the goddamn gig. Can you believe that? The kid is amazing, I tell you! He even beat out the local impersonator. Ever since then he's been doin' a lotta Sinatra, not just here, but in New York. I keep tellin' him, I think his real future lies in cabaret. That way he can do a little Frank but not only Frank." I heard Luke Jonas ending his invitation to the audience to fly with him, the velvet voice giving every syllable exactly the right intonation. It was the end of the set. The applause was thunderous.

"What a story, Al. Listen, I've got to make a deadline. I'll call you." I turned away, eager to avoid coming face to face with Luke Jonas. Now that the set was over, I knew the performer would seek out his agent for a report on how he made out selling J. J. on Luke. I didn't think it would be good for my health for Luke to know that I'd been pretending to be a reporter who was very curious about his future in film.

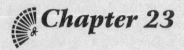

Chapter 23

To: Bbarrett@circle.com
From: Eafallon@juno.com
Re: Childbirth today
Date: Sat, 01 Aug 1998 16:18:09

Dear MOB-to-be,

You're right. Having a baby now is different than it was in our day. Back then as soon as we started barfing up breakfast, we went and panted through those Lamaze classes and then thought it was a big deal if they let our husbands into the labor room. I remember one cranky OBGYN didn't show up until after I'd been shaved, had an enema, and been in labor for about two weeks. When somebody finally dragged him off the golf course, he just wanted to knock me out, drag the baby out, and get out himself so he could finish his golf game. I've been there and done that. Recently I've watched my three girls have their babies, and believe me, it's a whole new ball game.

My girls love midwives. They're highly trained and caring and spend lots of time with the moms. Midwives do not play golf. The Bradley Method is what they're into today. It's about early prenatal care, good nutrition, and a comfortable drugless delivery. The woman in labor is supposed to focus and move around a lot. That's where the pool comes in. They've found that sitting in water reduces the pain of contractions. A lot of women prefer to have their babies at home now. For others, there's the birthing center, a Martha Stewart version of a delivery room/cabana club.

Your daughter may change her mind about giving birth with a cast of thousands on candid camera. My Sue did. She settled for having just two of us there. But about six of us welcomed Valerie's son, who smiled for the camera before he was even half out. And when Ellen's daughter was born, it seemed like her whole neighborhood was in the room, including Oswald, her collie.

I called Luke Jonas and the other people I'd scheduled to speak to my class on Monday night. They would provide my students with useful information from recent college grads in the white-collar workforce. Although I'd already written to each speaker, I reminded them of the time and date as well as the address and room number where the class met. I also reminded them to dress as they would for an interview, and to bring twenty-five copies of their résumés and any other printed material they planned to use. I repeated my promise to reimburse them for copying and parking expenses since on-street parking near RECC was very difficult to come by. Something about Luke Jonas's card struck me when I took his phone number from it, but I couldn't connect the dots then. I was getting used to waiting for my brain to catalogue and interpret information, so I knew whatever it was would eventually surface.

As it turned out, my car wouldn't start on Monday, so I took the PATH train to work while Sol tried to get my old Toyota going. There was still a lot to do to prepare for the evening if it was going to be both informative and pleasant. I stopped by a deli and ordered some iced soft drinks and a couple of trays of cheese and fruit to be delivered just before class. I would serve these after the talks when I hoped students and speakers would chat informally. Once in the office I typed up and printed out a simple program identifying the speakers in the order I wanted them to talk. The first, Harold Noyes, taught elementary school, the next, Jignesh Singh, managed a Baby Gap in Manhattan, the third, Latifah Matthews, an entrepreneur, designed websites, and the fourth, Luke Jonas, a singer and actor, performed in clubs and musical theater productions. All but Luke were RECC graduates.

To my great relief, all of them showed up. I seated them in a row across the front of the classroom. Dressed neatly in a summer suit, Harold gave out copies of his résumé and explained how he had to take state and national exams, fill out papers, be interviewed three times, and teach a demonstration class before finally landing a position in a private school in Newark. He said he loved his work and that the effort to prepare for teaching and search for a job had finally paid off.

Also wearing a suit and tie, Jignesh Singh passed out copies of the résumé that had landed him his promotion to manager at the Baby Gap store he now ran. He spoke about the process of applying for an in-house position, what it was like to be interviewed by people who know you, and how he was one of the few men managing a Baby Gap. Somewhere in the middle of Jignesh's talk, Tomas got up and left the room, catching my eye and holding up a coin when he got to the door. I knew he had to feed the meter or face a costly ticket. I hoped Jignesh would remember this dismaying aspect of academic life at RECC and not interpret Tomas's departure as a lack of interest in the trials and tribulations of career advancement at Baby Gap.

Latifah was dressed in cut-offs and a T-shirt because, as she explained, she got most of her work via the Web and conducted almost all of her business via e-mail and fax, so every day was dress-down day for her. She began her business when she was still a student at New Jersey Institute of Technology, and she now earned enough to pay most of her own grad school tuition. She gave out a résumé she had downloaded from her website and a business card.

There was no trace of the Chairman in Luke's apparel or demeanor at first. In tight black jeans, a black T-shirt, and sandals, he resembled a fugitive from a nineties version of *A Chorus Line*. His long reddish hair gleamed, and he continually pushed it back off his face with his hand. Like the others, he gave out copies of his résumé, which, unlike theirs, was stapled onto the back of a headshot. At this point Ndaye flew into the room. With her usually sleek hair winging her oval face and wearing her white uniform, she resembled an African angel. As she took in the unfamiliar faces, she looked perplexed until she realized that she was, indeed, in the right class. Luke acknowledged her with a nod.

He went on to recount how he had only recently acquired an agent to represent him, without mentioning that said agent was a friend of a relative. He then described how he prepared for auditions. From the black shoulder bag he carried, he took out a few pieces of sheet music, explaining that he had to be prepared to sing various types of songs. Then Luke took out the rudiments of his Frank costume—the fedora, the wig, the blue contact lenses, and white dress shirt—and explained that at an audition he would try to resemble the person whose part he was playing and that he occasionally auditioned for gigs impersonating Frank Sinatra. He did a funny imitation of how a director simultaneously scanned a singer's résumé, gave his appearance a once-over, listened to him sing a few bars of a song, and said, "Thank you; next please" all within the space of a moment or two. My students were charmed.

I had decided to serve the refreshments during the question-and-answer session because I knew that after class, people would be unlikely to hang around no matter how fascinating the speakers were or how appealing the edibles and potables. Two other people ran to feed their parking meters and three diehard smokers left to enjoy a furtive cigarette on the fire exit stairwell or in the lavatory. Most everybody stayed in the room though, and soon we were all sipping soda and munching on cheese and fruit.

The speakers were making an effort to mix. Luke had approached Ndaye and was showing her his portfolio. Tomas had boxed Latifah into a corner where I heard him grilling her on our prospects for surviving Y2K. Winston and several other students were quizzing Jignesh about the pros and cons of a career in retail management. And a bevy of women, all early childhood education majors, surrounded Harold. I wonder if their curiosity would have been quite as keen had they known about the wife and daughter waiting for him at home in Bayonne.

After about fifteen minutes, I stood and said loudly, "I'm sure our guests have provoked much curiosity. They've graciously agreed to answer specific questions, so let's come together again and have some of those questions now. And please, I want everybody to keep right on enjoying the goodies. I don't want any leftovers."

Latifah was besieged. "How did you figure out how to start your business?" "How do you know when it's quittin' time if you work for yourself all by yourself?" "How do you decide how much to charge people?"

Harold drew a few queries, mostly about teaching a demonstration class. "How did you know what to do for a whole hour with a bunch of kids you never saw before with all those people watchin'?" "What if the kids don't listen to you?"

Jignesh fielded a few inquiries about the logistics of his work. "How can you stand a schedule like you say you got? Man, you change your hours every other week it seems like." "How can you get promoted if, say, the other manager got an attitude about you?"

There was only one question for Luke from an aspiring rapper, who had given his résumé a close reading. "It says on your résumé you have a four-year degree and you have a lot of experience singing in different shows and clubs. Why wouldn't they cast you? Is it politics?" I had to laugh at the question, a logical one here in Hudson County, where patronage politics is as omnipresent in the culture as pollutants are in the air.

That's when Luke flushed and said with a shrug of his shoulders, "Not usually. The truth is most of the time when I don't get a part it's because there's someone else who the casting director thinks can sing better or act better or just look better in the part. There's a lot of competition out there. You have to beat out a lot of other actors to make it." His mouth twisted momentarily.

Tomas asked somewhat rhetorically, "Didn't you sing at the festival in Hoboken Saturday night? I seen you there." I hadn't seen Tomas at the feast, but I was glad he was doing something with his time besides sitting around worrying about Y2K.

Luke smiled and said, "Yes. I get a lot of gigs now doing Frank Sinatra. He's real popular still, especially in Hoboken."

Winston said, "Frank Sinatra was a short skinny Italian guy with dark hair. My grandmother has these antique records with his picture. And I seen him on TV. Before he died, I mean. You must be an amazing actor if you can impersonate Frank Sinatra." Luke flushed again. He didn't respond.

"You are szo much better lookeeng zhan Frank Zseenatra." Ndaye's candid appraisal brought a smile to Luke's face. He winked at her.

Shortly after that exchange, I thanked the speakers and ended the class. Delighted to be leaving ten minutes before our usual dismissal, the students rushed for the stairs. Even though they were getting out early, they were still the last class left on the floor. Most of those who taught in the evening routinely shortchanged their students by dismissing classes long before they were scheduled to end. The administrators, although aware of this problem, had failed to solve it.

I stayed to wipe off the desk that had doubled as our buffet table and put the cups and glasses in the trash. That was my first mistake, but I was conditioned to doing what I had to do to stay in the good graces of RECC's maintenance staff. They would have my head if they thought I expected them to do a lick of extra work just because I wanted to make the evening a little special for my students. Cleaning up after class fetes was not in their contract, and if it wasn't in their contract, they wouldn't do it. Of course, catering wasn't in my contract either, but hey. Pondering for the umpteenth time the ongoing conflict between my literal job description and the spirit of my work, I switched off the lights and turned in the direction of my office to drop off the unused paper cups and napkins. That was my second mistake. "Can I give you a lift back to Hoboken?" Luke Jonas waited in the deserted corridor, lounging against the wall.

"Oh no, I have a ride. Thanks anyway. That's very kind of you." I reached the door to my office, unlocked it, and piled the paper goods on my desk. Too late I realized I should have taken them home with me rather than enter my office. Luke followed me. He stood blocking the door, trapping me in the cubicle.

"No problem. I'll wait and walk you downstairs." He let his shoulder bag slide to the floor and took a step toward me. His voice seemed to bounce off the walls of the boxlike room, his words separating and coming together and echoing crazily. I could feel my heart racing and hear it beating louder and louder. I hoped I wouldn't faint. Just as the room started to spin, I pulled out my cell phone, pushed a button, and said, "Hi sweetheart. I'll be down in a sec. Luke Jonas is walking me down. He was great." My mouth was dry and my voice was reduced to a frantic squeak, but I didn't care. I had let Luke know that somebody was aware that he was up there with me.

Wordlessly he moved back toward the door, picked up his bag, and stepped back into the corridor. I locked the office door and joined him, almost giddy with relief. "You heard me tell my partner what a great job you did tonight. I'm sure my students appreciated learning about your experiences. And they enjoyed your sense of humor too. Thanks so much for coming." I continued to babble all the way down the stairs.

Luke held the door to the building open for me, saying tersely, "No problem. Are you sure you don't need a lift?" He looked up and down the street, presumably to see if my ride had shown up. He had.

"Thanks, but my chauffeur's here. And again, I really appreciate your coming to our class. Good night." Sol leaned over to unlock the door for me, and I waved goodbye to Luke and got in the car. As soon as I closed the door I said, "Go around the block, please." I locked the car door.

"Jesus, Bel. Why?" Sol asked, steering the car along

the nearly deserted street in downtown Jersey City. His voice was sharp with worry and irritation.

"He's parked in the lot on the corner. I want to see what he's driving. By the time we go around the block, he'll be just pulling out of the lot. He'll be ahead of us. He won't be watching his back. Just do it, please." I spoke urgently, fumbling in my purse for a Post-it, my distance glasses, and a pen. I was relieved when Sol turned the corner without comment. The combination of moonlight and streetlights had turned the familiar buildings a silvery gray. I felt my chest contract when a small black pickup truck pulled into the street in front of us. Wearing my glasses and squinting into the glare of our own headlights, I could make out only three letters on the license plate. "Can you read the license number?" I asked.

"DMJ 44Y." Sol rattled off the letters and numbers. "It's a black Dodge, '97 maybe. Now can we go home?"

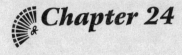

Chapter 24

Luke Jonas
Agent
Hirsch & Walker, Ltd.
Al Hirsch 212-555-9649
Ahirsch@starworks.com

Height: 6'1"
Weight: 180
Hair: Auburn
Eyes: Brown
Voice: Baritone

CABARET

Swing for Your Supper, New York, NY
Red Blazer, New York, NY
Starlight & Roses, Grafton, OH
Festival of St. Ann's, Hoboken, NJ

CLARENCE COLLEGE PRODUCTIONS

Oklahoma
The King and I
Grease

NYU MUSICAL THEATER PRODUCTION
(MFA PROGRAM)

A Chorus Line

We sat around the table at Betty's on Friday night, pondering copies of Luke's résumé. Illuminada was the first to speak. "I'd like to know what is going through that steel-trap mind of yours this time, *Profesora*. These show-biz résumés don't say much. No references, no dates. This is really just a list of stats and performances." She eyed the sheet of paper disdainfully and then waved it at me, asking, "What are you seeing here that the rest of us are missing?" She took a long pull on her Corona and waited for me to speak.

"Well, I just thought it was interesting that he was only in three productions in college, that's all. Usually college drama departments put on a play a semester. Maybe he changed majors after sophomore year or . . ." I let my voice trail, partly because I wanted to see if anything else had struck them about Luke's résumé and partly because I was listening hard for the doorbell, which would signal the arrival of our dinner.

Betty was on the same food-centered wavelength. She stared at the door as if willing the bell to ring and, to no one's surprise, it did. "Praise the Lord," she said, jumping up to answer it. We spent a few minutes in compatible silence chowing down on our barbecued chicken, slaw, and corn muffins.

Then, having placated the beast in my belly for a little while at least, I took a deep breath and began, "Okay, here goes. I've put it all together, and I'd like to run it by you. To make a long story short, I think Luke Jonas killed Louie Palumbo."

"*Dios mio*, Bel, I appreciate your wanting to condense for once in your life, but this is not the time. We actually would like the unabridged version this time, God help us." Illuminada raised her eyes heavenward. "Why on earth do you think Luke Jonas killed Louie, and how did you come to that conclusion?" She spoke slowly, patiently, the way she often did when she felt like screaming.

"Oh, Illuminada, you're so unreasonable. Why would Bel want to bore us with those details?" Betty's sarcasm was hard to miss.

"Okay," I said, taking a deep breath. "Just remember, you asked for the uncut version. I don't know if I told you that when I availed myself of the Palumbos' bathroom, I noticed a copy of *Movieline* magazine there. When I bought that issue at a newsstand, I learned that Back Room Productions, an indie studio, is making a musical film based on Frank's early life and coming of age in Hoboken. It dramatizes his transition from Dolly's boy to Dorsey's boy wonder. I didn't think too much about it when I read it. Then the reference librarian in charge of the Sinatra archives told me that a screenwriter had been in town a while back doing research for a film. This guy interviewed Louie at great length, so Louie definitely knew about the project."

Pausing for a swig of beer, I took a deep breath before continuing. "Illuminada faxed me last week to say she found out that Jack Dawson, the guy whose bill was on Louie's desk, teaches acting in the Village. When I called him, Dawson confirmed that Louie had been taking acting classes with him for a few months. Also, Danny Palumbo said that Louie told him he expected a big break soon."

"Speaking of Danny Palumbo," Betty interjected, "I've been doing a little research on identical twins. Every now and then, one or both can be homicidal." I couldn't believe that Betty had just interrupted me. When she continued to speak, I found myself seething. "There was a British twin who tried to strangle her sister, who, in return, tried to drown her. They were in love with the same guy. And a Korean-American twin tried to arrange to have *her* twin sister killed. She wanted to assume her twin's life because it was better than her own. So identical twins are not always simpatico."

"True if you say so. But, hello? Do you mind if I finish? You both wanted to hear this," I reminded them, not wanting to let Betty's intrusion go totally unmentioned. I tried to pick up my story where I had left off. "Anyway, a few days ago I got an e-mail from Mark about sending in a demo tape and getting a gig at a bar in Hoboken without even auditioning."

"*Caramba*, Bel! Are we totally shifting gears here? Are you having a bad patch day or something?" Illuminada asked, finally pushing her plate away.

"How do you think Mark'll feel if his mother's posse shows up in force?" asked Betty, her eyes agleam with mischief. "I'd love to hear him play in public." Now Illuminada glared at her.

While I was talking, Illuminada and Betty had managed to reduce the contents of their plates to chicken bones, a few shreds of cabbage, and some cornbread crumbs while my dinner was still barely touched. This went against my grain, so ignoring them both I hurried to finish my tale. "Well, after I read Mark's e-mail, the word *audition* stuck in my head and there was something about the idea of a demo tape lodged in there too, but I didn't know it until everything came together for me at the feast." They looked perplexed, so I hurried to explain. "Ma recognized Luke's agent and Sofia recognized the guy he was chatting up as a Hollywood type. He was here arranging to rent a house, from a friend of hers actually, in which to shoot scenes from Frank's childhood. Anyway, as soon as I heard Sofia say *Hollywood*, a lot of little things fell into place."

It was hard to keep the excitement out of my voice now. "Remember the letters *FFBRAUD* on Louie's desktop calendar?" Illuminada nodded. "Well, they *could* stand for *F*rank *F*ilm *B*ack *R*oom *AUD*ition. Louie was going to audition for the film about Frank's early life by Back Room Productions on July 28." I managed a bite of chicken before I sat back, pleased with my own cleverness.

But my dinner companions were too busy demeaning the dead to appreciate the genius behind my code cracking. "Say what, girl? How could that dude expect to get a role in a musical? He could hardly carry a tune." Betty shuddered for emphasis.

Illuminada began to hum the refrain to "It Was a Very Good Year" in a deep falsetto. She was doing Louie Palumbo doing Frank. The resulting noise was not a compliment to the late tribute bard's vocal range or tone.

"That's what's so interesting. They've got tapes of Frank or CDs or what-have-you, so they don't need a singer. They need somebody who looks, talks, and acts like Frank, and Louie Palumbo did. They can use recordings of the real Frank and dub the songs, don't you see? Louie Palumbo had a good shot at getting that part, damn it. And the fact that he was a B&R as in Born-and-Raised Hobokenite would make for marvelous spin too. I can see it now: 'Hoboken Homeboy Plays Sinatra. The Legend Lives.' " Once again I attempted to ingest a few mouthfuls of food. Betty went into the kitchen and returned with three cold beers. "Luke Jonas wanted that part. He knew Louie was his most serious competition. When he got the chance, he killed him."

"What about the guy in the black truck who's trying to kill you?" asked Illuminada. "Are you going to tell me Luke Jonas owns a black pickup?"

I updated them on the events of last evening, when Luke Jonas had cornered me in my office and I had foiled his assault on my person. By the time I finished, they were both wide-eyed. Illuminada recovered first and raised her beer, "*Dios mio*, it's a good thing Sol made you get that cell phone."

"Praise the Lord that you had the wit to use it," echoed Betty, "and that Sol got there on time."

"Wait a minute, I want to ask you something before we get totally carried away." I knew Illuminada would have more questions. She probably asked questions during sex and childbirth too. That woman was born with a silver question mark in her mouth. It was one of the first things I'd noticed about her when we met. But I was fortified. I had finally finished my dinner, and I washed it down with a gulp of Corona. "First of all, how do you know Luke Jonas meant to harm you? Did he actually attack you?"

"No, he didn't have a chance to attack me. But he would have if I hadn't made that phone call." I was sure about this, but I could tell that Illuminada wasn't convinced.

"Let's leave that for a minute. How did he find out you were on his trail?"

"One possibility is that his guilty conscience has made him paranoid, and he's heard about my sleuthing. So he got suspicious after seeing me at Swing for Your Supper talking to his agent at the feast. I mean I'm not

really invisible. And if Luke asked his agent who he
was talking to and the agent told him I was Sarah Wolf,
Luke would have had good reason to be on guard. I
never should have lied about who I was," I said, shaking
my head. "That was dumb."

"Well, you've been pretty smart about everything
else. You're entitled to do something dumb once in a
while," said Betty. This was generous of her since Betty
had zero tolerance for mistakes. Maybe she was trying
to make amends for having cut me off before.

"*Dios mio*, if you're right, it was not only dumb, but
also dangerous," said Illuminada. "I keep trying to get it
into that head of yours, you don't want to get on the
wrong side of a murderer, Bel."

"Too late. Get this. He also bopped me with a cinder
block." They both looked quizzical, so I added, "He
lives on Sixth Street in a house that's getting an addi-
tion. By Louie's old band buddies, in fact, but that's neither here nor there. And I was walking by. He must have
seen me approaching from the window and reached out
and pushed a cinder block off the scaffold. It landed on
the sidewalk directly behind me. The damn thing grazed
my back on the way down." Now it was my turn to
shudder at the memory of what a close call that had
been.

"Bel, did you see him? How do you know he lives
there?" This time it was Betty throwing questions at
me. I could tell that they weren't buying into the notion
of Luke as Louie's murderer.

"No, I didn't see him, but I heard him. Listen. This is
so bizarre. Just before the thing landed behind me, I
heard Frank singing 'I'm Walking Behind You.' At first
I didn't think anything of it. I mean if I had a dollar
every time I heard a tape or CD of Frank in Hoboken,
I'd be a rich woman." Illuminada and Betty both smiled
at the truth of what I had just said. "But the weird thing

about it was, and I didn't realize this until much later, it was a cappella. Frank sings that song with an orchestra. There's only one person around here who could have done that." Neither Betty nor Illuminada answered.

"Less interesting but also true, I know that Luke Jonas lives at that address because he gave me his card when we met in the library. He's also in the phone book at that address. And, are you ready?" Sipping my beer, I looked at each of them in turn.

"Come on, Bel. No dessert until you tell us," said Betty. She was really pushing my buttons tonight.

"Okay. You won't believe this, but after the block just missed me, I noticed a black pickup truck double-parked in front of the house. I left and then after a few minutes I doubled back and checked the plates." Reaching into my bag and groping around just a little, I pulled out the Post-it on which I'd scrawled the plate number that Sol had read off to me and the one I had copied myself. They were identical. "See, the numbers are the same." I handed the Post-its to Illuminada, knowing that she could check out the plate numbers in a matter of minutes. "There used to be writing on the door of the truck, but it's painted over. It's a 1997 Dodge." Illuminada was staring at the two Post-its, incredulity crinkling her features.

"*Como mierda*! Have it your way, Bel. But what a coincidence that two suspects have black trucks. It's hard to believe, but I guess it's easy enough to verify." She sighed and stashed the Post-its in her purse.

We sipped our beers quietly for a few minutes. Betty's fingers tapping on the keys of the laptop were the only sound in the room. When she had caught up, she said, "So I don't suppose anybody wants a Häagen-Dazs ice cream bar with dark chocolate over vanilla ice cream, right?"

I smiled at her and said sweetly, "I'd kill for one."

Illuminada looked up and said, "I'll have one just to be polite."

Soon the three of us were ripping the paper off our ice cream bars and nibbling away. Pushing her laptop out of range of the inevitable drips, Betty said, "We have three things to do. We have to find out everything we can about Luke Jonas. And I mean everything. Like why does a wanna-be actor drive a pickup truck? Is he the type to kill for a part in a movie?" I raised my hand, indicating that I accepted that assignment, and with the same gesture acknowledged Betty's predictable leap into leadership. I resisted the urge to compete as she continued, "But I also think we ought to see if there's anything we're missing in Danny Palumbo's background. Maybe he wanted a part in the movie too. He seems like a much more viable suspect to me than Luke Jonas. Maybe it's not grief that's making him look so bad. Maybe it's guilt." I wanted to strangle her, but I refrained.

Illuminada's next contribution to what was supposed to be a joint effort didn't sit much better with me. "I'm going to check out Gio a little more thoroughly. I know you two think he's harmless now, but I'm not so sure. His own sister thinks he could have murdered her boyfriend."

Ignoring both of them, I said firmly, "After I find out what skeletons are stored in Mr. Jonas's closet, and I bet there are some, I'm going to work real hard figuring out how to implicate him. I don't even know if he has an alibi for the time of death. The police have probably never even considered him a suspect," I said, wondering if the annoyance I felt showed. I sensed that something had shifted and our usual collaboration had degenerated into competition. But there was no way to deny the advisability of checking out each of the three main suspects, so I kept my feelings to myself and concentrated on my ice cream bar. Sadly I noticed that I had eaten all the chocolate coating on mine, so I raced to finish the ice cream before it melted and dripped down my wrist. For a fleeting moment I recalled summer nights when I was a child, and keeping an ice cream stick from dripping down my wrist had been my biggest problem.

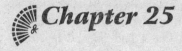

Chapter 25

Hoboken Municipal Court
Traffic Division
Hoboken City Hall
94 Washington Street
Hoboken, NJ 07030

Barrett, Mark
205 Park Street
Hoboken, NJ 07030   Case No. 44472SRGB31

The Court is returning your personal check, money order
or credit card *authorization for the following reason(s):*
    *CREDIT CARD INVALID. SEND CHECK OR MON-
EY ORDER.*
    *Please comply with request by AUGUST 15, 1998, to
avoid additional fees and/or license cancellation.*

Thank you.

Francis L. O'Connell
City Clerk

For about two seconds I had debated opening the letter from the Hoboken Municipal Court addressed to Mark before I slashed the envelope. Had he gotten another speeding ticket? A parking ticket? Had he maxed out his credit card again? Would he sulk for a week when I confessed that I had opened his mail? Should I call the court, find out the amount, write a check, and perhaps save his license? Or should I e-mail him about the letter and let him handle it in his own time frame that might not jibe with the court's? And what would this ticket do to my car insurance?

These questions as well as the less-familiar one about how to get the goods on Luke Jonas were very much on my mind when I stopped off at the mailbox on the way to my last class of the semester. That must be why I dropped the overdue rental movie that Mark had left for me to return into the mailbox instead of into the slot at the nearby Blockbuster's. The young people working at Blockbuster's were very understanding when, frazzled and red-faced, I explained what I had done. They would not require me to pay for the movie. I offered to call the post office and arrange for the video to be held for me to collect and return. As soon as Sol dropped me off at the office, I did that, glad that the kindly postal worker could not see my red face. I tried to recall the signs of early-onset Alzheimer's. What did it mean that I couldn't remember them?

It was the night of final speeches, usually the most rewarding class of the semester for the students as well as for me. They had already given three speeches, so their confidence level was considerably higher than it had been when the course began. I was sure that their final speeches would be their best so far. I was almost relieved when Ndaye didn't appear. She had already missed more classes than she had attended, and there was no way for her to pass even if she had come and turned in her take-home exam and given her speech. Her situation saddened me, but I assumed she would retake the course with a better understanding of the attendance requirements. Perhaps she would wait until she had a job with predictable hours around which she could build a schedule of classes that she could attend regularly.

Winston's speech was impressive. One of his visual aids was his identical twin brother, Harris, who stood beside him throughout part of his talk on the social and psychological advantages of being an identical twin. Harris was the spitting image of Winston, diamond-studded tongue and all. None of us could have easily distinguished one from the other had they not worn different T-shirts. Winston spoke smoothly, referring to his notes with great panache, neither reading them nor reciting them by heart, but using them to guide him to his next point. He sounded as if he had been giving speeches for years. Having his twin beside him seemed to give him added confidence. Listening to Winston speak about how close and alike most identical twins were, I better understood the full extent of Danny Palumbo's loss. Betty's anecdotal evidence about twins doing each other in was negligible in the face of what Winston was saying. In fact, Winston and Harris really got me thinking about Danny and Louie in a new way.

But before I could dwell on the concordance of the Palumbo twins, Winston had finished and it was Tomas's turn. Tomas had been absent the night I went over students' speech outlines and when they rehearsed with partners, so I wasn't sure what he was going to talk about. However, I had suggested strongly that he find a new focus for his final speech. Unlike Winston, who had approached the topic of twins differently each time, Tomas always seemed to end up prophesying about the devastation ahead when the old millennium

would give way to the new. I thought he needed to
expand his research techniques and had encouraged
him to look beyond cyberspace for his supporting mate-
rials. He strode to the front of the room carrying a pil-
lowcase. Reaching inside, he pulled out his arm with an
enormous brown and white boa constrictor writhing
around it like an oversized animated bracelet. I couldn't
breathe. The room began to whirl. I don't care what
Freud says, I don't do snakes.

Holding his outline in the hand that was not hosting
the snake, Tomas began his introduction. But, as if they
had rehearsed, his classmates stood in perfect unison
and made straight for the door, taking care not to venture too near the lectern. In about five seconds, the
room was empty of everyone but Tomas, his much
larger-than-life writhing bangle, and me. By virtue of
my role in Tomas's educational program, I felt obliged
to stay and hear him out. Not only did I have to stay, I
had to keep my wits about me so I could fill out a feedback sheet while he spoke, enumerating his strengths
and weaknesses as a public speaker. Unfortunately, my
dizziness had evolved into paralysis, and I couldn't
move anyway. Nor could I take notes or smile or nod
appreciatively as I listened. I just sat there frozen with
terror, afraid to look at Tomas for fear of seeing his
visual aid while his words raced round and round the
room. After about a million years, I finally did hear
Tomas say, "Thank you for your attention," and saw
him stuff his slithering sidekick back into the pillow-
case.

As Tomas headed for his seat not too far from mine, I
came to life and said stiffly, "Thank you, Tomas. Now
please take that snake out of here. It's alarmed your
audience. I'll be in my office tomorrow afternoon doing
grades. Perhaps you'll stop by and we can chat again
about appropriate visual aids."

"No problem," said Tomas, relieved that his speech was over and that he'd once again faced down his own demons. From the doorway he turned back to ask, "Was I okay? I wasn't too nervous once everybody left. And I had a lot of research, didn't I?"

"You spoke well, Tomas," I said, marveling that he was oblivious to the fact that terrorizing the audience into flight is incompatible with the goals of effective public speakers. *Where had I gone wrong?* When the students huddled in the corridor saw Tomas exit with his sack slung over his shoulder, they returned, and we finished class.

"No. Get away! Get off me! No! No! Help!" I awakened snarled in the sheets, dripping with sweat, certain I had been screaming. "Sol!" I called. I guess I had only dreamed the screams. "Sol! Wake up!" Why was he snoring while I was in a snake pit? It wasn't fair.

"Now what, sweetheart?" he mumbled, reaching out to pat me on the shoulder but patting the pillow instead. "What's the matter?"

"I'm dreaming about snakes again," I said, the whine in my voice in keeping with the childishness of my desire for him to stay awake and talk to me so I couldn't fall asleep where the dream reptiles would certainly reclaim me.

Sol pulled me to him but he didn't really wake up. "They hate snoring," he mumbled this time. "I'll frighten them away. Listen." In an instant he was snoring again just as if there were no serpents slithering down our bedroom walls and across the floor. I dozed fitfully. Finally when even the rhythmic breathing I'd learned in yoga failed to soothe me, I thought about Eve. Like Eve, I could look at the damn snake as a server announcing the house special and get up and get a piece of fruit.

Quietly I got out of bed, went downstairs to the fridge, and took out a bowl of ripe peaches Sol had brought home from the Hoboken Farmers' Market. As I stared at them, the events of the day, including the horror of class, replayed themselves in my head. Mechanically I rinsed the biggest peach and took a bite. With peach juice dripping all over my nightgown and the voices of students sounding in my ears, I suddenly knew how to get Luke Jonas. I just had to work out a few details. There's something to be said for eating fruit from the tree of knowledge. Grinning, I rinsed off my hands, dropped my nightie in the hamper, and went back to bed.

The next morning I took Ma to her opthalmologist, Dr. Frazier. The timing couldn't have been worse because I felt very pressured to work on trapping Luke Jonas, but I also felt pressured to get Ma to her eye examination as I had promised I would. Dr. Frazier called me in after he examined her. This was never a good sign. "Your mother has a cataract in her right eye. She needs laser surgery. I'm trying to explain to her that it's just an outpatient procedure that we do right here in the office. She doesn't seem to understand that it's simply a routine procedure." He was talking as if Ma weren't in the room, irritation clipping his words. Explaining to this frightened elderly woman why she should even consider letting him apply a scalpel-sharp beam of concentrated light to her eyeball seemed to annoy him. As she sat across the desk from him, Ma's shoulders had rounded and her skeletal fingers were tapping out a silent song on her thighs.

I let him finish, and then I said, "Thank you. We'll talk it over and get back to you, okay Ma?" My mother's shoulders squared and her fingers came to rest in her lap. Back in the car, I said, "So where do we go for lunch?" There was no way I could drop her off now.

Sofia was at Long Beach Island with her daughter until the weekend, and Ma was on her own contemplating Dr. Frazier's mandate. In a brief but intense battle, my inner good daughter defeated my inner sleuth.

"Piccolo's," Ma said without hesitation. "Sofia took me there once. They're famous for cheese steak and Sinatra. And let me treat you to lunch for once, Sybil. Today would've been your dad's and my sixty-fourth wedding anniversary, remember?" Of course I hadn't remembered. No wonder Ma seemed a little down. She had more than cataracts on her mind today. I was glad that I had not abandoned her.

"Sure, Ma. I'll let you. And speaking of Sofia, let's find out who did her cataract surgery. Dr. Frazier rubbed me the wrong way this morning. What do you think?" I reached across the front seat, patted her shoulder clumsily, and began to search for a parking space.

"Good idea, Sybil. I didn't care for him either." Ma smiled sideways at me, making me an accomplice in her understatement. I felt good about being able to suggest a next step that would make the journey to surgery a little less threatening. Grading exams, sensitizing Tomas, and even checking out Luke Jonas would have to wait another hour. Besides, I hadn't been to Piccolo's since the food police had declared both cheese and steak off-limits to those with even the slightest desire for self-preservation. I couldn't wait to go back.

I found a meter on Observer Highway and as Ma and I walked slowly up Clinton Street to the luncheonette, I heard "Angel Eyes" half a block away. Frank's lament was amplified by loudspeaker from Piccolo's to the sidewalk. "Beautiful song, right Sybil? One of my favorites," Ma said dreamily, squeezing my hand. We were in yet another room with photos all over the walls, but here the photos were of the owner and his customers and friends. Only a couple of posters of The

Voice were in evidence. "Come inside. Look!" Ma was
dragging me by the arm into a second room behind the
first. This was the real heart of the place. And here in
this inner sanctum, photos of the familiar face crowded
the walls. "Sofia brought me here last year on Frank's
birthday," said Ma. "The owner and his son throw a big
all-day party every year for Frank's birthday."

We seated ourselves at a table in the cheery front
room where the lunch counter was crowded with aging
bikers, construction workers, and office workers. I went
up and ordered us two cheese steaks, hand-cut fries,
and a couple of iced teas. Our cheese steaks came, and
Ma immediately hacked hers in two and wrapped one
half in a napkin, saying with her usual mordant wit,
"By dinnertime I'll have forgotten I had this for lunch
and it'll taste new to me." I was so pleased to see a
gleam in her slightly clouded eye that for a moment I
forgot my own impatience.

"Tell me, Ma. What was your favorite wedding
anniversary? Was it the one you spent at Niagara Falls?
Or when Daddy took you to Paris? Or the party we had
for your fiftieth?" I thought it would be good for her to
reminisce a little now with me rather than to go home
by herself and brood.

"Actually it was the weekend we spent in New York,
our twenty-fifth anniversary. We stayed at the Plaza and
went dancing at the Rainbow Room." Of course, the
famous weekend in New York. I'd heard the story many
times. I loved it. "That was some place, that Rainbow
Room. I heard they're going to sell it, but, Sybil, it was
so romantic. You went up in a special elevator, and
there was a beautiful bar where you waited until they
called you to your table. The tables were arranged in a
circle around the dance floor. And all around was that
view." I think I inherited my addiction to the spires of
Manhattan from Ma. "We were in the first tier, right up

close to the band and the vocalist. I felt like a movie star." Ma's eyes closed for a minute. Mine widened as I realized how I could use the information Ma had just given me to expose Luke Jonas.

Trying to keep the excitement out of my voice, I asked, "What did you wear? Do you remember?"

"A gray taffeta cocktail dress with a dropped waist, a scoop neck, and long tight sleeves. It was perfect to dance in because the skirt swirled. Your dad wore a dark suit. We took a picture. I have it somewhere." Listening to Frank reminding us of the value of little things, I resolved to remember to ask Ma to show me that photo sometime, sometime soon. In the meantime, I had a murder to solve.

"So get to the important part. How was the food?" I asked, keeping my voice light.

"We had a marvelous dinner, Chateaubriand and baked Alaska. Everything was delicious and so elegant. The waiters all wore tuxedos. Can you imagine? They were very formal and attentive. Your father ordered champagne. And we danced all night. Your dad was quite a dancer, remember?" Frank was singing "You Make Me Feel So Young," and Ma's face was aglow with the light of pleasure recalled. I felt guilty for being eager to end our mother-daughter moment so I could begin to weave the web that would ensnare Luke Jonas.

"You both must have saved up for ages to pay for a room at the Plaza and dinner at the Rainbow Room," I commented in between mouthfuls of my truly memorable and very messy cheese steak. Ma had taken hers off the roll and was disposing of it deliberately and neatly with a knife and fork. I glanced surreptitiously at my watch. "Sounds like you two had yourselves quite a blowout," I said, wondering how long it would take for me to metabolize all the cholesterol I had just consumed with such relish. As Ma and I finally left Piccolo's arm in arm, Frank was singing, "I'm a Fool to Want You." And, thanks to Ma's anniversary memories, I was another step closer to nabbing Luke Jonas for the murder of Louis Palumbo.

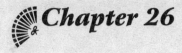

Chapter 26

To: Bbarrett@circle.com
From: Mbarrett@hotmail.com
Re: Traffic ticket
Date: Tue, 11 Aug 1998 11:08:37

Yo Ma Bel,

Sorry I forgot to tell you about that ticket and using your credit card. You won't believe how I got the ticket. I was double-parked in front of Grandma and Sofia's house one afternoon after I spotted the two of them walking home from the Farmers' Market lugging all this fruit and corn they'd bought. I gave them a lift, of course. I yelled at Grandma Sadie and told her she should call us when she wants to go shopping, but she said she didn't need to call for every single thing.

So anyway, I double-parked for like two minutes while I carried their stuff into the house. When I came out, the damn cop was writing out the ticket. I was so pissed. He wouldn't rip it up either. I figured you wouldn't mind if I used the credit card you gave me for emergencies, so I did, but I forgot to tell you. But your card must be maxxed out or something. I'll send the court a

check since your credit's not very good right now, so don't worry
about it.

Everything's smokin' here. Dad and Cissie will be home in a
week. Aveda and I may camp at the Cape for a few days before
we resurface in Hoboken.

Love,
Mark

I called my bank, only to learn that for the last two
months I'd neglected to pay the bill for the credit card
Mark had tried to use. Annoyed with myself, I went to
RECC to meet Tomas, read exams, put together final
grades, and do a little background checking on Luke
Jonas. Instead of Tomas, Ndaye waited outside my
door. "I want to geeve my szpeech now. Iz okay?" she
asked, smiling her lovely smile and waving a sheaf of
papers at me. I assumed they included her take-home
exam and speech notes. This was going to be difficult,
but, a veteran of many such scenes, I was both determined and resigned.

"Ndaye, I'll read your exam and comment on it and
give it back to you so you'll know how you did, but you
will lose points for turning it in late and—" I could read
confusion in her eyes, so I interrupted myself to
explain. "You had extra time that your classmates
didn't have to work on the test and that's not fair.
Remember what it says on your course outline." I
pointed to the place on the course outline where late
work is discussed. Eyes down, Ndaye handed me her
exam, neatly stapled. I added it to the pile on my desk.
"But I won't hear your speech. As you know, it had to
be given last night in class. And, as I told you several
times, you've already missed too many classes,
speeches, and assignments to pass the course. I know
you had a scheduling conflict, and I'm really sorry."

Her eyes were filling. She looked at her notes and spoke. "But I had to work last night. Now I have everyzhing for zee zpeech right here." She flipped through the papers she still held. "I szay eet for you now."

"Ndaye, I won't hear it now. Reread your course outline. It's very clear about all this. You have to repeat the course. That's not negotiable. I'm very sorry. Next time you take Speech, choose a section that will not conflict with your job. You have the ability to do very well in this class, but you have to attend regularly." This is the part of the semester and of my work that I find most discouraging. I hate the way my students' responsibility to jobs and families sometimes poses obstacles to their academic progress. But for every one who, like Ndaye, hadn't yet learned to juggle school, full-time work, and family, there are many others who have and do it with energy and even grace.

"But you don't understand, Professor, I have to pay for zeez clazzes double. I am foreign sztudent, remember? I am not even zee ceeteezen. Zere ees no financial aid for me. I have to pay. I cannot take zee class over and pay again." She was crying softly now. I felt like crying too.

"Ndaye, I'm sorry, but I cannot pass someone who has missed the number of classes and the amount of work that you have. You should talk to a counselor before you plan another semester." Suddenly her shoulders straightened, and glaring at me through her tears, she snatched her exam off my desk. She turned and stomped out of the office, slamming the door behind her. Slumped over my desk, my head cradled on my arms, I tried to tell myself that I'd done the best I could. I reached in my drawer. This was an M&M's moment if ever there was one.

Wendy arrived just as I was about to pick up the phone. The empty M&M's bag was on the desk in front of me. "I can see it's too late for sharing," she quipped, dumping her pile of papers and books onto her desk. "Fortunately I brought my own and one for you too although you don't deserve it. It's going to be a long day." She tossed another bag of M&M's onto my desk. She was right. An afternoon of paperwork stretched ahead of us.

As soon as Wendy left the office for a meeting, I figured I could make a few phone calls without bothering her. I got the number of the Drama Department at Clarence College, poked the phone in the appropriate places, and asked the obliging department secretary for the chairperson's name and number. I left him a voice mail message and then, after thinking a moment, called the secretary back. "Hi. Sorry to trouble you again, but it occurs to me that Professor Reid may not be on campus this summer. I'm Professor Bel Barrett. I teach English at River Edge Community College in Jersey City, New Jersey. I really need to get some information about a former Clarence College drama major. He's applied for an internship with me at a community theater I run in Hoboken, New Jersey. We need to fill the position immediately. I just have a couple of questions about his résumé."

"Perhaps if you tell me his name, I can look up who he studied with and give you a few other faculty members to contact. That's what Professor Reid would do," she said in the manner of one long accustomed to dealing with the rituals of the academy and the vagaries of the academic calendar. In the time it takes to click a mouse twice, she gave me the names and numbers of two other faculty members with whom Luke had worked, and I left urgent messages for both of them. To my amazement and relief, one returned my call later that very afternoon just as I was recording the last few grades on my roster.

"Professor Ryan O'Toole here. Just checked my

messages and heard your cry for help. And how might I be of service?" The man sounded jovial and relaxed, the way a faculty member should sound during August. I could have kissed him for returning my call so promptly.

"Professor O'Toole, I'm very glad you return calls," I gushed. "Thank you. I teach English at River Edge Community College in Jersey City, New Jersey."

"Oh, you have my sympathy, madame," he interjected. "I taught community college English for a few years in the seventies. Big classes, small paychecks, and students with lots of talent and no time to develop it. I couldn't hack it. My hat's off to you."

"Well, nothing's changed," I replied, grateful that this faraway colleague was so chatty. That was a good sign. "I also run a community theater in Hoboken where I live. That's why I'm calling."

"Oh, you must be a real martyr. The only gig that's more work than teaching full-time at a community college is running a community theater part-time," he cracked. I laughed appreciatively at his comment, willing him to continue his banter. After all, it was his nickel.

"You're so right," I said with what I hoped was an endearing chuckle. "But the good news is we're taking on a paid intern in cooperation with NYU's Drama School. We need somebody in this position who will be able to fill in when necessary on stage, backstage, and even in the office. We're looking for somebody who's a real team player. I have several candidates to screen. One of the top runners studied with you when he was an undergraduate," I added. "Tell me, is Luke Jonas a team player?" I injected Luke's name into my palaver suddenly, hoping to surprise my listener into a revealing reaction. My effort was rewarded.

He guffawed and echoed my question in a mocking

tone, "Luke Jonas? A team player? Not on your life. And I don't mind telling you that either. It's common knowledge thanks to his own overdeveloped ego."

"I don't understand," I said blandly, hoping he would elaborate.

"Listen, even in a field like musical theater that is rife with egomaniacal narcissists, Luke Jonas is a standout." Professor O'Toole made this pronouncement with such alacrity and spirit that I got the impression he'd been dying for a chance to share what he knew about Luke. I was beginning to feel I'd done him a favor by calling him. "Get this. When Jonas didn't get to play Lancelot in a student production of *Camelot*, he wrote a letter to the school newspaper denouncing our casting policy, which, naturally, advocates spreading the parts around among our majors. If you ask me, that's part of why he left here before he graduated." He paused. "I can fax you a copy of the letter if you like."

"That would be very helpful," I said simply, suspecting there was more and that he would continue. To encourage him, I added, "According to his résumé, he's in grad school at NYU. I assumed he had an undergraduate degree."

"If he does, he didn't get it here. Jonas left in the middle of his sophomore year right after the *Camelot* debacle. He threw a real hissy fit backstage and walked out. And . . ." he paused. I waited, willing him to say more. "And while normally we're always sorry to lose a student, we said good riddance to Luke Jonas."

Now I was sure this man knew something else about Luke. The joviality that had warmed his greeting was gone and his last few words were clipped. But a stage-struck youngster angry over not getting a part cannot be that unusual for a drama department. Dealing with disappointed and angry students was, unfortunately, something college faculty sometimes had to do. I thought fleetingly of Ndaye's anger. *How could I get Luke's former mentor to reveal whatever it was that had really soured him so on a gifted student?*

I didn't have to do anything. In a tone once again collegial rather than angry, Professor O'Toole said, "Bel, forgive me for sounding hostile, but that kid had a kind of poisonous effect here. You said you have other candidates for your internship?" His use of my first name was not lost on me.

"Yes, a few, but . . ." I stammered in response to his question, annoyed that I couldn't recall *his* first name.

"Well, no buts about it, save yourself a lot of grief and award it to one of them. Luke Jonas may come across like *A Chorus Line*, but trust me, Bel. He's really *Sweeney Todd.* The kid who got the Lancelot role in *Camelot* that Jonas wanted was found bludgeoned to death in his car. They never figured out who did it, but . . ." Now it was Professor O'Toole's turn at the meaningful pause, the telling hesitation, when, by saying nothing, he revealed everything. "I'll fax you a copy of that article too."

I gave him my fax number at work, expressed appreciation for his candid responses, and put down the phone. In a few minutes, I was in the department office hanging over the fax machine the way I used to sit by the phone as a teenager, willing it to ring. Before too long, as if by magic, the machine began to hum and spit out sheets of paper. I rushed back to my office to pore over them in private. After reading them twice, I called Betty and Illuminada.

The three of us got together that evening at my house. Sol had promised to pick up some vegetable quesadillas at the local *taqueiria* before he left for his CCPW meeting. Betty and Illuminada arrived together, both looking tired and hot. When I saw them dragging in, I was thankful for the window air conditioners we'd installed last summer and for the fridge full of beer. I greeted them each with a Corona. "Okay, *chiquita*," said Illuminada, kicking off her shoes and sinking into the corner of the love seat that she liked. "What's the big rush?"

"Yeah. I could have been having dinner with Vic, but instead . . ." Betty whined as she yanked the beer out of my hand and plopped down in the chair across from Illuminada. I couldn't blame them for being annoyed at my last-minute summons, but I felt a great sense of urgency. Before I could answer, Sol brought in our dinner and turned to leave, saying, "Remember, don't do anything stupid or dangerous." In unison and without discussion, we raised our beer bottles to him and made faces. After he left, we brought our beers into the kitchen and gathered around the sink island to eat.

Betty jumped right to the subject at hand. "I had a brainstorm this morning and called Father Santos. I asked him to check with Father Sebastian, the Palumbos' priest at St. Joe's in Hoboken and see what, if anything, he knew or could find out about Danny Palumbo." Betty glanced around to see if we appreciated her inspiration. Since I was still annoyed with her, I wasn't about to gratify her with a compliment, although I had to admit tapping her Catholic connection was a damn good idea. Betty's close relationship with Father Santos, her parish priest, had proved useful before. She was the most religious of the three of us, and although Illuminada and I ribbed her mercilessly, I think we envied her the certainty of her convictions. I know we envied her access to Father Santos, who was as well known for his big heart as he was for his liberal interpretation of Church doctrine.

Illuminada, whose classiness and professionalism enabled her to transcend the petty hostility Betty sometimes inspired in me when her inner tsarina got out, exclaimed, "*Caramba!* What a great idea! I love it."

Betty preened a moment and then went on, "Helena Riccio, the woman who cleans for Father Sebastian, is a good friend of Louie and Danny's mom. According to Helena, Danny was usually a really good kid. The worst offense she could come up with was once in a while he'd tie a pair of sneakers together and throw them up on the power lines. And she said one mischief night he got caught tossing eggs at cars."

"Ho hum," I said, imitating a yawn. "What Hoboken kid hasn't done those things? When I first moved here, I thought the sneakers just grew up there like some kind of urban flora. And throwing eggs? Standard operating procedure for the local kids. Some don't even wait until mischief night."

"There's more," said Betty with a grin, indicating that she too realized Danny Palumbo's adolescent capers were hardly going to rock the tabloids. "She also said that after his bachelor party he and some buddies got stopped rolling garbage cans down Washington Street. They didn't get arrested though because one of the ushers in their wedding was a Hoboken fireman whose brother was a cop." Betty paused and then added in an exaggerated whisper, "Are you ready for this? It's a biggie. She remembers gossip from her daughter who's been best friends since Catholic school with Anna Deloia, the woman Danny married. Danny Palumbo and Anna had sex before they were married. For two years!"

Illuminada crossed herself and quipped, "*Dios mio!* Was this before or after he rolled the garbage cans down the street? Is that some kind of foreplay we should know about?"

Ignoring Illuminada's crack, Betty continued, "She

also said that Anna was worried that Danny was having
an affair."

"Isn't everyone?" I snapped, remembering the pert
student teacher who had just happened by Danny
Palumbo's office during my visit. In the Year of the
Intern, I wouldn't have been surprised to learn that
Father Santos himself was getting it on with somebody.
Now ignoring my interruption, Betty went on, "Any-
way, I asked Father Santos to find out if there had been
any change in Danny after his twin's murder and . . ."

Here Betty paused dramatically. A little food, a beer,
and the starring role in the conversation had perked her
up. "Danny Palumbo told his wife he feels responsible
for his brother's death. See, Danny was supposed to
meet Louie on the night he was murdered up at Stevens
at the overlook. Louie wanted to talk to him privately
about something. Danny was late because after he left
home, he stopped off to see his lover. When he finally
got to the overlook, Louie wasn't there. Danny waited
for an hour and then went home. After Danny heard that
Louie had been killed, he broke down and told Anna
about the affair. He told her that if he hadn't been
screwing around, he'd have gotten there sooner, and
Louie would still be alive today."

I thought again about the student teacher who looked
like Toni Demaio. What a heavy price Danny Palumbo
had paid for an extramarital roll in the hay. I figured his
survivor's guilt would probably make him very eager to
do what he could to atone for straying from the straight
and narrow. That was not a bad thing. "Well, you sure
got a lot of mileage out of Father Santos. He really
came through again," I said, unable any longer to
begrudge Betty the praise she deserved.

"Of course, you don't know any of this. Father Santos said Father Sebastian is determined to protect his
source. I swore on my mother's grave I'd never repeat a

word of what he told me." Betty's eyes moved from me to Illuminada.

"Scout's honor," I said, raising the requisite two fingers. I felt an urge to prick my thumb and take a blood oath like we used to do when I was a kid in Passaic.

"My lips are sealed," said Illuminada. I stood up and took the empty beer cans into the kitchen along with our now empty paper plates. When I returned, Illuminada sat up and said, "Well, I didn't come up with much on Gio, but what I did find was interesting. The night his sister lost the baby he let all the air out of Officer Montegna's tires and was waiting for him. *Dios mios*, he was actually picked up stoned in the parking lot at police headquarters late that night. The cop took a statement. Seems our Gio was miffed at Montegna for questioning his sister about Louie's murder. Said the interrogation had caused her to lose her baby. Officer Montegna decided not to press charges on account of how much the Palumbos and Nancy Deloia had already been through." Illuminada shrugged at the selectivity of the police officer. Then she added, "I got this all from Giselle, who works the switchboard at headquarters and who owes me for tracking down her ex after he skipped the state last year, leaving her and the baby to fend for themselves." Illuminada shook her head. The fecklessness of deadbeat dads never failed to amaze her. "Sorry, but that's all I got on him."

"Well, I learned a whole lot about Luke Jonas this afternoon," I began, not knowing how else to respond to Illuminada's not very helpful revelations about Gio. I gave them each a copy of the letter to the editor and the article Professor O'Toole had faxed. As they scanned the pages, I explained the gist of what he'd said. "So you see, I think Luke's some kind of psychotic with an entitlement issue. He thinks he should get the part he wants and when he doesn't, he strikes out at the person

who does if their paths happen to cross. I'm not sure
it's premeditated even. Listen, 'Jeffrey Stemple's body
was found behind the steering wheel of his car in the
parking lot of Clarence College's Hayes Hall. Cast
members and the Wheeler drama coach Ryan O'Toole
report that Stemple never appeared at Hayes Hall for
the rehearsal of a Drama Department play. Death
appears to have been the result of a blow to the head.
An autopsy is being performed . . . ' "

"*Caramba*! You think he's some kind of serial
killer?" Illuminada asked, her voice tinged with
incredulity.

"What's with the psychobabble mumbo-jumbo about
entitlement issues? Are you trying to say the dude turns
deadly every time he gets thumbs-down for a part?"
Betty shuddered, her gesture undermining her attempt
at skepticism. I could tell she had grasped the sinister
implications of Luke Jonas, psychotic killer of his competition.

"Actually that's exactly what I think. And if you want
a little more psychobabble, I think he acts on impulse
like he did when he tried to brain me with that cinder
block. I was just in the wrong place at the wrong time."
Now I shuddered, remembering the crash of the heavy
piece of concrete hitting the ground behind me. "He
could be one of those types with little control over
impulsive behavior. Who knows, maybe he hears
voices? Louie was up at Stevens waiting for Danny. He
was alone. Luke happened along, saw Louie, saw his
chance, stabbed Louie in the back, and dumped him
over the railing. With the competition eliminated, so to
speak, Luke probably figured he'd ace the audition and
get the movie role. And the cops were so preoccupied
with Louie's lovelife that they never even looked for
another motive so they never connected Luke to the
case." I waited for their reaction.

"Now Luke's not going to get that part, so . . ." Illuminada had already moved on to the logical conclusion.

"He's a menace to whomever they do cast. When are they actually doing screen tests or whatever they do? We've got to stop him." Sitting up on the edge of her chair now, Betty looked like she was ready to take off after Luke immediately.

"I don't know, but based on the conversation I heard between Luke's agent and the film company rep J. J., they aren't even considering Luke. The agent seemed to accept this although I expect Luke's having a very hard time dealing with that rejection. But I have an idea . . ."

After a lot of note taking and Post-it writing, each of us was finally sure of what she had to do and when she had to do it. I was going to contact Danny Palumbo and explain to him how he could work off his guilt. Betty, who was unknown to Luke's agent, was going to call him after she had rented a suitable space for our own little drama. Illuminada, who had a staff that could be counted on to do what she told them to without asking questions, was going to have the tapes played and handle the other technical, legal, and safety details. She rushed out to her car to get her handy-dandy powerful portable recorder. I ran upstairs to get my *Louie Palumbo Sings Sinatra's Greatest Hits* CD, and Betty typed fast and furiously into her laptop so we'd each have a legible checklist and timetable to minimize the possibility of a senior moment screw-up. We spent what was left of the evening isolating and taping snippets of songs from Louie's CD. When we finished, we had about ten real killers.

Chapter 27

August 11, 1998

Dear Professor Barrett,

Sorry I didn't turn in my paper. After everything that's happened, I'm just not into finishing it. I don't have the heart for school anymore. My lawyer says the cops want to talk to me again next Tuesday. I may end up in jail in the fall instead of at State, so it doesn't matter anyway. For now I'm working in my dad's store like I used to. But I want to let you know how much I appreciate all your help, not only with the paper, but with everything. Even though you couldn't really do much about this mess, it was nice of you to try. I'll always remember you.

Sincerely,
Toni Demaio

I crumbled Toni's note into a ball and tossed it into the trash under the sink. That's how mad it made me. Then I snatched up the phone, got her number, and stabbed the digits into the handset. When her machine picked up, I spoke sternly: "Toni, this is Professor Barrett. I just got your note. Did Dolly Sinatra give up when things got tough? I don't think so. Be at 448 East Twentieth Street in Manhattan tomorrow night at seven. Bring your lawyer *and* your paper. You won't be sorry."

It would do Toni good to see for herself what a few women who refused to roll over and play dead when trouble came could pull off. And, if I had my way, the event we hoped to pull off would result in the arrest and conviction of Luke Jonas for the murder of Louis Palumbo. We were staging a sham audition for Sinatra impersonators who were interested in singing at the Rainbow Room on December 12, the date of The Voice's birthday and the night of the last performance to be held in the venerable Manhattan supper club before it was sold.

Betty had rented a studio in Chelsea where such auditions were frequently held. She had also called Luke's agent and left a brief and businesslike message inviting Luke to audition for this one-night gig and a callback number. It went without saying that impersonating Old Blue Eyes on the Rainbow Room's final night, which was also the legendary Chairman's birthday, would jump-start the performer's career big-time. Luke's unwitting agent had already gotten back to Betty to say his client would be there.

Illuminada had arranged for one of her staff to call Luke Jonas at odd times, but mostly in the early morning hours when he was likely to be home and answer the phone himself. The calls were to be made from different pay phones in Hoboken, so if Luke had call waiting, it would reveal nothing. We knew that Luke couldn't report his mysterious caller, nor could he very well change his phone number without missing out on other audition callbacks. Illuminada had instructed the caller to play a selection from the tape we had made of Palumbo singing snippets of: "I'll Never Smile Again,"

"I Get Along Without You Very Well," "Strangers in the Night," "Oh, Look at Me Now," "I've Got You Under My Skin," and, of course, "Don't Get Around Much Anymore."

According to her staff, Luke had responded to the first couple of calls with the predictable question, "Who is this?" At the next few he had slammed down the receiver. More recently he was listening and then asking, "Why are you doing this?" "Who are you?" "What do you want?" his voice trembling and his words rushed. Illuminada's operatives saw to it that whenever Luke checked his messages during the day there were one or two from Louie Palumbo. Whoever described Frank's renditions of these standards as haunting should have heard the late Louie Palumbo on a message machine at three in the morning. That voice redefined *haunting*.

My phone conversation with Danny Palumbo had been brief and to the point. After taking a moment to digest my request, he had agreed to the basic plan and promised to deliver the band except for the pianist. Not surprisingly, Nick was now tickling the ivories with an up-and-coming new group in the Fort Lee area. Danny offered to find another pianist, when I had the brainstorm to recruit Sol to sit in on piano. He jumped on the offer. Sol's repetoire was limited to Scarlatti and works for piano by other classical composers, so he had spent the last two days practicing "Don't Get Around Much Anymore," "I'll Never Smile Again," and "My Way" over and over. I thought he sounded pretty good, although, I must admit, the songs were beginning to wear on me just a little.

It was my hope that giving Sol a central role to prepare for and a ringside seat during the action would keep him from neurosing over everybody's safety for

the next crucial day and a half. It helped a little but
what really reassured him was the fact that Illuminada had arranged for a fair number of cops to be in
the studio. She had called in a few markers in Hoboken and gotten the two detectives assigned to the
Palumbo murder to agree, no questions asked, to
appear at the studio undercover and to arrange for a
warrant and backup that could lead to an arrest by
members of NYPD. Illuminada stipulated that the
backup be undercover cops posing as auditioning
impersonators.

Sol wanted to get there early to rehearse with the
band, and as it turned out, most of us got there early.
The studio was a rectangular windowless room on the
third floor of a former factory now housing small busi-
nesses and this one space used for auditions, rehearsals,
and, according to the posters on the lobby bulletin
board, a few select performances. Betty had chosen it
for its proximity to the PATH train as well as its small
size and limited means of egress. There was only one
door. Rows of folding chairs ten across filled most of
the room. In front of these were a piano and a small
space for the musicians. Behind this area was a platform the size of a postage stamp that would serve as
stage. Before leaving work early, Betty had borrowed
RECC President Woodman's mike and amp.

As an undertaker, Vic had considerable experience
and expertise in the art of transformation, so he had
acted as our wardrobe and make-up consultant. Raoul
had agreed to stay downstairs and act as the
doorman/bouncer. Staidly suited, clean-shaven, and
laptop laden, Raoul usually looked like the accountant
he was. That night Vic engineered a total makeover. In a
three-button cream-colored linen jacket, beige slacks, a
black, rib-hugging T-shirt, shades, and a day's worth of

bad boy stubble, Raoul became the quintessential low-level show-biz operative. He carried his cell phone and a clipboard. We wanted Raoul to make sure that Luke didn't get in before the cops and the band got there and before we had a chance to get everything and everyone organized.

The band members straggled in and set up with Sol. There was a new bass player replacing Danny and a guy on drums whom Illuminada assured me were both undercover cops. They took a while to get tuned up, but once they started, they didn't sound bad. And they looked convincing as hell, kind of the way starving musicians are supposed to look, somewhere between shabby and formal. Insisting that Sol couldn't appear in his nerdy summer uniform of chinos and gray T-shirt, Vic had dropped by and pulled out of the depths of our closet a dark suit and a white shirt for Sol to wear with no tie and sneakers. The other musicians turned up similarly attired.

Of course, Betty was going to act as our emcee, the rep from the Rainbow Room running the audition. She wore a simple navy blue short-sleeved linen dress and carried her Palm Pilot. Illuminada had agreed to video the "audition" ostensibly so Betty could review the various singers' performances with the rest of the Rainbow Room team, but really so there would be a record of whatever Luke said and did. She was dressed in jeans and a baseball cap and was fiddling with her equipment like the pro she was.

I was supposed to stay in the background and make myself invisible since if Luke recognized me, it would spoil everything. My disguise, a blond wig courtesy of Vallone and Sons Funeral Home, a simple black sleeveless dress, and Ma's pearls, was an added precaution. Except for staying in touch with Raoul by cell phone, I was sworn to silence. Trying to be quiet and inconspicuous would be a reach for me, but the cause was worthy.

When Raoul beeped me to inquire about letting in Toni Demaio and a male friend, I realized I'd forgotten to include her on the list we'd made up. I okayed Toni and, presumably, her lawyer, pleased that she'd made the effort to attend and hoping that everything would go as planned. So far so good. The band members were playing "Don't Get Around Much Anymore" for the fourth time and they sounded as if they'd been playing together forever. I felt as if I'd been hearing them forever. They ran through the other two songs a few times until they were satisfied. The other undercover cops had filtered in and seated themselves as if by accord in one corner just behind the front row of chairs. Clutching fake résumés and chatting nervously, they looked, in their rented tuxedos, white dress shirts, and flat-top wigs, exactly like the Frank Sinatra wanna-bes they were impersonating.

A few minutes before seven, Raoul beeped to tell me that Luke was in the elevator. I gave Betty the high sign, and she whispered to Sol, who signaled the band to stop playing "My Way" for the fifth time. In the ensuing silence, he played the opening bars of Beethoven's Fifth, our agreed-upon starter. Then as if nothing had happened, the band picked up "My Way" again as Luke Jonas entered the room.

Looking around, he quickly spotted the small collection of other men dressed as he was. Smoothing down his wig, he walked over to them and took a seat. Without preamble, as if the audition had been going on for some time, Betty strode to center stage, consulted her Palm Pilot, and called out, "Hanson." One of the undercover cops straightened his tie and swaggered to the stage in his best imitation of someone imitating Frank. He handed Betty his résumé, and she seated herself in

the front row. The band started "My Way," and the
phony impersonator opened his mouth to sing. He
could carry a tune and his voice actually had a gravelly
quality that was not incompatible with Frank's. Thin
and dark-haired, he was a plausible imitation. Briefly I
wondered what leverage Illuminada had with the Hoboken police to get them to cooperate so fully with this
enterprise.

After giving Hanson a quick once-over, Betty
scanned his résumé. He had gotten through no more
than three lines of the song when she signaled the band
to stop, said, "Thank you" to the singer, and waved him
to the side of the tiny stage. You'd have thought she'd
been running auditions for cabaret acts all her life. Consulting her clipboard and looking slightly bored, she
called out, "Jonas."

Luke rose and made his way to the stage, smoothly
passing his résumé to Betty en route. He had apparently
decided to abandon his effort to mime the famous
swagger. When the band began this time, they played
"Don't Get Around Much Anymore," and Luke began
to sing. I closed my eyes. It was Frank. Betty let him
sing the whole song before she glanced at his résumé.
When he finished, she thanked him and waved him to
the side of the stage. He was swaggering now, no doubt
flattered by having been allowed to complete the song.
Then, glancing at her clipboard, Betty called out
"Palumbo." Luke twitched, his hand moving to rub his
eye and then reflexively moving once again to smooth
his wig.

No one rose to the stage. "Palumbo? Louis Palumbo?" Betty glanced in the direction of the pool of
singers. One who had taken his place among them
while Luke was making his way to the stage stood. He
was a dead ringer for Frank Sinatra. He was also a dead

ringer for Louis Palumbo. Luke Jonas's eyes widened, first in disbelief and then in horror.

A clean-shaven and poised Danny Palumbo swaggered to the front of the room, dropped his résumé in Betty's lap, chucked her under the chin, and winked at her, saying audibly, "Thanks, doll." Then he climbed the three stairs to the platform and casually detached the mike from its stand. When the band began to play "I'll Never Smile Again," he sang in the familiar and unforgettable voice of Louis Palumbo. He turned slowly away from Betty and locked eyes with Luke, who was now ashen-faced, bug-eyed, and twitching spasmodically on the edge of the small platform. Slowly, a ghostly smile on his lips, Danny began to move toward Luke.

"No! No! You can't be here! This is my gig! You can't be here!" Luke's voice came out in a raspy stage whisper. He shook his head from side to side, oblivious of the fact that his wig had slipped and now was perched like a rakish party hat atop his auburn hair. As Danny walked slowly closer, still singing, Luke covered his face with his hands and croaked, "No! You can't be here! You're dead! Goddamn it, man, I know you're dead! I put a knife in your fuckin' heart myself! Remember?"

Luke reached for his pocket. My heart stopped. I saw the drummer put down his drumsticks and reach into his own pocket. The bass player too had put down his instrument and was reaching toward his ankle. Several of the other supposed impersonators had their hands in their jackets. Sol, bless his heart, hunkered down over the keyboard and segued into the first bars of "My Way." Illuminada was zeroing in with her camcorder now, not wanting to miss a word or a gesture of what might very well be Luke's last act. Then Luke pulled out a large pocket knife still folded and, as if warding off a vampire, held it up between him and the ever advancing Danny. He flicked open the knife and lunged.

# Chapter 28

SERIAL KILLER SEIZED
Manhattan Cops Save Palumbo Twin
from Knife-Wielding Assassin

by Sarah Wolf

Undercover agents from NYPD collaborated with
Detectives Alphonse Montegna and Salvatore Reggio
to expose the confessed murderer of Hoboken singer
Louis Palumbo, best known for his impersonations of
Frank Sinatra, in a tense scene at a Manhattan
rehearsal studio last night. Responding to a timely
tip from private investigator Illuminada Guttierez,
Detectives Montegna and Reggio arranged for additional undercover backup from NYPD. According to
police reports, knife-wielding Luke Jonas, also of
Hoboken, was disarmed and arrested while attempting to stab Louis Palumbo's twin brother Daniel during a cabaret audition in Chelsea. Jonas confessed to
the murder of Louis Palumbo, his rival for a movie
role, and is being transferred to New Jersey to stand
trial as soon as the assault charges against him in

New York are filed. He is also being questioned in connection with the 1992 murder of another rival singer in Grafton, Ohio where he and the victim both attended Clarence College.

In an interview with this reporter last night, Joseph Palumbo, father of both Louis and Daniel, expressed his relief that his son's murderer has been apprehended . . .

"So where did you get the idea to enlist Danny Palumbo in this scheme?" asked Wendy, tossing aside the newspaper I had saved for her while she and her family canoed in the Adirondacks. A frown pleated her forehead. "Your buddy Sarah left out all the good stuff."

"It was Winston's speech. Didn't I tell you about the speech student who was obsessed with twins because he's a twin?" I didn't know when I'd had the chance to tell Wendy anything. As soon as she turned in her summer school grades, she and her family headed for the hills, the Adirondacks to be precise, for a couple of weeks of canoeing and camping. "He did all his speeches on twins," I continued, shaking my head as I recalled Winston's monomaniacal approach to the course. "On the last night of class, when he was standing in front of me with his twin brother talking about the closeness of many identical twins and how they often lead parallel lives, I realized how we could use Danny to smoke out Luke. I should have thought of it sooner. The kid talked about twins all summer." I leaned back in my lawn chair, and sighed.

"Okay, I've got that straight, but how did you ever get the moxie to stage a fake audition? What if Jonas had figured out that it was a fraud? Weren't you worried? And what about Sol? How the hell did you get him to buy into this?" Wendy pointed at the newspaper, sipped from her glass of white wine, and punctuated her final question with an arch of one eyebrow, a maneuver, I confess, I've never been able to master.

"The way Illuminada set it up, I felt as safe as I do right here in my own backyard." I looked around at the clusters of friends chatting and nibbling amid the flowers at our Labor Day barbecue. A more benign setting would be hard to imagine.

"What the hell did she do? Hire bodyguards? I know you, Bel. You have chutzpah, but not the kind that extends to going head to head with knife-wielding serial killers. You're a little ditsy, but you've never been stupid." Wendy's curiosity had obviously not been satisfied by Sarah's deliberately muted page one story.

"Ask her yourself," I said, throwing my arm across Illuminada's path as she walked by carrying a basket of nachos and a bowl of guacamole. "Illuminada, tell Wendy how you managed to get all those Hoboken detectives and the guys from NYPD to show up at our little psychodrama."

"It was simple," said Illuminada, winking and lowering the bowls so we could easily reach in and help ourselves. "Louie Palumbo was a local, from an old Hoboken family, one of their own. Luke Jonas . . ." Illuminada shrugged dismissively. "To the Hoboken cops, that *hombre* was an out-of-towner, another arrogant yuppie," she explained. "You know how it is here between the old-timers and the newcomers." Wendy nodded. The tensions between native Hobokeners and those who've moved in from elsewhere are legendary. The young newbies view the religious customs and politics of the blue-collar locals as quaint throwbacks and scorn the local public schools and polling places alike. The old-timers resent having their town turned into a mile-square unisex dormitory, housing narcissistic latte lovers biding time until they can afford homes in the burbs.

"As far as they're concerned, Luke Jonas was an invader to begin with, and when they heard that he was probably the one who murdered Louie, they really wanted to see him stand trial." Illuminada smiled as Wendy and I continued our attack on the nachos and guacamole. "And now, *chiquitas*, do you mind if I bring these goodies over to my husband before you two finish them all?" Illuminada grinned and ambled over to the grill where Raoul was transforming pork from mere pig meat to food for the gods.

"I didn't know you'd ever been to the Rainbow Room either," said Wendy. "But that was a great idea. I can imagine how badly Jonas would have wanted to perform there. What a résumé builder a gig at that place would be."

"Actually, Ma gave me that idea," I said, nodding in the direction of my mother who sat in the shade in animated conversation with Mark and Aveda. She had had successful cataract surgery the week before and ever since, had been light-headed with relief. Not only was the dreaded ordeal over, but it had gone well. Once again, in her terms, she had beaten the odds. She was probably telling the kids about her operation.

"Your mother?" Wendy asked, wistfully eyeing the nachos and guacamole now untouched on the other side of the yard. As if she had read Wendy's mind, Betty picked up the nachos and guacamole and brought them back to Wendy, who smiled her thanks. "Did Sadie know you were trying to apprehend a murderer?"

"No, I didn't want to worry her about it then. But she was reminiscing about her twenty-fifth anniversary celebration that just happened to take place at the Rainbow Room. And when I heard her mention it, something clicked. I knew Luke Jonas would want to perform there. As you just said, a gig there is a real career booster." Betty put the guacamole and nachos on the low wall behind our chairs.

"Your mother looks great. I bet she was pleased as punch to have been able to help in some way," said Wendy, glancing over at Ma.

"Yeah, she was. She had something to brag to Sofia about, and it also took her mind off her surgery," I answered. "I sometimes forget that she used to be a court stenographer, and she's still very interested in crime and criminals."

"Like mother, like daughter," said Wendy with a grin. "Maybe your predisposition to mess with murderers is genetic. And speaking of daughters, how's Rebecca? How was your trip to Seattle?"

"The trip was too short. I was there for less than a week, but Rebecca and Keith are doing very well. She feels terrific." I whipped out my Seattle photos, which I just happened to have in my pocket. There stood Rebecca with Keith behind her, his arms circling the swell of her tummy, both of them grinning. In another photo, Rebecca and her friend Louise mugged for the camera outside the greenhouse in Volunteer Park where the three of us had walked after having lunch on Broadway. And in the next, Rebecca posed alone, dwarfed by the statue of John Henry outside the art museum. Several shots of the new apartment followed, including the bookshelves Keith had built and the alcove where the baby would sleep. Finally there was a picture of Rebecca and me, arm in arm with Snohomie Falls as a backdrop.

Betty was looking over my shoulder, and she and Wendy were making all the appropriate noises in response to the photos. "So, Bel, did you finally see the place where the wedding's going to be?" asked Betty. "Is it as way out as you thought?" Betty was standing behind me kneading my shoulders.

"Yes. It's just what Rebecca described, a gas station museum, but I think it's going to work. As I told her father, it's very hip, very unconventional, and very informal. It's not what I would have planned, but hey . . ." I shrugged my shoulders.

"In other words, it's very Rebecca, which is as it should be, since, after all, it's her wedding," said Wendy somewhat sanctimoniously. Witnessing first-hand Rebecca and Keith's excited planning, I had finally come to terms with the fact that it wasn't my wedding, so I greeted Wendy's observation by forming my fingers into the familiar peace sign and lowering my head.

In the momentary lull, Betty fired off another question. "And how is the father of the bride? Still foaming at the mouth?"

I chuckled. "He's come around a little. Rebecca called him while I was out there and told him they were naming the baby after her grandpas, Lenny's father and mine. You know it's a Jewish custom to name a baby after deceased relatives. This was the first Lenny had heard that the baby would be a boy. He was predictably ecstatic about the gender and the naming, so he offered, actually volunteered, to pay all medical expenses not covered by insurance and to foot the bill for most of the wedding." I grinned.

"I don't even have to ask who orchestrated that maneuver," Wendy said, grinning back. "You're teaching that girl to manipulate men. For shame." Eyes twinkling, she gave me a big thumbs-up that belied her words.

"Forgive me for backtracking, but I still want to know one more thing about the Palumbo business," said Wendy. I nodded, used to the circular conversation pattern that had replaced the linear ones of our youth. Now we said what we remembered whenever we remembered it, sequence be damned. "Did the student who got you into all this ever turn in her paper? The essay on Dolly Sinatra?" I had to smile. Only another English prof would ask that question in the aftermath of a murder.

"You better believe it! She finished it right after the arrest and handed it in. It's excellent. She starts at State next week." The three of us clinked glasses, toasting Toni Demaio and her future academic career.

"But Toni's not the only one who'll be back in the classroom. Did I tell you Mark's starting that month-long course in teaching English as a Foreign language? He's going to learn in thirty days what I've been struggling to learn for thirty years!" I laughed, but I was enormously pleased that Mark had finally decided to get the training that would enable him to teach overseas. I'd always hoped he would put his linguistic talent and caring sensibility to work in the classroom. His students would be very lucky, and his father would get used to saying "my son the teacher" instead of "my son the CEO." We clinked glasses again. "And I picked up my fall rosters Friday. Guess who else will be going to school next week?"

"I give up," said Wendy. "Who?"

"Nancy Deloia," I announced. When Wendy still looked blank, I continued. "She was Louie Palumbo's longtime girlfriend. The one he was two-timing with Toni Demaio. The one who lost her baby and whose brother threatened me? Remember?"

"We all start this week," said Illuminada, ambling over with a full plate of food in one hand and some flatware in the other. As an adjunct in Criminal Justice at RECC, Illuminada would be back in the classroom Tuesday night. And so would I. The summer had gone. My paper for grad school was still in draft form, the novels I'd hoped to read lay unopened in a pile, and the closets I'd planned to reorganize remained black holes into which things disappeared forever.

Sighing, I said, "Well, I'm not going to start a new semester on an empty stomach." I got up and walked with Wendy and Betty toward the table where grilled meats, Jersey corn, and a salad of sliced Jersey tomatoes, fresh mozzarella, and basil from our garden spoke eloquently of summer's end.

Discover Murder and Mayhem with

~ Southern Sisters Mysteries ~

by

ANNE GEORGE

MURDER ON A GIRLS' NIGHT OUT
0-380-78086-0/$6.50 US/$8.99 Can
Agatha Award winner for Best First Mystery Novel

MURDER ON A BAD HAIR DAY
0-380-78087-9/$6.50 US/$8.99 Can

MURDER RUNS IN THE FAMILY
0-380-78449-1/$6.50 US/$8.99 Can

MURDER MAKES WAVES
0-380-78450-5/$6.50 US/$8.99 Can

MURDER GETS A LIFE
0-380-79366-0/$6.50 US/$8.50 Can

MURDER SHOOTS THE BULL
0-380-80149-3/$6.50 US/$8.99 Can

And in hardcover

MURDER CARRIES A TORCH
0-380-97810-5/$23.00 US/$34.95 Can